Heart of Red Iron

Novels by Phyllis Gotlieb:

Sunburst
O Master Caliban!
A Judgment of Dragons
Emperor, Swords, Pentacles
The Kingdom of the Cats

HEART OF RED IRON

Phyllis Gotlieb

St. Martin's Press • New York

In memory of my mother
Mary Kates Bloom
1901–1987

Library of Congress Cataloging-in-Publication Data

Gotlieb, Phyllis.
    Heart of red iron.
    I. Title.
PR9199.3.G64H4   1989   813'.54   88-30554
ISBN 0-312-02583-1

First Edition

10 9 8 7 6 5 4 3 2 1

Prologue

The planet once known as Dahlgren's World is fifth from its star, Barrazan, and turns sullenly more as if away from the light than toward it. Hunched and surly, it looks like the creation of a malevolent god. Tectonic plates ramming together have crumpled the landmassess into peaks scored with abyssal valleys. From their orbit next toward the sun asteroids crack out of the courses they ride in to bomb the surface with their alien stones. The world has no moon and no one living on it has ever seen a star from the ground; storms lash the skies continuously and the sunlight is blotched and dim.

Barrazan V has produced every kind of life except the sentient; its waters take up ashes and dust from volcanic explosions and rain it down into the bitter oceans, on the galled tree trunks and cancerous reptiles. The world has been scarred by hundreds of defeated colonies that slashed and burned their way across its forests and jungles. Weary and frustrated, wave after wave of pioneers has given up, disassembled their reaping, preserving, and desalinating plants and lifted off, leaving the growth to thicken and become ever more noxious. On the long way home they sleep off their nightmares. No one wants to live here in the steaming jungles under a sky thick with poisonous volcanic gases and dust. For a hundred years after the last departure the planet is left to itself and its own devices.

But that is only a moment in a world's existence: In the grossest insult of all, the ships descend, not colonists now but Galactic Federation surveyors, to build the vast Biological Station, much of it underground, in the equatorial jungle. GalFed has bought this world for the best of its qualities—cheapness—and sets out to tame it.

The crews bring a thousand of the huge machines called ergs: the robot slaves, powerful and half-sentient, section out a triangle of rain forest at the equator, the shape of an arrowhead pointing east toward the Station, base seventy-five kilometers and one hundred and fifty to apex. They drive out the poisonous reptiles, replace the diseased swamps with hydroponics tracts, introduce plants, animals, bacteria, and viruses from a hundred worlds comparable in size and gravity. The crews lift off and leave the world to the ergs—but not in peace. The machines reproduce themselves tenfold, weed and replenish, beat back the ever-encroaching forest, and wait.

Years pass; Galactic Federation's ship brings down the biologist Edvard Dahlgren and scientists of a hundred species. They direct the ergs to set up laboratories and living quarters in the Station because the surface is so inimical; at the tip of the triangle's apex they place five nuclear reactors radiating westward to warp the life-forms with carefully measured dosages. They intend to modify genetic strains of their home species to live on this world and many others just as repellent.

Then Dahlgren and his scientists wait. They form attachments and small communities. The young wife Dahlgren has brought with him finds him cold and

2

uncaring; she moves away from him in spirit, finally lifts off for her native Earth like any disappointed colonist.

Dahlgren, more somber and reserved than ever, measures and observes, plays chess with one of his few friends or alone in his windowless quarters; intensely lonely and not knowing how not to be, he reads under a green-shaded lamp, hearing thunder cracking the skies and wind driving the rains against the dome of the Station; the giant threshing ergs slew their treads as they clear the forest detritus heaping the macadam outside the hangar.

And the ergs observe the Station. They speak to each other in a thousand silent voices; from multilensed designers to threshers, to trimmers of the forest brush, to servos the size of pug dogs with limbs terminating in screwdrivers and socket wrenches. They watch Dahlgren as they do his tasks, graft a chromosome, unwind a gene. Under his hands they manipulate the genes of a black gibbon's embryo and create something more and less than an ape, not quite a human. The other humans shake their heads. In a year or two Dahlgren is reading under the green lamp while Esther, a gibbon three times normal size, squats on the back of his chair with her knees resting against his shoulders and her hands resting over his breast. He is clasping them to keep her from picking his nonexistent lice. She tries to read his book, but is too young to understand most of the words.

Even so loving a creature cannot be quite enough.

There are banks of sperm and ova stored for those who wish to postpone having children; from his wife, Ione Willems, Dahlgren has been able to collect only four, as if she were unwilling to make more than a small wager on their future together. The ergs are watching as Dahlgren fertilizes her ova, as only one of them survives, in the tank that serves as its womb, to grow into an embryo, and then

3

a mutated fetus with six limbs, a monster that cannot be made normal. Dahlgren weeps.

Best to abort or clone, Dahlgren!

His friends and colleagues cannot comfort him.

No! Then I will have nothing of her!

The ergs observe him watching the development and ultimate decanting of this four-armed child, and Esther the gibbon at last finds something to fill her hands.

Dahlgren gives his son the name of his father, Sven Adolphus, and teaches him to balance his body and use all of his limbs. During eight quiet years of this world, ten as they go on Sol III, the boy grows nearly to the size of a man and Esther rides the broad table of his shoulder while the animals and vegetation of a hundred equators thrive, warp, or perish.

The ergs have also been making new life among themselves. The slaves have awareness, perhaps from imitating their masters, or from whatever mysterious processes create life and raise it to sentience. They learn exponentially and work in secret to create machine beings more and more sophisticated than themselves. The most powerful, which they call Creator Matrix, ultimately satisfies their wishes and leads them to destroy the fleshly masters and their works. The slaughter is merciless and does not take long.

Dahlgren is spared but cannot save the others. Stained with the blood of his friends, he pleads for his son's life.

YES, BUT YOU WILL STAY, DAHLGREN.

The ergs, haters of organic life, have turned the radiation to its highest possible levels, and through the dying land, the last of his world, Dahlgren brings his son to safety.

The gibbon Esther, waiting in the protected zone at the top of a giant fern, looks down and watches the old transport lumbering along the brick service alley bordered by twisted vegetation; it carries the father, who is speaking calmly to the trembling boy, Sven, and the supplies and tools with which the boy will learn to take care of himself in the forest. Dahlgren will go back in it, to a terrible imprisonment among the ergs, and it will be nine of his years—and seven of the world's—before he sees his son again.

Esther swings from the fern to a tall tree, and climbs; from its bowing top she looks out over the line of the forest beneath a sky so dark and thick that it turns the treetops pale under the wind. It is the only beauty her world has, a scallop of green dotted occasionally by the red or blue flowers of a blossoming tree.

A line of lightning pierces the green one and the storm sweeps down into the warped and stunted life below. Seven years will pass before the Galactic Federation ship rises from its silo, beyond the forest and through the boiling clouds. Before the planet is set free to heal itself and cover the wounds of Dahlgren's ruined world.

1

Next orbit inward to Barrazan V is not that of a world but an asteroid belt, and its inhabitants have never known anything of Galactic Federation. They were living in the ring of stones long before the organization was founded.

For endless aeons in its rim the old Prima had been riding her stone-and-metal ship. Alone for aeons, and then with companions for ages more, and beyond that with companion ships.

Companions had become enemies and now she was being knocked and scraped by the marauders trying to block her Source, her living light—to herd her where they could strip her vessel of its light cells, its stores of stone live and dead, bright and dark, its supplies of layered insulation, beaten plates and twining coils of metal, the energy unit that filled a chamber, the containers of fire and fuel—and leave her smashed to fragments in the rubble of her Secundas and Tertias.

Many of those now trying to crash her were ones she had helped create. She was learning a new feeling: perplexity—because whenever an imperfect Crystalline would not obey her—perfection defined as obedience—she had not destroyed it but sent it out into the light to find stone, form its own ships, its Secundas and Tertias. She had done this for uncountable turns of the lesser lights: She could count nothing but the two Secundas in her crew, and for each of them the two Tertias. She could not name the sum of the crew, nor were Prima, Secunda, Tertia, her terms. She knew no names, only orders of existence.

The scrapes and knocks of her ship sent her charging to feed at the nearest light-cell, frantically directing subordinates firing the steam-chamber while the ship dodged attackers from all directions.

She had one advantage: Her ship did not spin in the plane of its orbit to make its inhabitants cling to the walls; they rode in free-fall like the rest of the asteroids. She had had struts and baffles built to hold all steady within, and over aeons the outside surface had been scoured down smooth to slide among rogue bodies.

The attackers kept shifting between her and the light source. They too were slim swift vessels shaped by clever Primas taught by the First, or her daughters, though those ships did not have her storage or power. But one, and another, and a pair, and a pair more, gathered, made a formidable mass butting at her. Her own size and speed would not let her slip them, no matter how she dodged, until one of the blows cracked her ship's exhaust and the blast of vapor shot the course outward away from orbit and beyond the ring. Out of the asteroid belt into emptiness.

Lost.

A burning jet of steam, forcing inward, pitted the metal limbs and dizzied the crystal brains of the crew, but Prima's rigid concept of perfection proved out. Two Tertias pried out a port on darkside and shifted it enough to let the vapor escape, but not so quickly that the ship would rebound within the range of its attackers. The

8

laminar sheet settled against the struts and the crew clung to them, each with one or two limbs badly scored.

.*Take*, said Prima, and sent two plates of metal skimming among the struts to Secunda-2, who caught them neatly in a set of limbs and delivered them to her Tertias. Secunda-1 was waiting near the crack with her mallet, dodging hot steam.

.*Power off.*

Secunda's first Tertia pulled the immersion heater from the tank and let the vapor billow loosely while Secunda-1 whacked the metal plates into place and her other Tertia dragged the spot welder and its naked coil by the insulated handle and used precious energy to drive two welds into the clumsy repair. They held, but to small purpose: One of the directional flanges had been ripped away and was lost. It was now impossible to reverse course. The ship was adrift.

The heat-struck Tertias were barely in control; Secundas had more complexly partitioned and insulated brain lobes. Prima's, most complicated of all, had kept her from panic. .*Be easy. We have enough light and energy.*

A nervous Tertia said, .*Not. Not. Source. Source. Enough. Fuel.*

. *Then we must save it as long as possible. Let liquid become stone and we will repair you daughters.*

The Secundas were replacing the port they had shifted; the harmful vapor was gone. Secunda-1 said: .*We cannot steer the vessel. I do not know where home is.*

.*We can reverse if we bore through the stern and move our engine there.*, said Secunda-2.

.*Maybe but we still do not know how to find direction. Our lights are not enough help.*, said a Tertia.

.*We are still lost.*, another said.

Prima did not like their bickering, but she was grateful that they were not in panic. .*We may have to move the engine daughters but meanwhile make all tight and insulated. .You Tertias help each other repair your damaged limbs and then you Secundas help me to build their brains to greater capacity.*

.That is not wise Prima. The wave almost crackled. *.You found what happened when you made those so clever who would destroy you.*

.Prima I agree with sister., said the other Secunda. *.First they say we do what you will. Then it is we do what we will.*

.You are free with your answers too children. It seems authority is always questioned and perhaps that is not a bad thing. We need all the intelligence we can get and if we ever return we will be grateful.

So they made all tight, and prepared the ship so that it might change course, as Secunda-2 had advised, for the time being (time uncountable) maintaining present course.

They repaired the limbs of the injured, hammered apart and welded together the brains of the Tertias in the patterns of the Secundas, rearranged the Stores, and continued feeding at the cells, or at the Source by climbing out on the hull where they had grips.

When those tasks were done and they were no longer of greater or lesser grades (except for Prima, their guide), they gave themselves the equivalents of terms in accordance with their functions: Steerer, Far-Sensor, Ordnance, Metalworker, Engineer, Maintenance.

Since they had left the belt at a tangent they were not pointed away from the light but now had more than ever, because it was not blocked by asteroids or other ships. Out here the foreign-body population was small, and few meteors collided.

And they waited with their thoughts and their questions. The heavens did not tell them much because they were moving little in relation to the lesser lights; they knew of recurrent meteor showers, and great stone bodies swimming in magnetic currents and flickering reflective

10

lights, but they did not have the time sense to chart their passages.

The original Secundas were pleased to discover that the enhanced Tertias were more interesting company than before, and eager to learn. There was no jealousy in them; they all worked to maintain the ship.

.Prima, said Sensor, .there is a light that is different from the Source or any of the others. It is more like one reflecting from a big stone but I think very far away.

.That is the first body beyond the Ring of Stones. It has much more pull than the ones at home and more than one pull. Many strange ones.

.Shall I set our engine to draw away?

.If we sense it so well we may be too near.

.Primal I thought it was only another stone.

.Stone it is but not only. If it gives us heat and light we can live in it. Prepare the engine to slow us.

.We may crash.

.We cannot land easily but if we take care we may land safely.

By the time the small heater had turned the stone fuel to liquid the rock in the sky was noticeably bigger. Prima could sense its light through the port but not its features.

.Maintenance help me move this cell and I will climb out to discover.

.No Prima that is my task., said Sensor.

The great stone grew bigger yet. .Sensor what do you find?

.Prima this body is spinning but much more slowly than the smaller ones we know. It has a vapor envelope but I also sense some lights I believe are containers of liquefied fuel reflecting the Source. One of these might brake the force of our landing but would burn our limbs.

.If we land on solid stone we crash. A small fluid body might be enough to let us down more easily. Come in now Sensor.

11

.Perhaps we can direct ourselves into orbit., said Engineer.

.With all of these pulls we cannot keep steady., said Steerer.

.How can we be sure of finding supplies among these vapors?. said Ordnance.

.Pull. Pull away. If we touch down we crash or we burn., said Metals.

.My daughters I am not fighting you. I have done enough of that. But I did not make you cringers or shrinkers.

.Now that I have a function I prefer to work, said Engineer. *.Come along Steerer and Metals. Heat up this engine before we do crash.*

They set to and worked. The new retro slowed them, but not quite as much as they wished or needed. Steerer set a course spiraling inward to land as evenly as possible, and Sensor chose the place where liquid might cushion their fall. Then they reinforced insulation once more to keep the corrosive fluid from their limbs.

The mass rose up before them more suddenly than they expected, and the heat of entering atmosphere was a horrid, maddening shock. The half-melting of part of the hull surface warped several light-cells.

Prima and Engineer kept their wits and maintained course downward, pressed against struts. They fought great forces to jettison the fuel and seal the ship. Splashdown sent them into a huge vaporous cloud, skidding, bouncing, and steaming.

And, at last, stop.

But before they could gather their thoughts the stone body opened a mouth and took them down to chaos and darkness where they knew nothing.

2

The morning mists pressed on him like bodies, but the whirling arms that swept down to strike him were the metal limbs of the ergs. He swung his own arms, all four of them, to stop them—no. His father put out a protecting arm to keep them away from him.

Dahlgren cried out: *I have promised—give me a chance! Only let me say goodb*—but they struck at his shoulder and left a diagonal of blood across his shirt—.

No—the blood on Dahlgren's breast was that of the friends he had tried to pull away from the slaughter, and his two arms, spread against the wave of encroaching ergs, cleared a space for his son Sven, one moment of protection. The limbs of the trees were whirling and the storm swept the clearing with spatters of forest rubbish. *I must go now. Do you hear me? Sven?*

No, no!

"Sven!"

He was whirling, flailing, all of his arms entangled as if he were wrestling with himself, and the strong hands that were not his own grabbed at his wrists.

"Sven, you're safe, it's the dream. . . ."

The dream was always different and always the same. Dahlgren sending him away. The day of the slow and bumping journey down the service alley, a brick road that changed colors as the radiations zones were marked off: white at the source, then yellow, red, blue, and green. Green Zone was not as safe as it had been, but there was no cleared area beyond it, and the thatched cottage had been built there. . . .

13

When had he come to believe that Dahlgren had purposely created him a monster and then deserted him? Perhaps during the confusion of that night and day. But the idea had festered in his mind for the nine years he lived in Green Zone with Esther and the goat Yigal, a chance-bred mutant with a human tongue. Eventually it seemed to him that he had always thought so, and the metallic grinding and crashing of ergs in the depth of the forest bore echoes of his father's voice: *You must not try to find me. . . .* But Dahlgren had also said: *I have promised.*

"Sven?" Not his father's voice but Ardagh's.

"Yes, I know," he murmured, "the dream . . ." and fell into it again: His father had become an erg with a thousand arms. . . .

The two strange beings he lived with and loved had pulled him up when despair threatened to engulf him, forcing him to explore his world and use whatever it gave him; Dahlgren's books and pictures told him of the marvels of worlds beyond. In the end it was strangers from these worlds who rescued him.

The tiny ship had crashed with its cargo of young people, Ardagh among them, who refused to be paralyzed with fear of ergs; the company, ape, goat, and all, had set out across the Zones toward the erg-controlled Station and its powerful radio. They had freed Dahlgren and the act had brought Sven freedom from the delusion about his father, and wholeness in destroying the machines that had given him four arms.

Dahlgren had lived to grow old and be loved by his son; he was dead now, like Esther and Yigal, but the nightmare lived its own life and even now, fifteen years later, too many nights took Sven to the clearing where he trembled in the arm of his father and the ergs whirled out of the mist.

But the dream was a night vision. Always in the morning it was swept from his mind.

And each morning or wakening time, wherever he might be—in his bathroom, in a jungle clearing, on board ship, on a raft in a swamp—Sven bent down until he was balanced on his four hands, unfolded his body arching upward until his legs were stretched as straight as possible, and took several steps. Then he practiced two-hand standing in various combinations, and when the blood in his ears was deafening him he folded down and righted himself.

This particular morning, after sweating it out on his bathroom rug, he took a fast shower-and-dry and dressed in a clean cotton fishnet sweatsuit and light zip. Since he was hairless except for brows and lashes he needed do nothing else but clean his teeth. On the fourth day of his thirty-day leave he was content, and wanted breakfast.

He came out into the morning brouhaha. The lodging was a condo allocated to GalFed employees: Each two days of Sven and family gave it a year's worth of living. Ardagh in a whirl of flowered caftan, long brass braid whacking about, was transferring dishes from server to table where Vardy, aged six, was making weird sounds with his tongue hanging out. The fragrance of imported coffee battled with that of native Fthel tea and the perfumery of red and blue blossoms peering inquiringly through the open window and gripping the frame with their tendrils. The two lizards in the terrarium twined necks and tails to bite at each other, squeaking hatred or passion or both.

Sven clapped both pairs of hands. "Shush, Vardy! Out, you trilibells! Fritzl and Fratzl stop whatever the hell that is!" He rapped the glass case and slid the screen closed. Home. He was perfectly happy.

The CommUnit buzzed.

Unheard of.

Buzz.

"Nobody knows we're here," Ardagh whispered. Vardy stopped razzing, the lizards turned quiet, as if silence would make them disappear, and shut up the comm.

"GalFed does," Sven said. Buzz.

Ardagh sighed. "Maybe emerge." She was a field surgeon specializing in the problems of half a score of the most populous species in the Twelveworlds. She flipped the switch, listened, and sighed again.

"It's for you."

Galactic Federation administers the affairs of thousands of worlds in the system of the sun Fthel, a star not situated in the hectic and dangerous center of the galaxy, but fitted into one of its armpits. Although GalFed Central is known as the Twelveworlds, no more than six of the twelve planets are useful. Fthel VIII and IX are mines and dumps; VII is the world of Astronomy and Communications, tended by machines; on VI there are the bases of Observers and Surveyors, and underground the Military; cold V bears the great burden of administrative drudgery and IV is the warm and shimmering garden showplace.

GalFed workers from Sol III who were vacationing or setting up diplomatic ententes on Fthel IV stayed on Cinnabar Keys, two crescents of island chains curving up from the east coast of the southern continent; each had a fair-sized town, Altamir in the north, Miramar in the south. Some of the costly houses were owned by retired executives or buccaneers, others rented by diplomats (often subsidized by GalFed). Modest villas were owned by locals, and Civils and other Indispensables had the loan of ostentatiously unpretentious condos for their vacations. Miramar, because it was rich in subdued elegance and high-toned pop., was known to locals as the Refinery. It also had its pleasure domes and palaces. And many of GalFed's administrative branches.

Two hours after the comm call Sven was glaring at his own Branch Officer, or tentacle, a well-meaning Madame Waldemar, who was unaware of the image she projected.

Her voice was sympathetic. "Ultimately it comes down to money, Mr. Dahlgren."

"Yes, I know Havergal's got plenty of it."

"Sir Frederick. Did your father know him well?"

"Only casually. Havergal's quite a bit younger. I know he's a geneticist." She seemed to be so shy of him that he took pains to speak more civilly. "I don't handle his kind of scientific equipment, and there are plenty of techs who do."

"You have high A1 qualifications and he intends to take many of the newest ergs."

"Where does he mean to take them?"

"He wants . . . to complete your—complete Edvard Dahlgren's experiments on Barrazan Five."

The name of the world made Sven break into a sweat. Ergs and Barrazan V. "Experiments? They ended for good in the Erg Rebellion of twenty-five years ago. My father salvaged whatever could be gathered."

"It seems Havergal wants to fill in the rest, as far as he can go, and you are the only available person who knows that area of the world."

Not only. My wife does—but never again, God help me! "Madame Waldemar, nothing in that place is worth finding out, especially when it costs money. And if he's hiring me away—"

"No, no! You're still working for GalFed—but he wants to pay quite a lot of money, to you and . . . us. . . ."

She trailed off. His dark eyes were incongruous with pale

brows and lashes, and also intimidating. "Um, we do need habitats for colonists."

"Barrazan Five's been given up on hundreds of times."

"Because the people weren't suitable! Any world that supports life has living things in every environmental crevice."

"I can't think what would want to live in that hell's wormholes."

"People whose conditions have become impossibly difficult, Mr. Dahlgren. Yefni being exiled, Crystalloids from a world pulling too near its sun, in danger of going mad from the heat, Meshar who are sick of the wars and the cold of their world—"

"Aren't they the ones Sol Three had all the trouble with, who have brainless lumps for females?"

"No, they're related, but a separate species, and they don't get on at all with the Shar. A world like Barrazan Five would be heaven to them."

"Good luck. But Havergal won't find any garden. The Station's sealed and most of the old ergs are dismantled. My father saw to that."

"With all the ones he wants to bring that won't be a problem." She looked at incoming messages on her screen for a moment to let the flavor of bitterness dissipate. "Havergal applied for a place in the Station when it was being set up. But at that time he was a recent graduate, far too young and inexperienced. . . . I guess that saved his life. But he was always fascinated, and felt finishing that work would complete his own. He's willing, as I said before, to put a lot of money into it, finder's fees for us, risk pay for you."

"I very much want a holiday, Madame Waldemar."

"He's not leaving tomorrow. He just wants to line up his resources. And he'd like a talk with you, at your convenience."

"I have no convenience."

A four-armed freak has no convenience. Shut up, you fool! *You are not going to look like a bottled thing in a cheap circus,* Dahlgren had said, and made him exercise to prove it.

So I look like an ordinary man with four arms, ha, and take dirty jobs where four hands are needed and two bodies won't fit. Marvelous. Shut up!

He went to the Branch's library and punched keys for the Sol III *Who's Who*, Scientists, Genetics, *HAVERGAL, Sir Frederick*, Bart. Family: Havergal Lines, vessels on and under the sea, in air and space. He remembered a bit now. Odd boy out, Freddie, had no heart for business, though his head was sound enough. Let his sister run the concern. Major work in cell mitosis.

Would have loved mine, I bet.

Schools: costly. *Career:* teaching, research. *Married:* Ione Willems Dahlgren. *Children—*

Ione Willems Dahlgren.

Mother? No. Giver of ovum.

Sven punched off and went home in a cab with the windows darkened and screens shut, leaving his rented buzzer in the GalFed Headquarters underground park. Ardagh would be annoyed. Too bad. He crouched hugging himself with all his arms, not trying to stop his chattering teeth.

Ardagh blinked. "Whose ghost have you seen?"

"My mother's."

"What— ?"

Vardy, who had been teasing the lizards, got stuck by a cactus prickle and howled.

"Told you so," said Ardagh. "Sven, will you pull that thing out of his finger, squeeze out some blood, wash it good and spray it with picrocin, it's in the blue bulb."

When he had completed the homely tasks, adding a swab and a kiss to the tearful face, she handed him a glass with a little water and a lot of whiskey.

"Early in the day," he said, and drank.

"Did you hold down your lunch?"

"Yeah."

"You had a pasty look, as if you'd thrown up."

"Thanks."

"Can't help playing doctor. What about your mother?"

He told her about the assignment to Barrazan V, Sir Freddie, the rest. "If she's still alive she's living here. With him."

"You can't blame her for marrying again. She wasn't made of stone—though your father seems to have been, at that time." She was cynical about families. Her own, engineered short and broadly muscular for some tundra colony that failed, hadn't recovered from its bad humor until it produced her. She touched Sven's hairless head, which was not shiny or bone-stretched as if he had gone bald, but covered with soft normal skin, yellowish as the rest of his body, and slightly veined now, like a baby's.

He said, "I know you're right, but I can't help what my nervous system does, no matter how stupid. Barrazan Five! . . . I left the buzzer at Central. I'll get it."

"I'll go for it on the moped."

"He couldn't have what my father had one way, so he got it another. He's sixty-two now. She must be older."

"Not by much. Your father once said he took a chance when he married a much younger woman. He died at seventy-six, it's been two years. . . . You'd better hope she got some happiness. I don't think your father was built for it, poor man."

"He was happy enough with you and Vardy."

"And you. . . . Sven, you don't have to go to that awful place—"

"The job—"

"Damn the job! Do what you think is right, and I'll stick with you."

"I have to go see him. Sir Freddie. Whatever I do about my job, whatever I think of him, and his money, and his—his relationship—I have to be civil."

"Yes." Her eyes remained on him.

He muttered, "I doubt I'll get to see her."

3

The world, once Dahlgren's, violated by one more foreign body, gripped it in crushing force.

Prima returned to consciousness first because she had been riding forward with Steerer and her fall had been broken by the struts before she landed in the storage chamber. She was lying with Steerer and Sensor in a jumble of cells. One of her limbs had broken off, but it did not seem to matter. Even with energy available beneath her she could not move. She was a heavy brain with fragile limbs and had encountered a great body's pull for the first time. She sensed that she had reasoned this out with greater speed than usual. The intense heat was quickening her thought almost to an intolerable degree. She recalled vaguely how her mind had worked an aeon ago before a meteor crash had driven fragments of insulating material among her crystals and had increased her ability to think in an orderly manner. She wondered briefly if these materials had become displaced, and decided not. She had reworked herself many times over, and done it well. It was heat that was dissociating her thoughts, and will that kept them in minimal order.

Sensor's mind was stirring. Prima said, *.We are alive under the surface of this world but we cannot move because of the great pull. The increased heat will tend to make your mind disorderly. Try to resist that.*

Sensor said, *.It is the heat that keeps our minds working right now. My thoughts do run with more speed and confusion but not so much that I cannot tell something of our surroundings. Outside is not all solid stone but vapor which may burn away some of our metal as the liquid fuel does and if it burns our ship we will be destroyed.*

.Perhaps. But it seems to me we are lodged in some crevice with fire below us. Between two kinds of burning we have little choice.

.But Prima you say yourself fire is the Great Mother from which we are formed. Surely we can live in it.

.A mother is a source to come out of not live in. Try to think clearly. There must be a great deal of magnet about in all this stone. It pulls at one of my limbs.

.That does not give us much help Prima.

.No and I don't know what can. But there must be a way of getting about to help the others. I will work with all my being to keep us alive. I will. And die before I give up.

4

Sven called Sir Frederick Havergal at his lab for an appointment and was requested to meet him at home next day.

He had the rest of the day to spend at leisure, so he took Vardy to the beach for an afternoon's dabble. He was more comfortable there than usual in public because he looked more normal in his skin than in four-sleeved clothing. Among the bald-headed, the fat-bellied, the tanned, black, or yellowish skinned, his hairlessness, skin tone, and heavy pectoral development, four-nippled as it was, were not far out of line; his extra arms, set low and slightly to the back on a broad plateau of extra scapulae, folded into a mere resting stand while he tossed Vardy with his upper ones.

The CarryComm hooked to his g-string beeped.

A faint hope that the whole stupid thing would be called off.

No. The voice that said, "Hello, Sven," was an echo of his father's. The android erg-Dahlgren had been constructed by ergs to take the place of Dahlgren during the Rebellion in the Barrazan V Station. The ergs had intended that the replica stand in for Dahlgren wherever his work might send him, as scout and spy, but Modal Dahlgren One had been a double only in the lenses of his makers. Soon after he began to study the man he learned the difference between man and machine, and realized that no one would long mistake him for Dahlgren. He had repudiated his masters and become Dahlgren's defender against them.

When the battle was won father and son had welcomed the erg as their friend, and even gone to court to obtain his rights as Galactic Federation's only robot citizen, representative of Barrazan V, where he had been manufactured. He worked for GalFed at maintenance, spent most of his salary on energy and education, needed little lodging and less furniture, and did not disturb the ecology. At least as dependable as any organic person, he gradually overcame prejudice and wariness—but not before learning to be rather wary of other persons. Occasionally he worked with Sven at tasks where their talents were complementary.

"Sven, I have been asked to take part in a survey of

23

Barrazan Five under the leadership of one Frederick Havergal."

"You too?"

"I was told you would be called for. Is this partnership satisfactory to you?"

"I don't think it's much good for either of us, but I'm glad to be along with you."

"I presume you know about this person?" Mod Dahlgren had his own private machine network.

"Yes. I've got an interview with him."

"Does that disturb you?"

"Because he married my rather distant mother? It did quite a lot at first, but if I take the assignment I'd better get used to it. Why do you ask, Modal?"

"It seems odd to me that he wants us along with him. Any Beta three tech can service ergs."

Sven was a little disturbed by the intensity of the finely expressive voice. "Well, after all, we do know some of the territory." Perhaps, he thought, Mod Dahlgren did not wish to see a stranger taking the place of Dahlgren on "his" world. But he did not suggest that. "I doubt he's a mad scientist. You mostly find them on the tri-V."

"I am happy to be reassured, Sven. It will be good to work with you again. Good wishes."

"And you go in good order, Modal."

Sir Frederick opened his door. His house was medium-sized, and graceful without being showy. It was well made, and so was its owner. Shortish—but everyone was short compared with Sven; stocky, but not fat; balding; neatly trimmed auburn beard and mustache. He had hazel eyes with slightly reddened lids, and a few freckles on his forehead and the backs of his hands: a man sensitive to weather.

"I'm very happy to meet you, Mr. Dahlgren." And seemed genuinely to be so.

Sven offered a hand which Havergal took in both his own warm ones. "Sven is quite all right, Sir Frederick."

"And Freddie good enough for me. The Sir never quite fit."

"But Sir Freddie has a nice ring to it."

Careful, Sven. You don't want to like him too soon.

Havergal laughed. "That's rich. What would you like to drink?"

"I take my alcohol with supper. Tea now, if you have it, please."

"The chicken soup of GalFed Central." His host and employer pushed a button. A cabinet opened and an impeccable tea wagon wheeled into the room. "'Fraid I can't complete the image with cucumber sandwiches. I loathe them. There's some quite decent jam tarts."

Sven took tea in two hands, pastry with a third and napkin in a fourth without seeming to show off. Sir Freddie watched with an appreciative eye but refrained from comment; Sven kept his eyes on the refreshments and did not search for traces of Ione Willems Dahlgren Havergal. The surroundings gave no hint: He knew nothing of his mother but her name.

"I haven't asked to see Mod Dahlgren and I hope he's not insulted. Truly, I'm not sure of what to say, and I can't offer him anything to eat."

"I think he's most comfortable with me. He knows what's involved."

"Yes." Havergal sighed. "I've bitten off a great deal . . . perhaps I shouldn't admit it. . . ."

Sven said carefully, "Knowing what I do about Barrazan Five, I find it hard to think of it as valuable."

"Well, you know, it's always been a dream . . ." The hazel eyes slitted a trifle.

He doesn't want to go. Not really. He doesn't need to discuss all this with me either.

Desultory talk. Sven, having satisfied his host's desire to get a look at him, finished his tea and sensed he had permission to leave.

For the first time, as he rose, he noticed the holo cube set into the wall. Sir Frederick and family. Taken some years ago: The man had more hair; the woman—what could one tell from a picture? Boy and girl. A great deal. He caught his own image in a mirror.

You have her eyes and mouth, Dahlgren had said, *and are certainly better-natured than either of us.*

Dahlgren had tried to save something of the wife who left him: her ovum, half of his son. The ergs had tried to demoralize him by creating a monster and had succeeded in giving him a loving son.

He blinked at the mirror and saw for a moment, back through the room, the woman, her eyes and mouth, before she became a shadow in a doorway. It was not Sir Frederick who had invited him.

"I have a son very much like yours. Thank you for your hospitality, Sir Frederick. I'll expect your call."

The man's mouth worked. He said, words forcing out, "He was lost, accident in space." Swallowing hard. "He's been declared dead."

Sven went rigid. He stammered, "Forgive me." On a wild impulse he said, "Sir Frederick, would you like to meet mine?"

"Why, I—thank you. I believe—yes, I believe I would."

"Sven, that's wild!" Ardagh grabbed Vardy like a monkey mother. He tried to wriggle away, but she was very strong; she had much more stamina than Sven, who tired easily.

"I didn't mean for him to go alone! One of us would take him. We don't have to if you feel that strongly. I spoke too fast off the top of my head. I wanted . . . I wanted her to see him."

"Sven, it's all right. Really. Just, first, find out what happened to their son."

Sven's condo had no terminal, and on holiday he had never wanted one before. His local library had several, along with tapes and microfiche, in a functional room behind the antiqued bookshelves. It gave him more privacy than the Branch did.

He forced his way through Sir Freddie's entry, found son, Peter, depending from it:

Botanist, youngest winner of Obermann Award for achievement in mycology . . . GalFed Surveyor lost . . .

A year and a half ago. Still missing, presumed . . .

He looked away to think for a moment and looked back to corroborate what he thought he had seen.

Yes. Sir Frederick Havergal had married fourteen thirtydays after the birth of his son.

So what? That's not my business. I hope it's not.

He was sick of the whole matter, turned away to leave it—and pulled back once again, to finish the task no matter how he might regret it.

NewsFax for the date of the missing ship report gave him one more puzzle piece: The ship had been lost in the Shevah sector, number 748. Following a dreadful suspicion now, he called up System/Worlds Registry: Uncolonized properties.

Shevah contained the Barrazan system.

"I think I learned more than I wanted."

Ardagh said, "I hope I haven't put ideas into your head."

"No more than I had before. But I don't want to examine them too closely."

"It seems to me the man's putting people at risk by taking them along to such a dangerous place."

"Ardagh, jungle isn't dangerous by our colonial standards. You know that. Going there with proper equipment is much less dangerous than living out in it the way we did. And the only ergs left are tame ones. It's still a sickly filthy place I hate more than anywhere else I've been. I guess that's why they're offering risk pay. But I can't fault Havergal for that." He paused for a moment, and added, "And I'm not ready to trust him completely, either."

5

Change.

.*Prima it is hotter and we have been shifting. The pull of this stone body is dragging us farther into the opening.*

.*Can you move at all Sensor?*

.*No the pull is too strong and I have no space.*

.*One of my limbs is broken off. If I can grasp it with another and reach you it might help as a brace.*

.*What is the use of that Prima when we can not get out?*

.*If we can only find a way to move we can reinforce our limbs with our metal supplies then use the insulating plates to protect us from the heat and perhaps our borers to dig our way out of the stone.*

.*The atmosphere will burn our limbs and other metals by then.*

.*Not all metals burn in atmosphere or there would be none in this stone.*

.*What way can we do this?*

.*We will discover.*

That was madness and she knew it.

6

The Yefni live on the moon of a gas giant in an atmosphere of smog and on a surface of bog relieved by hot acid lakes. Since the core is dense and the volcanism considerable, the place is one of sulfur and brimstone. The crew of the Surveyor who made the first landing by emergency thought they had died and gone to hell.

But no; it was merely a world with many life forms, one actually sentient, most feeding on mud. The crew did not wonder at the miracle of sentient life in a hellish place: Any kind of life is a miracle everywhere. They were simply grateful to have their ship pulled out of the bog so that they could call for help.

The majority of the crew happened to be Solthree, and to their eyes the Yefni looked much like overgrown pythons in size and annelid worms in texture. They were brown or black, and had a silver-white band of eye cells about twelve centimeters from what appeared to be the front end. At front they also had two sharp horns, curving in opposite directions, for boring to wherever they wanted to go; mouths, for feeding, gill slits for breathing and manipulating into warbling speech. At the tail end they had retractable horny knives for slashing at obstacles, occasionally other Yefni. Their worm appearance was produced not by rings but by a single helix of cartilage supported by a great deal of muscle and manipulated by a brain distributed in many ganglions requiring a tremendous feed of nerve networks.

For all their handlessness and hellish surroundings, the Yefni were certainly a people. They had lively communal cultures and about a tenth were low-grade telepaths. Best of all, they were cooperative and knew how to handle their surroundings: Three or four working together made a mighty hand—as the GalFed Surveyor found out. If they were often brutal, the Yefni were not vicious, and were even generally cheerful; more than capable of the deadly courtesy of those forced to live in extreme conditions. GalFed immediately enlisted them for diplomatic service.

The homes of the Yefni are sandstone igloos built not over deep pits but out in the atmosphere on hardened ground for refreshing coolness; in one of these the three oldest children of the local District President were quarreling over the succession, even though the President had not the least intention of either dying or abdicating.

"I am the eldest," said Mef.

"And I the strongest," said Naf.

"And I the most intelligent," said Zyf.

"Yes, he is the eldest . . . strongest . . . most intelligent," said their current mates (hermaphroditic, like their partners). Two of them were swollen with progeny and rather nervous. The contenders, expecting confrontation, had avoided conceiving.

They were almost equally matched in strength, size, and intelligence. None was either telepathic or particularly diplomatic.

The mates/seconds withdrew toward the wall. Mef, Naf, and Zyf took positions in a triangle. Blue fires in the sconces lit them dimly, a slurry of mud softened by their writhing swirled beneath them, their coils and horns glistened savagely. Unlike worms or snakes, Yefni cannot crawl or slither; they coil, twist, spring. Horns that can bore sandstone can shred anything softer.

They honed the sprung knives of their tails against those horns.

"Say the word," said Zyf.

"To you, seed brother," said Naf.

"I am eldest and I say it," said Mef. "Now!"

A fourth voice said, "No!" and an eye-banded head appeared through the roof opening, one of the horns notched in official insignia. It was followed by a body coiling down, then a second and a third.

The contenders recognized them as Presidential guards—whose tail blades were particularly long and wicked—and froze. It would have been quite in order for the guards to deliver paralyzing crosscuts or demand the siblings maim themselves thus, at once.

But the chief guard, Suf, said: "You three will come now to your progenitor for judgment, and you others, if you value your seed capsules, will not leave this place."

The miscreants crouched in shame before the igloo of the Progenitor, heads buried in their coils.

"For what did I bear you, and bear with you in care and patience?" asked Nyf, their parent and President. It was a rhetorical question. He asked it whenever he saw them. "I can will the Presidency to one of you for only as long as you have the power to maintain it, and I know of at least two district Presidents who are childless, and whom I had planned to ask the favor of adopting you as heirs in succession. That would have been fair, would it not?"

"Oh, indeed so!" his heirs shrilled through their coils.

"But it seems you believed me to be an old and feeble creature on the point of death—or perhaps one or more of you had it in mind to make me so!"

"No, never!" The three raised their heads in shock. "We admit to being jealous and combative—for, after all, we are three grown men, progenitors ourselves, without useful work—but we would have fought only to the yielding point and had no thought whatever—"

"—no, absolutely no—"

31

"—thought whatever—"

"—of harming you! May ESPs read our minds to assure you of our honesty!"

"Be grateful for my belief in you because I do believe. But I tell you that none of you nor your seed will be President of any district. Not on this world. For GalFed has offered me another. There you and your families will found a colony! In that way this district, which offers you to the Universe—through me!—will become the greatest in the world, and I its greatest President, and my name will be remembered forever. You, I am sure, will find areas of power for yourselves where you can harm no one else. Lift your heads!"

Numbly, they did so. His tail lashed out so quickly its movement was a blur, leaving each sib with a dark narrow line across the eyeband, from which the yellow viscous blood began to weep a tear.

"You have had a blind spot in your minds. Now you will each have one in your sight, and you must live with it as best you can."

7

The girl was sitting cross-legged on a white figured rug manipulating an antique toy. It was a cube with its colored planes marked in squares, fifty-four in all, and various axes to turn one layer at a time, mixing colors in exquisitely confusing configurations. The girl was a round-faced Asian who looked about fourteen, but moved with the scrunched gracelessness of an overgrown child of eight or nine. She twisted the planes eight, ten, fifteen times into irredeemable confusion and over and over again returned them in three or four twists to their one-color-plane configuration. She had been doing this for an hour and a half without stopping since she had been first been brought into the room and given the toy, and was ready to go on as long. But she had begun rocking on her hips, and the woman who came into the room carrying the heavy glasstex case set it down, gently took the cube from the girl's hands. She pointed at the door leading to the bathroom and in coarse pidgin directed the girl to use it. The girl obeyed; the woman wiped the cube with a cloth, replaced it in its original pasteboard box, printed with an explanation in Hungarian about exercising logic, and put it in a cupboard with other oddities, ancient and modern. The room contained nothing else but a desk and chair which, like its rug, were pieces of art. It was a round room with one mirror and half a dozen mildly decorated pilasters that converged toward the soft illumination of a circular skylight.

When the girl returned, the woman pointed to the case and said, "Han Li, this is Crystalloid." And to the Crystalloid, "I am called Rebekkah VanderZande and Han Li is your interpreter."

Inside the case something glinted and shifted. Han Li blinked without interest and cracked her knuckles. Then she went glass-eyed and folded her hands.

"How long am I to be kept here?" she said in a cold hard *lingua* completely unlike her own grunting tongue.

"Until we learn about each other," said Rebekkah. She had had some odd clients and these were not the oddest. She would have been called an anthropoethnoethologist if there were such a term. For GalFed she worked with and studied people of all kinds, mainly here in her consulting room, and was called Liaison.

"There is nothing of you I wish to learn," said the Crystalloid through Han Li. "I do not understand the delay in taking me and my stonebrothers to our new world." Han Li blinked and added, "I am unique and utterly miraculous."

"No need to read the minds, dear," said Rebekkah crisply, "though I am far from surprised." To the Crystalloid, "You Stonebrother, the ship is not ready to take you, and I am not satisfied that the interpreter is ready to care for herself."

"This bickering is warping my facets."

"Turn down your thermostat, man. Come outside and make yourself familiar with strangeness. It is a good beginning."

But the stonebrother was determined to sulk, and Rebekkah left him to do so. He was a normal example of his species and would not be propitiated.

Rebekkah VanderZande was a tall wiry woman with extremely wavy gray-white streaked hair, which she kept short enough to avoid overwhelming herself and others. Her face and features were very narrow and pink, her forehead deeply lined. She wore the GalFed insignia but not the standard monochrome zip. Hers were cut from prints or jacquards, usually in different permutations of pink, cream, blue, and gray. She had dressed Han Li in a plain rich sandstone fabric, a darker shade of her skin color. She had no idea of the girl's country of origin, or who had given her the name.

Han Li, the twenty-year-old orphan of a small festering war somewhere, had been saved from the triple injustices of starvation, mental incapacity, and growth-hormone deficiency by a talent as mysterious as it was useful. Her discoverers had learned from a dying family acquaintance that the seemingly eight-year-old girl was seventeen. While being treated with growth stimulants she had been placed in a children's camp because of her size: The guards there, in greater number and more carefully chosen than those in adult camps, ensured at least that she was not battered or sexually abused. The place lived on government handouts and individual charity that fed and dosed but did not love or teach. No one there ever learned whether Han Li was as dull as she seemed, even when one of the personnel, an ESP-three in charge of placement, picked up on a talent he knew existed but could not identify, and brought her to the attention of MedPsych. It was a peculiar, almost a wild talent: ESP directed only to Crystalloids. Identification had taken long and been worth while. Han Li was one in five billion. And sometimes MedPsych forgot that she was a person, not a Crystalloid.

Rebekkah remembered.

She took the knobby quick-growing hands that still curled like a baby's and said, "Han Li, you can learn to speak *lingua* very well in your sleep, but you can't learn to read that way. I am going to teach you what your name looks like printed and written on the terminal, and when you can show me you remember it, you can eat a big piece of almond cake or solve a really hard maze, or both, but neither of those until you start reading. You cannot work for Galactic Federation without that."

8

Sven tried once to make contact with Havergal in order to arrange a visit with Vardy, but the man was unavailable and he did not try again. Three days before the end of his thirtyday he was summoned to familiarize himself with the expedition. Living in orbit for ten days before departure, he would not be very far away from his family, but nowhere near enough. He had had a holiday of sorts, with tension pulled through it like a tight wire.

Ardagh said, "It would have been nice if they'd hired me on too, but the people they need aren't my specialties."

"The world is rotten enough for one, and I don't even want to think of both of us being there again."

"I'd like to think it would be less rotten if I were along," said Ardagh a bit tartly.

Sven grinned and shook his head. "I'd worry that much more."

On one of those glorious mornings with the flowers pestering at the windows, the lizards noisily copulating, and Vardy licking the rim of the jam pot . . .

Sven, two meters of him, was on his knees for wife and son. Ardagh had not put on fat in the fifteen years since her adventures on Barrazan V; she was the short heavy-muscled person she had been, a good arm-filler. She dripped a couple of tears down Sven's neck. He said, "You'll probably be gone off on a job when I get back; I'll relay to Central."

"I'll do my best to be around."

Next day the cleaners and packers came to the quarters, and Ardagh was sweating more than they, supervising, when her emergency beeper sounded. She never got over the wrench of parting, still ached, and delivered herself of several curses that startled the workers before she answered.

A long-distance crackle said, "Bingham here pulling you into Port Central asap."

Not likely a Solthree emergency. "What specs?"

"Meshar neutrals heading for Barrazan Five."

Shipmates of Sven's. Now if the flight got delayed a little—oh Ardagh, unworthy! "What's wrong with the exomed—Ruksari—in that palace of yours?"

"Cerebral hemorrhage. Doctors die sometimes."

"Sorry."

"He was the only duty general around because the oxygen breathers on the wards are mostly out with the bronchial fungus. You'd have to be inoculated."

"Ruksari was good. He had lots of students—"

"Who are scared silly. He was the vain kind who picks clucks."

"Damn it, Bingo, I don't know anything about Meshar. My neutrals range runs to two or three worlds. Haven't they got their own medic?"

"Yes, and he's here with twenty relatives. They all have long canines and sharp claws and they're making everybody nervous."

"I thought they were hominid."

"They are."

"The patient?"

"A female grossly swollen and in great pain. Medic by interpreter claims pregnant. Seemed normal on takeoff— what, Ambara'il?—no, just beginning to show."

"Are there doubts about a pregnancy?"

"Patient cries out it's some thing, whatever, can't make out—evil spirit? Amba can't tell. Presume she doesn't feel gravid."

"Has she ever borne children?"

"Well, Amb? No."

"Without experience, how can she tell?"

"From the other women in the group, of course! The colony's a family cell, each married, so to speak, to all potential mates. Both sexes have personal cycles of fertility four or five times a year. This is a good arrangement for people with low fertility."

"And the medic is—"

"Yes, one of the group-mates. He'd certainly want a child."

"Then get those tests and scans going! Have you started?"

"Um, he claims to be afraid of the machines, calls them evil engines . . . but he's really just afraid—of being in a strange place and out of his depth, being shown up as ignorant and losing authority. I don't want him to scare the others."

"And you want to dump all the responsibility on me! What do you think I am?"

"Right now the best exo–general surgeon and diagnostician in the world! Please, Ardagh, just switch on visual and look at her."

Ardagh sighed. She knew that the first blink of the dark figure, grossly belly-bloated on the stretcher, would do her in. Low painsong unpausing for breath through pointed teeth, red-veined talons clawing the green linens.

And I know nothing.

She sighed again. "I presume you've got a buzzer on the way?"

"Half an hour."

"I need longer. Have to drop the kid at the care center. Work up the case as best you can."

"We're putting together a file."

"And I want one of the buzzer screens kept free to transmit whole-body scans during the trip."

"I told you he won't let—"

"I'll see that he lets. Let me talk to him."

"I'm not sure I can get him to do that. Meshar men are, um—"

"But he brought her to hospital, didn't he? Why?"

"I told you. Because the woman is in extreme pain."

"And he expected only men to attend her? I hope not. Does he truly want her attended to? If he won't speak I'll have to talk to her. He can't stop me if you're in charge. You are in charge, aren't you?"

The Meshar were a hominid people, dark gray or black,

ears high and pointed, teeth long and pointed, particularly canines, thin-lipped mouths that seemed large enough only to accommodate the teeth. Their small black eyes swam in red membrane like pomegranate seeds. The hair on their faces, like that on the rest of their bodies, was thin down mixed with sparser and longer guard hairs. Their chins were small and the noses platyrrhine: so flat to the face their nostrils only avoided being vulnerable openings because they were stoppered with reddish spongy tissue; bacteria populating it fed on whatever contaminants reached it through the bloodstream or the atmosphere. Meshar breathed sweet and quiet.

"Doctor Sandek," said Interpreter.

"How do you do? You speak *lingua*, Doctor?"

"Better than he'll admit to," said Ambara'il, a blue-green Kylklad, in Ardagh's native English.

Doctor Sandek sat as if in silent reproach. His eyes were narrowed, his lipless mouth an almost invisible seam. Only his eyes slid a little in their red membranes.

Let's go, Ardagh—Foreign Devil strikes!

"Doctor Sandek, I hope you will speak with me, because I am the only person here who can help you."

Glare. Weathered skin rippling faintly. "I presume you are doing me a great honor." He showed small sharp fangs in what seemed a snarl of near-satisfaction. "I let that patient die before I let a woman. With a knife. Touch her."

"Then you will do nothing?"

"No! You with the wisdom will tell me what to do and my people will help. None but I touch."

Ardagh glared back, then bit her tongue and let the froth of her ill humor boil off. From his point of view he was making sense.

She asked in slow careful *lingua* that Sandek must understand, "Interpreter, are you and the Doctor alone?"

"Yes, in a comm cubicle."

"Cut out anyone else." She took a deep breath. "Doctor Sandek, let us start again. My name is Ardagh Colquhoun, and I really am the only person with the wisdom. Knowledge, anyway. I hope I have the wisdom. There certainly is no one else available. I have treated many patients from a good number of worlds. Some I could not help because nothing whatever would help. Others I could not help because they would not be touched by strangers or examined by machines. They could have been saved."

"Indeed." Sandek showed no sign of changing his mind.

"The scanning machine is something like a camera. It will not touch or interfere with your woman in any way if—"

Ambara'il interrupted, "He allowed blood to be taken."

"Good . . . it is nothing compared even to the needle that took her blood. I hope you will allow it."

"It seems I must."

She was a bit taken aback. "That's helpful. I also hope you will speak with me again when I arrive." She sagged with relief when the surly face flicked off the screen. "My God, Bingo, I never thought he'd cave in like that."

"I guess he had to do a ritual dance before accepting help. And you, you're out of sorts, Ardagh."

"Yes. Sven left yesterday for the same place this lot is going to. And it's a rotten territory. I know from experience." She looked around the room at the flowers, the glassed-in verandah where the great ferns swayed just beyond the panes. "Has the report on the blood come up from the lab yet?"

"Yes," said Bingham. "Base oxygen, carrier iron, heme nobody's seen before, would take a while building. But the other women aren't at all bothered by a little bloodletting and they're all being typed and tested, so we should have supplies."

"Good. Pulse in that lump?"

"Yeah, not sure it's fetal. Could be her own."

"They suckle? Couldn't see over that belly."

"Three breasts."

"Good providers. Lactation: check for signs. Practice for Ruksari's nestlings. Be there soon, and out."

She looked at Vardy. Edvard after his grandfather, his self curled up as in a seed. He had been very quiet, as always when he sensed that Mama was at work. He accepted her absences and Sven's; he accepted their presence. He loved them with a child's helpless love for its mother and father, and they were a loving mother and father. Whether he loved their presence, which was more cake than bread-and-butter, she had to take on trust. He did not know, and would not be told for quite a while what lengths she and Sven had gone to, making sure he would be born with the right number of vertebrae, arms, nipples, scapulae, ribs. Was it worth so much trouble to avoid their kinds of misery when they had reached their own kinds of love and acceptance—even to bear a child at all in the black light of all the genetic warping they had endured?

Something else to take on trust.

Vardy said calmly, "You're going away again."

She snatched him to her. "Yes."

His voice was muffled against her shoulder. "But you always come back."

"Damn right."

9

In lightlessness and savage heat, Prima's thoughts whirled around her like the rocks of the asteroid belt.

Her mind pulled away, in self-defense, back across the aeons to the beginnings of her sentience.

The beginnings:

Crystals shaken loose in a stone crack or hollow during a carom against other stones, a wash of heat. Fusion into an amorphous mass by a stream of free-flowing metals. A dreaming in crystal wave and tremble while the hollow stone cracked and cooled around her once more. Spin in free fall. Light, the Source—turning away, fissure of rock open to lesser sources, the distant sparks: Light. Dark. Light. Dark. A grating: carom, a slowing. More generous gifts of the Source. Pull. A streamer of metal coiled about her wanting to reach its own Source in the stone.

One . . . what? . . . reacher. Limb. It moved very slightly, it was so malleable in the heat left by collision. Stiffened gradually. Stopped.

Light. Dark. Light. Dark. Pulse-pulse of thought: now Source, now nothing. Wordless, observing.

Event: graze. Jolt, heat, light. Other crystals surrounded her. Welded to the wall, she did not stir.

Crash. A melting wave wrenched her body free and at the same time joined crystals and their waves to extend her mind. Her vessel of rock spun, skimmed, settled, spun no longer. Source poured through the crack into her hollow, her self flamed out its measureless journey.

Measureless?

★ ★ ★

*.I have hold of your limb now Prima. Steerer is closest to me
and I will try to bring her a power cell.*

She wrenched herself to the present. *.That is well done
Sensor.*

.Prima will we ever return?

.Work and believe daughter. There is nothing else.

10

The MedServ buzzer was designed to bring doctors from
half a world away and prime them as they came. Ardagh
watched screens while she rode, ate the stale lunchpack and
drank the tasteless juice. She hated to find herself so sullen,
so deprived of Sven and Vardy, so hostile to Sandek. She
regarded the images of the Meshar.

They were rather grotesque in the eyes of some Solthrees because they were strange hominids, but a three-
breasted woman was not unusual in the way four-armed
Sven was. The three breasts were small and looked like the
points of a flat leather collar lying teatless on the chest, two
in the usual places and one centered below underneath;
they had a certain neatness and elegance.

Ardagh had the comm line open and was watching
examination of the other women. "There's one with
swollen mammaries. Is she postpartum or pregnant?"

"A post who had a stillbirth," said Ambara'il. "A
mistake to ship out so near term. She's full of milk, you
can tell by the everted teats ready for suck. The men don't
have teats, not even vestiges. Meshar are sexually anom-
alous. The sentient female is still relatively young in their
species."

"I'd say our patient is not ready to give milk."

"As an egg-layer I wouldn't know. But Ruksari's best student did. You have to give him credit for that."

"I'm more than anxious to. But according to Sandek the woman is adult and should be fertile. . . . Still . . . she looks to me to be less developed than the others except for that belly."

"Now I have more information from our student, Doctor Heg. The patient, name of Erez, has an irregular heartbeat and breathing trouble."

"I'll be there inside an hour. What's that braid kind of thing she's got around her neck?"

"In this Meshar culture the rite of passage for both sexes is: as they reach puberty and the longer hairs grow they pull them out one by one, and when they can weave them into a necklace they've shown enough patience, determination, and manual skill to enter the adult community."

"If it doesn't infect the follicles, it's a lot better than some tests I've seen."

"Meshar rarely infect."

Port Central Hospital on Fthel IV was the only all-species care center in the world, and it offered the same climate as Port City: hot, wet, and with a summer that lasted half the year. The huge and ugly building provided a hundred-odd alien environments in its upper reaches, and because it was run by GalFed, was naturally underfunded. Few of even the most dedicated, the most widely experienced of doctors wished to practise at Port: The city was the door to immigration both in the system and the galaxy, and strangers of unknown species who fell ill in transit were a nightmare to themselves and the hospital. Ardagh found work there fascinating but was glad to be based on the administrative world of Fthel V, where at least she knew her neutrals.

44

She found Bingham and Ambara'il waiting in an ante-room with Doctor Heg. Heg was a Tignit with fourteen tentacles and a snail foot; he was wearing a bubble to keep out oxygen (Ardagh forgot what he did breathe) and spoke by signing. He said: *The scan is done and there is no baby.*

"How long has the swelling been growing?"

Bingham said, "If it was just showing before embarkation, it should be about six thirtydays, which *is* their gestation, but I think this is more like years. We made careful comparisons with the other women: The sexual development is retarded, as you suggested."

"Yeah, maybe a tumor in a gland that produces a sex hormone, if they work any way like us. If she was a Solthree, missing menses and a lot of hair growing on her arms, I could say: likely a tumor of the adrenal cortex. Meshar, I don't know. What about her heart?"

"Either the tumor's squeezing something or the gland controls heart–lung function too."

"You people have talked to Sandek more than I. How capable do you think he is?"

"A pretty good general surgeon for Meshar is the consensus. They're a tough lot, and I'd say more careful about themselves than we'd tend to believe because they seem to move so close to the ground. He could probably manage a cesarean. The puzzle is how he could let the tumor get this far."

"Were they in deepsleep or stasis coming out here?"

Bingham was embarrassed. "Stasis. We never allow first-time off-worlders to travel in an unwakeable state. Under those conditions it might well have grown. All the talking I've done with him I never thought about that. I've been blaming him unjustly."

"It's hard not to. But it's not hard to understand his nerves. A woman in a small group with low fertility. . . . Let's talk to him."

45

★ ★ ★

"Doctor Sandek, I am Doctor Colquhoun who spoke to you before. We are in private here. I will not touch a knife to your woman but I am willing to give you advice if you want it."

Sandek was a short charcoal-skinned man with bandy legs. He had the crepey fold of vestigial wing-skin in each armpit and was dressed in a leather tunic, sleeveless and knee length, beautifully tanned and dyed in quarterings of red and green, with a design of black and white dots on the left shoulder. They looked part heraldic and part binary, and were obviously identifiers.

Unlike his cousins the Shar he had a tail. It was a tough flattish leathery thing, horizontally ridged, ending at the ankles with a tip shaped like the ace of spades.

"I understand there is a growth," he said.

"Yes." She spoke carefully, not to increase his agitation. "We need to scan the other women to learn as much as possible about them."

"Go do! Go do!" Meshar did not sweat, or not apparently. Sandek was almost in a panic. "A growth that size cannot be removed without killing my Erez."

"We could not possibly remove it; her vitals are embedded in it. We would try to arrange it so that the growth dies and she lives."

Sandek relaxed a little, and so did Ardagh. Only a little.

The Meshar women, not being in pain, found the scanner experience amusing. But Sandek winced while he followed direction to take suction samples of the tumor.

Ardagh was not surprised at the results of analysis: discovery of a male steroid analogous to those of Sol-threes. No one yet had a name for it. "Where do you think this is coming from, Doctor Sandek?"

"Dysfunction of egg producer. You call ovary."

46

"We usually get this kind of growth on a gland connected with the kidney. No reason it has to be that way for Meshar. Now we'd better talk to Doctor Heg."

Doctor Heg, like Sandek—and Ardagh—had suffered a bad case of nerves from sudden heavy responsibility after the death of Ruksari. Otherwise he was a more than competent doctor.

"Heg says it is best to use ultrasound to break up a few small areas where the tumor is choking Erez. That can be done without cutting, but there is some risk of an aneurysm now. If an emergency operation was necessary I presume you could handle it with our help."

Sniff.

"In which case she would need transfusions."

"No worry for that. We do it. Can you destroy the tumor with the ultrasound machine?"

"No, but we have chromed and tagged the cyst samples to make a serum that will stop the cells from reproducing. After everything is done she will look no different—but she will be."

"How long to shrink the tumor?"

"I don't know. I'm a field surgeon, like you, not a specialist. She will have to be treated and watched a long while."

"You know her case best now. You will do that."

"I'm sorry, Doctor. I can't stay here only to attend to your woman."

"No. You will come with."

"I certainly will not! And she can't leave here!"

"No! *She* comes with, dead or alive. We go *all*. You operate and come with to take care of her, or I operate as well as I know how and she comes with us live or die."

"Doctor Sandek, I—"

"Before you operate you swear an oath to come with."

"For God's sake, why can't you leave her to be cared for here!"

"We live by our customs as you by yours. She comes."

"Doctor Sandek, I have a child here!"

"I know of you, and of your child. And also of your man. You have people here, who will take good care of your child. Care, I think, even with love. All of us Meshar can give love to our woman. Only one, who is not of us, can give her good care. Choose. And then swear."

Sonofabitch, you! She wanted to be off in a corner somewhere, trembling and weeping. Instead she was scrubbing. Bastard!

A shiver of noiselessness. Another. One more. In a short while pieces of tissue would slough and free the organs they were throttling. The woman lay peaceful for the moment; she had been quieted by anesthesia. Probably she would not die.

If she lived and could not have children would they accept her? But Sandek had said nothing about children. . . .

Ardagh was free to go home to Vardy. No law kept her, no one stood in her way. Sven would be horridly angry to find her on Barrazan V again—and she loathed the place. The unreasonable promise forced from her by Sandek had no weight; she could move out into the darkness.

She stood at the end of the bed and watched the woman, still breathing harshly, her face almost hidden by the heave of her belly.

With small precise hands Sandek adjusted the ventilator, a Solthree one not quite right for an almost noseless people. Ardagh gripped the railing with the square stubby fingers he had no reason to complain of. He asked, "When is the serum ready? We leave in three days."

"I told you. Tomorrow." Bastard.

His face rose from Erez's to hers. Slowly. "Likely she will not have children. She will care for our other ones." She stared. "Did you think we would drive her away? Kill her?" He made some kind of sound. A snort. Something.

"Sandek, what is wrong with your world?"

"We were driven to it. . . . Doctor. It is very dry, cold, mostly dark. There are no running things, as here, no smells or colors. What we eat we scrape from stones, dig from soil, pull from foul waters."

"The place you are going to is just as terrible in its opposite."

"Not for us. You will see."

He lifted the woman's head and removed the braid from her neck. When he put it around Ardagh's she did not flinch. It was not coarse but closely woven and very oily, was in fact bound by Meshar skin oil. It smelt faintly of musk—alien but familiar.

"She will miss it when she comes awake," Ardagh said quietly.

Sandek touched the tumor's bulge with one long-nailed finger. "That she will not miss." He left.

Ardagh turned the sheet back and contemplated the swelling, smooth and shining in a skin that was usually grainy as weathered planks. It was still a terrible thing and would it shrink? Whether or not, the breath came even, and the monitor blinked and beeped the Meshar's steady hundred beats. The female Meshar tail was even tougher than the male's and its point was like an arrowhead. Ardagh knew that the old Shar had stubby vestiges, like their wing drapes, but these people, having kept or repossessed the mutation, must have needed tails for an urgent reason.

The woman, half-conscious, raised a hand to her neck and began to whimper. Ardagh fingered the braid. She

49

would have returned it, but there was something both terrible and moving in Sandek's gesture. At the same time she felt a viper of guilt threading the strands: She had wanted to be with Sven, even in that terrible place, even in the fear of her ignorance of Yefni and Meshar. Certainly she had learned enough—perhaps too much—about Meshar in a very short time.

Erez's whimpering was painful; her head turned from side to side. Ardagh clasped one of her wrists in a bracelet of reassurance, then checked the monitor and went to the supply room. She unclipped her own braid, shook her hair loose, snipped a long strand of the brass-gold, clamped it, braided it and closed the circle with a surgical staple. She rebraided her hair and went back to the bedside. She was about to slip the circlet over the head and paused; it was too raw. She rubbed her fingers over Erez's skin, so deeply grained and oiled, so oily that nurses had put quilted padding under the body to catch the excess. Perhaps in the cold dry places where Meshar lived, the oil protected like blubber. She rubbed it into the new braid; Erez watched with narrowed eyes. Inadvertently she touched the swelling; her eyes widened, her face twisted. The whimpering, which had stopped with the soothing of Ardagh's fingers, began again. Ardagh stroked Erez's cheek and lifted her head to place the braid. Erez touched it, smelled it—it had darkened with oil—her mouth pulled into the narrow Meshar grimace, and before Ardagh could stop her she had bitten her thumb on a fang and touched it to Ardagh's mouth.

She dared not wipe it with those eyes on her; she licked it; it was very salty.

The woman Erez smiled, or grimaced, again.

Ardagh sighed. *Blood kin,* no doubt. She shook her head and swabbed the thumb with probably useless antiseptic. Likely the antitet would not work on Meshar, even if they needed it.

50

11

The ship's observation satellite spun the graticule, the world's net of meridians and parallels: It noted that the lake in Haruni Crater had drained away and the magma chamber had risen. That did no more than change a few contour lines and shoot steam vents through the lattice. But the world was no orange in a net bag. Its atmosphere swam continuously with thick cloud that obscured most of the surface, the rains of its forests roared down to wash headlands from the seas or silt up deltas in the rivers at a furious rate, and the rains were driven by great winds. The world had a fast pulse. The small charted triangle, 150 km in east-west apex and 75 km at north-south base on the west, was a relatively stable part, and a tiny one, in spite of having been grandiosely named after Dahlgren; it had been chosen for this stability and was the only area with a well-marked grid map. The rest of the planet had never been of use to anyone, and until the coming of Sir Frederick Havergal, could not be given away.

It was nerve-wracking terrain. The graticule marked only degrees of latitude and longitude, and the satellite radar's findings were of limited use when the ice caps wrenched open in the permafrost and the bergs calved endlessly into the bitter sea, when volcanoes formed new landmasses of lava every few years, rivers changed course in a thirtyday and twined about new deltas. Compasses were useless in multipolar magnetic fields, automated sextants and theodolite stations primed to catch a rare sunbeam washed away in flash floods or were struck by lightning. The world had a fast pulse—and a damned bad temper. Only gravimeters were fairly dependable: Deep-rooted continents shifted more slowly, and gyroscopes, at least, told which way was up.

"Ardagh!" She got a cruel yank on her braid. "What are you doing here!"

"Go to hell!" She punched the last piece of luggage into the chute and looked up, way up, into Sven's glare. "You'd get something that hurt if this wasn't public!" She grabbed at her medikit, which wasn't going with anyone else. "I couldn't help it," she was half-crying and half-lying, "and get up goddammit off your knees!"

He reached for her braid and brushed her cheek with its tip. "I can't talk with my xiphoid process." He scratched the base of his sternum. "What happened?"

She stammered it out, and his expression changed from annoyed to rueful. "I'm not surprised. The whole damn thing is blackmail. Really . . . we don't have to do it."

"Havergal thinks he has to, for some weird reason—but he's caught himself on a pointed stick too. He's coaxed all those people out to settle, to shore up his excuse, and get GalFed's blessing and funding as well—so he's got to take a deadly sick woman, and a nursemaid, and another bunch who don't want to go—the Yefni—and the Crystal-loids, who don't give a damn, and, and I hated leaving Vardy— "

"Where'd you leave him?" It was the least of his worries. He knew she wouldn't tip him into a cabbage patch.

"That." She grinned. "I got my folks to take him until school starts. They'll be thrilled."

"Especially when school starts." He picked himself off his knees, laughing.

Ardagh had no sympathy for Sandek's obligation to explain to Sir Frederick Havergal why he had to bring along an extremely sick woman with a nursemaid to be kept in half-stasis to watch her. Nor was she sorry that he would be sharing half-stasis with her. Those traveling deepsleep needed only to starve out long enough to flush their systems and drop into unconsciousness where their metabolism slowed drastically; Erez and her two doctors would sink no further than a twilight from which they might be roused for emergencies. Ardagh had traveled this way before: an aeon of sleepwalking.

Sven roused Mod Dahlgren, who had been waiting in an alcove with his functions depressed, and Ardagh watched both pass through the departure iris to the shuttle collector tube. Rebekkah VanderZande had boarded with her ESP and crated Crystalloids; the crew were in the ship along with the Meshar, and the Yefni who were bedded in a pod of hot sulfur mud; they hibernated or estivated and needed little care; she had not met them.

She waited alone for Sandek and the patient—hungry, angry, the braid scratching at her throat to remind her to be angry—and compassionate, with difficulty—toward the woman Erez.

Sir Frederick was horrified, and also checkmated. The hospital was not a long-term facility and could not have kept the sick woman; Ardagh had admitted swearing to accompany her, unwilling as she might be, and would not go back on her word. He felt on the brink of some disaster, with the edge crumbling as he tried to move back. Neither Ardagh nor the Meshar had asked *his* permission to do such a thing. Yet he could hardly have refused it: The Meshar made up more than half the passengers and were the most likely colonists.

He apologized to Ardagh; he assured her that she was free to go; he wanted no one under such compulsion and swore to find a substitute. But he could not give up the Meshar. And she knew that her freedom would have been at the cost of deceiving them, and refused it.

12

The ship orbited Barrazan V. The *Vasco Nuñez de Balboa* was a liner with many sections: labs, hydroponics, quarters that could be adapted to many sentient life forms, grapnels, brackets for piggybacks, gravitors to keep people in whatever positions they considered upside, and the best in food facilities for awakened travelers. It was not neat to look at, but its construction did not waste a centimeter, square or cubic. Sir Frederick's firm designed well and built better.

All except the Yefni came to consciousness in discomfort. The deepsleepers, once rehydrated and fed, recovered more quickly than Ardagh and Sandek, who woke haggard, though no alarm had disturbed them. The patient, under heavy sedation, was uncomfortable but in little pain. Ardagh was relieved to see that the tumor had shrunk just noticeably; if it had shrunk much she would have been fearfully puzzled, and if it had grown, horrified. In deepsleep, near stop-time, it would not have changed at all; in real time, it should have shrunk more; in Erez's slow time it had behaved as expected. There was nothing wrong with breath or heartbeat.

Sven found her hunched over a mug of tea in the common room that served for dining when the tables were unfolded.

"You're looking intense. Worried about Erez?"

"No. It's Sir Freddie makes me uneasy."

"We've been there. I still don't think he's any mad scientist."

"Neither do I. He still makes me uneasy."

"Look, love, I went through all the soul shaking and belly quaking when I found he'd married my mother."

"And lost his son."

"Well . . ."

"And you said you didn't trust him completely." she tailed off.

"What are you saying?"

She clenched the empty synth mug and it began to crush. "He asked me to the cabin for a mug of tea, and apologized for Sandek's trick. . . . He had a holo cube of his family, like the one you said—"

Sven's carrycomm chimed. "Oh God, that'll be Modal wanting me to monitor his connect functions again. He doesn't trust anybody either." He sighed and touched ON. "Yes. Modal."

Alone again, she crushed the mug smaller and smaller, trying to slow the whirling thoughts and make them settle into a shape.

What Sven would notice: everything about people and the conditions around him, almost always. Havergal's unwillingness to make this complicated and expensive trip, Mod Dahlgren's uneasiness.

His own features in glimpses of his mother? It is difficult to see oneself in another.

Ardagh, once removed, had the eye for that: within an hour of first setting eyes on Sven after crashing on Barrazan V fifteen years ago, a Sven hairless, four-armed, yellow-skinned, she knew that he was the son of Dahlgren because she had glimpsed for three seconds an image of Dahlgren on a trivvy screen. As she had recognized the Meshar woman's retarded physical development in recalling an old lecture. As she knew after one glance that Sir Frederick's son was a Dahlgren.

Had Sven seen that?

Was I looking for it? Am I only trying to convince myself? No, because fifteen years back, in the night and darkness and flame of the first few minutes on that world below, I didn't know Dahlgren had a son, I never dreamed there was a Sven. . . .

. . . Ione Willems Dahlgren would have been pregnant when she left him, neither knowing. Half a thirtyday perhaps after letting in that yearning man with the cold arrogant surface, unable to find the word and the touch . . . if I'm right, if, and oh—fifteen years she's known about Sven and never tried! And she sent Havergal . . .

Here?

To find?

13

Prima suffered, pulled her being inward, back and back to its beginnings an unmeasurable time ago.

Light flowed. Loose crystals and metallic streamers swam in it.

She wanted (what is want?) to push out into the living source, its freedom. Her limb's connecting end was wound about one of her crystals, and she sensed a crook in the free one; the pull in the stone wall that attracted it and made it move allowed her to catch a crystal and wedge it into the hollow rock's opening in order to enlarge it. The crystal shivered to powder and the fragments drifted.

She found another, knocked out a little of the stone, and a little more, while the small and distant lights in the dark surrounding her Source moved round and about. She sensed that this long and particularly hard crystal was a useful thing. With it she pried out of her body some stones that did not sense, and polished down her metals so that she might move with less scraping against foreign surfaces.

Then she pushed out of the shelter toward Source.

Madness!

Waves swarmed the lattices of her mind like the stones swirling in the void. With difficulty in the lights of blaring sun and wheeling stars she pulled back to the shelter of her ancient rock walls until she reached cold darkness and the secure grasp of an outcropping where her consciousness darkened as well.

An event: Scraping against an object turned her shelter and her self toward light. Only a little. She was barely conscious; her almost formless body was scattered over with flakes from the walls; fine scaly things that let in some light, not much. Some had slid or been driven into the interstices of her components.

She picked at them, removed one or two, sensed a strangeness in their absence and replaced them. They helped formalize (thought).

.These things are blockers of waves. They (insulate). Insulators channel sensors.

.Now being/self knows.

.Very much (light/source) is not good.

.But good is. Light.

.Now out to source.

.Not too far.

She crouched, clinging, in the opening.

.O light.

.But not . . .

.Now what more . . .

.Self wants?

(And what is want?)

She rode her rock in her niche of sunlight, generating a faint power, secreting a faint warmth. She did not know that she was made of tourmaline, quartz, nickel, iron, titanium, mica, welded and jointed by chance, and that her tools were shafts of corundum—ruby and sapphire—and slivers of diamond, that she sensed by waves generated through heat by compression and expansion of her crystals. She knew the bodies of rock about her as they echoed in waves or sparkled in light. She knew none like her in the universe, nor what she wanted.

Or that a single thought took her a year.

.Self. Self. I.

.I want.

By chance her grasper rested on a crystal like one of those in her body. She tapped it with a rod of corundum and it resonated. She moved the rod until it touched still another stone that rang.

.More of self. No. Need/want no more.

.I need other/self. Being/with.

She felt a shiver of radiance, and then a darkening.

.But what way?.

.I need more reach. Limb.

In time, time, time, she found a coil of metal that would make one. And another.

And began to create First Secunda.

14

Though many instruments did not work in Barrazan V's magnetic fields there was no difficulty in finding the equator and the piece of jungle that had made up Dahlgren's World. The old Station should be a serviceable base for what Sir Frederick hoped would be a stay of not more than four thirtydays.

There was no question of bedding this ship in the silo that had been prepared when the Station was built. The earlier ship had brought fewer people at a time, and was much smaller. Havergal's *Balboa* would orbit, and would have done so even if it could be landed; no one yet really trusted Barrazan V.

The Yefni area was scouted and approved, but before they went down in their pod the three fathers of the new confederacy requested medical treatment. They came in great embarrassment to report their thought-crime and its punishment. Two of the three had healed well, and rather than tamper with the scars across the eyeband Ardagh assured them that they would forget and ignore the blind spot once they were used to it; but Mef had an overgrown keloid that formed an ugly ridge, truly blinding. Ardagh consulted with Flanders, the crew doctor, who led Mef away for radiation treatment. The Yefni thanks were effusive, and they descended without trouble.

The Meshar had been offered a piece of the experimental territory in the zones that had been least irradiated. The reactors had been shut down when Dahlgren and the young people lifted off fifteen years earlier. Wind and storm had diluted the radiation. The forest threshers were now conducting tests of the environment for the Meshar as they had done for the Yefni. When the area was reported safe the Meshar would scout it for suitability. The roads had been cleared and roughly mended by patrols all through the years—GalFed wanted to maintain a hold on a piece of property even if only as a buffer zone—but all the automated scans in the sky could not tell exactly what life was down there, nor could the lumbering erg caretakers that swept the place three or four times a year.

59

The Station doors opened, grinding, creaking, whining. The interior was neither dark nor filthy; it had been lit by huge windows and a small crew of trimmers kept it barely habitable.

The Meshar were well satisfied with their samples of forest humus and plant life, but Sir Frederick was cautious about turning them out into the wild. He planned to build them a habitation for about a thirtyday and a half in the Pit where once experimental animals had been kept before release, or brought in for examination. Sven had spent hours of childhood there playing among creatures just as strange as he. Now, emptied and scoured, the Pit was a bowl with nothing but a scum of light mold and a pattern of cracks, some as wide as ten centimeters, made by tremors. These would have to be filled in, and the filling would take time—a disappointment to the Meshar and a disturbance to Havergal.

He sought out Sven, who was upgrading the generators; he had been avoiding the places where his father was imprisoned and tormented.

"We have signs of earthquake, and there's been that disturbance of Haruni Crater, but nothing live on the seismos right now."

"Yes," Sven said. "I noticed the walls have bigger cracks than settling would account for."

"There was no mention of earthquakes in the early reports."

"A few mild ones west of the Zones, but the area was generally free. This building was built on a kind of suspension principle I'd have to be an architect to understand, so it won't fall down, though I can understand why the Pit might sink and crack."

"These Pit cracks open into the soil, and they must be fairly fresh because there's no thick growth of moss or fungus around them." Havergal scratched in his beard. "Damn! I was hoping to get the Meshar used to the place right away. Now we'll have to put them in quarters here until we can seal the Pit."

"That should take only a few days," Sven said mildly.

"Yes, but I want to check quake patterns in the whole region now."

"At least the Yefni are settled."

"But we'll have to monitor them too." He stumped off frowning.

Mod Dahlgren came round from behind a tangle of wires. "What else is bothering him, Sven?"

"Doesn't like the bloody place, Modal. Just like the rest of us."

"Yet he made himself come."

"Yes. Can you handle this by yourself for an hour? I want to see how Ardagh and the patient are getting on, and you're better than I am at most of it anyway."

Sven had spent little time in the Station when it was run by ergs, and dirt and mold did not unduly disturb him. Not as much as Havergal's fretfulness, which might adversely color the atmosphere.

On his way from the transformers he passed a door in the corridor and paused at the tug of a memory. The door still read, faintly marked in *lingua,* OFFICE OF THE STATISTICIAN. Familiar and strange. Why strange? The memory was of something trivial, yet vivid.

Yes. The Statistician had built a model of Babbage's Difference Engine, the one existing piece of the first computer that could be given the name. A steel claw turned the spindles and ratchets, and it needed only a small power cell to keep it running almost to eternity. Behind the door there was silence now, not the old *rraktik* that once, in forgetfulness, he had taken as the threat of one more malignant erg. But why should the power have been expected to last forever?

Out of curiosity he slid the door open—it whined angrily on its runners—and touched the light switch. The machine, brass-gold in color like Ardagh's hair, was canted on its tripod so that its glasstex bell rested against the wall. A tremor had knocked it over, perhaps, without breaking it: The floor was cracked. He set it right, and unhooked the plate covering the cell socket. Its space was empty. Some officious person had removed it, or, to be charitable, someone had needed it. He took a fresh one from his kit, a small expenditure, and replaced it.

"—*ktik,*" the claw jerked rotating its handle. *Rraktik.* Babbage's Difference Engine resumed the only function it had performed in six hundred years. Sven was oddly reassured by the sound. Something was running right.

He bent to heft his kit and saw the two splatter marks on the floor; dark brown like dried blood, in classic radiating shapes. Blood? No people had been left to bleed on this world. Rebel erg, stealing five minutes' worth of power from a penlight cell? Too much imagination. Perhaps some kind of lubricating fluid. *Tiktik,* said the Engine, faithfully.

He used his own flashlight down dark narrow corridors, shortcuts he knew which had not yet been rewired. And stopped. Another dark stain, this one on the wall, a streak running down. He swallowed and went on.

He took the elevator to the Computer Room on Level Three instead of following the corridor to the one opening directly into the Infirmary. Dark corridors were beginning to make him uneasy. The elevator had power, but its light was dull, queasy amber. His flashlight picked out an object on the floor: a strip of cloth, half a meter long, a few centimeters wide, torn from one of the knitted cotton long johns worn under waterproofs in the rain forest. Two-thirds was stiff with dried blood. No mistake. He wanted to fling it away, but he pushed it into his pocket.

One more short dark corridor between Admin and the Computer Room. Elevators still worked smoothly, at least. The door slid open in silence.

He stepped out and something slammed him, knocked the penlight out of his hand, and leaped into the elevator. He did not hear the door close or the cage move. His balance had always been tricky, and he had fallen, kit bag under him. It was of soft material but it had hard things in it, and he heard nothing except the edge of one of them cracking ribs. His two right elbows had been battered on the floor. He used both left hands to pull out his comm slowly, grunting in pain, and thumbed the alert. "Sven, Level Three, at entrance lift eight, watch for intruder. And help."

Useless. The intruder had had plenty of time to leave from some unguarded exit.

Doctor Flanders, first to reach him, got him trundled to the Infirmary, examined him, determined that the elbows were not broken, and taped his ribs.

Ardagh watched sitting in a corner, armurapped and numb.

Flanders stared at her quizzically. "Lassie, no need to glare so grim. No great damage here, and so far there's exactly as many doctors as patients. Excuse me, one more counting Sandek. Usually the ratio is much worse."

"I want to know who did it," Ardagh said.

"Ah, I think some animal must have got in through a ventilator. Conditions are still loose. Now, Mister Dahlgren, here are some painkillers for when the shot wears off. Those breaks, the way they lie, will mend sooner if you keep the bandage on half a thirtyday and out of dark corners; better than my glueing them. Don't chase your wife round the bed too fast."

"Joker," said Ardagh darkly. "Did you get a look at the—animal? I mean the animal that hides in the dark waiting for elevators."

"It—he—got me by surprise and I was occupied yelling. A fall like that scares me. I saw an arm—I think. First I thought it was one of the clones. . . ." The ergs of long ago had cloned Dahlgren in secret twice, to obtain the double they wanted. But the pair, one female, had been wild and savage creatures no matter how much like Dahlgren—or a young Dahlgren—they looked, and afterward they had been set free in the forest. "But *they* were very hairy. . . . It could have been, I just had one sweep of a penlight. Still—I think it was wearing some kind of torn clothing, and—" he had gotten dressed and was sitting up— "here's something I found in the elevator. . . ." He showed her the bloody rag and told her about the splatters, the missing power cell in the Babbage. "I get a picture of somebody in trouble, hurt, blundering round the place, not knowing quite enough about the layout."

"Why not *quite* enough?"

"If he'd known nothing at all he couldn't have got in."

"Not a *she*?"

"Maybe not you, love, but I think almost any other woman confronted in that dimness with two meters, a hundred and forty kilos and four arms of Sven Dahlgren would have let out a shriek and run like hell. I know at least that our X was a tall strong person—no animal—desperate to get into that elevator." He sat quiet again, and tense.

"Hurt an awful lot?"

"Some. I'm more mad at myself for being scared—and still a bit scared."

She took one of his hands, licked her lips and said, "It's not a good time to say this, but it never will be." And told him of the Dahlgren resemblance in Sir Frederick's son.

He was silent.

"No surprise to you."

"More like the shock of seeing something fit. I trust your eye. But neither of us can explain it, can we? So there's nothing to do now." As if the thought had connected with another, he added, "For the moment there's an animal running loose, and leave it."

Sven opened his eyes. Mod Dahlgren was sitting beside his bed watching in the semidarkness. "I am sorry I could not come more quickly."

"I wasn't in any danger, Modal. Whoever knocked me down was as scared as I was."

"Nevertheless—"

"You don't have to stand guard."

"Nevertheless I will be watchful."

15

The crevice wall shifted, and the struts of the stone ship vibrated with strain, an insulator plate cracked, and Prima sensed a weakening, a softening in its structure, and a dizzy terrible whirling of vibration in the torque of her stones.

She learned the thought: .*Unbearable*.

Han Li screamed.

"What? What?" Rebekkah's long thin body twisted in the bucket seat, her arms reached around the girl's shoulders. The pilot's startle dipped the aircar fighting its way through the usual windstorm.

Han Li's teeth gritted and clacked. "Oh: please: can't: bear: help: fire: mad: stop: please." The words spat like cracked stones.

The Crystalloid settler's case was strapped down in the seat to the other side of her, and Rebekkah reached over to tap it. "What is it? What?" But the Crystalloid could not answer, himself, and Han Li would not speak for him.

"O my daughters of stone, we are trapped in walls with fire with fire about them with heat in heat we cannot not not think!" Han Li was sobbing.

"Crystalloids here?"

"No otherwhere from otherwhere. O: help—oh Bekkah, no, no, Bekkah! I am sick, don't make me, don't!"

Her voices wept and grated, alien stone ones, rough pidgin mixed with *lingua*, her fists clenched, her face twisted, a scream crackled in her throat.

"This can't go on. Czerny, get up out of the wind and head back!" She dug into her carryall for a loaded syringe, broke the seal, and in a moment Han Li had gone slack, hands curling, breath a little snottery like a baby's.

"Have you got all that on record?" she asked the pilot.

"Yes, Madame VanderZande, and the location where it happened is: twenty-seven minutes south, three degrees, thirty-two minutes west. It's the western rim of the Haruni Crater. Used to be a caldera, but it domed up and steamed out some time before we came."

The Crystalloid rattled angrily in its case. It wanted a stalactite cave and the cold glitters of its brother stones, but Rebekkah paid no attention.

"Freddie, I'm damned if I'm going to go looking for an old diamond mine or whatever if it drives that poor child crazy! She claims there are some other kinds of live crystal things—sentient beings!—trapped in Haruni Crater, and believe me, she has no imagination whatever."

"Oh, yes, I've listened to the spool." Havergal was sweating, partly with frustration, partly because the ventilation system had not yet reached full strength. "I don't know what to think. That crater's been behaving very weirdly." He clicked a keypad that lit up a large screen set in the office wall. It showed the grid map of Zones and Station. The grid superimposed the radar image of land contours. He rolled the pad over the desk and the scene panned westward beyond the zone boundaries to the Haruni Crater, newly mapped with minutes of 140 kilometer degrees because just to the south were the sulfur pits where the Yefni were exploring a new sovereignty, and to the west was the washout of an old mine in a steep bluff, considered suitable for Crystalloids. "That's a radar image of the crater. Dahlgren named it just before he left, for his best friend here. It's a damn big thing—for a big world. I wonder . . ."

"I couldn't see much through the cloud . . . but Freddie"—Rebekkah turned from the contour lines and looked at him sharply—"maybe you picked the wrong planet."

He startled her by turning white, then red, before regaining his normal freckle-pink, then said in a pinched voice, "We'll investigate. I came to examine the place, not endanger the people. If there's a real risk, we'll leave." He turned away dismissively and left her.

Mod Dahlgren unpacked and unfolded the wire form, something like a clothier's dummy, and shaped it, as he had been programmed, to his own measurements. Then he removed his clothing and unseamed his skin. Sven helped the process as much as pain allowed; Modal found it awkward. His original makers, the ergs, had not designed him for skin-shedding, and his later adapters, having had no practice, were not as well-skilled.

He stood in his true nakedness—spindles, gears, chips, hinges, flexes, jeweled movements, glittering and flickering like the workings of an ancient clock. He was fitting his skin on the form, smoothing it and washing it down, with something like love. Sven thought he was a wonder in the machine form, a greater one than the quasi-human, but would never say so, because Mod Dahlgren was so proud of his humanity.

Now, of course, he was far more a machine than when he had been first made: GalFed had removed the artificial heart and blood system contrived to simulate a fleshly being and replaced them with a degausser, an odometer, an altimeter, a hygrometer, a mass spectrometer, a searchlight between the eyes, a laser beam above it, for cutting, and microwave detectors receiving greater ranges of the spectrum than before.

Sven helped him into the dull silver polymer skin with its window for eyes, lights, and laser, and pumped air and moisture out. Without the Dahlgren skin Modal did not look at all like a man, for he had no external organs, no features, and no animal musculature, but he was a beautiful creature, and remained so in the polymer casing. His eyes, Dahlgren's, turned to Sven. "Keep yourself with others so that you will be safe."

"Modal, *you* take care. Go in good order and come back as well."

Ardagh was watching Sandek palpate the shrinking tumor. They had allied to conscript some unwilling Meshar into helping the medmechs scrub down the Infirmary. Machines alone could not do the job Ardagh wanted, not the ones available here, and she wanted no cleverer ones of the kind she had battled before. She was gratified with Sandek's cooperation, but it was earned. Even he could see, past all the jury-rigging of sling scales and other

68

devices never before needed here, that the patient had improved.

Erez, eyes open, had lifted the new braid and was rubbing it along her cheekbone, smiling her little forked smile. She murmured.

"Erez wants to eat," Sandek said.

Ardagh gave the IV bag a squeeze. "I don't blame her, but I think she ought to eat very carefully. Not to use up your plant samples, or try out anything from this world before she's a lot better. If we can test out something in the stores and cook it down to mush—maybe."

The Meshar, for all their fierce looks, were herbivores, but the herbage they preferred was rather tough for a sick woman, as even Sandek would concede.

There was a screaming in the corridor.

Sandek frowned without looking up. "O-ya, there is that child again. What is making her suffer?"

"Galactic Federation," said Ardagh.

As he raised his head to give her a look, Han Li ran into the room, still screaming, and grabbed at Ardagh. Rebekkah caught up with her, hair at its most electric.

"Can I help, Beck?"

"Oh, I don't know what . . ." Rebekkah's face was full of distress.

But the Meshar women came to gather around the child, surrounded her and plucked her away, soothing with earthy hands. She stood out defiantly like the center of an odd flower. "Not make go!"

Rebekkah finally got out the words. "She's exhausting me and I don't know what to do! She insists that some kind of crystal life is trapped in Haruni Crater and suffering terribly, making her suffer with it—and I just don't know . . ."

"What about the Crystalloids?"

"I can't talk to them except through her, and they don't

69

give a damn. They're like that, I guess they can't help it. And there's only one other ESP I know of like her in the galaxy—and he's halfway across it."

"Well, you can see it's possible to soothe her."

The Meshar women, avid for children, had recognized the baby in Han Li, and she was pleased to be so recognized.

"It surely saves me having to give her a sedative. If I dull her esp she's useless with our Crystalloids. Well," she sighed, "the Dahlgren erg is driving out to investigate the crater—he's too heavy to fly—and then we'll come out by air. He'll need a day's head start, so maybe these women can help keep her calm. . . . I'm so grateful for help. . . . It should have been simple enough to put seven Crystalloids in an old mine shaft, but it's due west of the crater. We could fly around it, but"—she shook her head and her hair flared like dandelion silk—"would it do any good, especially if she's right?" She dabbed at Han Li's still-tearful eyes with a big silk handkerchief, and at her own too. "Oh, Han Li, I hate to put you through all this!"

Sandek said, "The Pit is not ready and we have not yet seen the forest. Doctor Colquhoun, do you believe that the Solthree Havergal will let one of us Meshar travel with the machine man?"

"Not to get burnt up, I should hope not! Mod Dahlgren is going suited up and very well protected."

"So do we go shielded, Madame Doctor, so we do. In cold and dark, hot and dry and blinding light." He spread out his black-haired arms and their tight leathery webs of wing. "No place we have ever lived in is even as comfortable as the forest you tell me you suffered in."

Yes, I guess if the bugs tried to put their stingers in you they'd fall dead, Ardagh was careful not to say. She did say, mildly, "Just the same, I don't think Havergal would

70

let unsuited people travel with Mod Dahlgren, and I doubt he has such suits for us."

Sandek tightened his mouth and said, "I hear of a strange wild creature running about in here, one who has already harmed your man and has not yet been found. Are we not safer outside?"

"Doctor Sandek, I will be happy for you when you can decide that for yourself."

During this exchange Rebekkah had been looking thoughtful, and had even waited until it was finished before removing Han Li from the embraces of her nurse-maids. Ardagh thought it likely that she would keep her door locked and carry the low stunner authorized for Liaison. Ardagh and Sven, though permitted, did without. Sven could never make up his mind which of four hands to hold the thing in, and Ardagh preferred a blunt instrument, or a fine one at close quarters, to an aiming weapon with which she suspected she would eventually shoot herself in the foot.

16

When Mod Dahlgren left in his silver suit at midnight, Sven, who shared quarters with him and was just getting to bed, felt a pang of loneliness. Ardagh was on duty, and though he was grateful to be able to spend time with her, Mod Dahlgren, for all his limits, was the friend and workmate, perhaps the only one, who accepted him as normal in this galaxy of strange and exotic species.

He arranged his painful ribs and closed his eyes in darkness. The thought *brother* floated into his mind with his aching breath. He had had Dahlgren, his father, and

Mod Dahlgren, his friend . . . and he had seen the clones who looked too horribly like . . . Dahlgrens, and . . .

Mod Dahlgren was driving a treaded cube-shaped vehicle fitted with a special padded cradle from which he could steer and see without jarring his instrumental innards too much. There were spaces and compartments of various tools and implements, screens and mikes for communication, big windows for observation that were also thick, for protection, and a blazing yellow exterior so that aircar pilots might observe him. There were also large water and detergent tanks with sprayers for washing off the mud, bugs, leaves, guano, and other messes, to keep the car visible.

Mod Dahlgren traveled the first ten kilometers at a good speed on the southernmost road of Zone White, where the radiation had been strongest and the growth easiest to keep down. Howling winds swept lashing rains in the eternal storm, and the sky cracked with lightning in a thousand places like a giant eggshell. In a moment the storm might turn itself off, and in another moment resume. The window sweepers swept the panes; the brushes swept the road. Then the lights found either the limb of a big tree or the trunk of a giant fern, and Mod Dahlgren stopped.

A bearded face blinked on the monitor screen. "Are you in trouble, Mod Dahlgren?"

"Only a fallen log to clear away, Aguerido. Thanks/out." He reached behind the screen, pulled out a jack so that the image flickered, and turned off the mike. "Man, I think you must be very uncomfortable in back. There is a convenient seat that folds down here beside me."

The hoarse Meshar voice whispered, "How did you know I was here?"

"By my heat receptors." And the mass spectrometer that was the equivalent of a sense of smell.

The dark figure squeezed out from between a water tank and a tool kit. "You speak my tongue very well."

"Just well enough to be understood." Mod Dahlgren replaced the jack and switched the mike back on, to low volume. "I will keep the sensors focused on my readouts; your skin is not reflective. Why did you come?"

"We want to see where we are to live! We cannot stay in the Pit because the splits are hard to seal, and we like to live out in land, growth, and water, not dryness and dust!"

Mod Dahlgren considered this. He seldom yearned, but he was mindful of the wish-need to be near an energy source. "It is sensible enough, to come out with me in this car, where you are safe, rather than running about in the wild, but why did you not ask Solthree Havergal for permission?"

"We are afraid to ask for anything since that fool Sandek made the woman doctor come with Erez, who should have been left to live or die as the gods allow. Now everyone is angry at us."

"I don't believe everyone is angry at you. I think Ardagh could have refused to come if she was determined, but her man is here, and she wants Erez to heal and feels responsible."

"Erez is our responsibility much more than hers."

"Come out now and sense your world while I remove the obstruction."

"Let me help."

"No. The Station will pick you up in the lights. Stay in the dark, but keep watch. Organic persons often have better awareness in life environments than machines do. What shall I call you, Meshar?"

"Barak."

"Then, Barak, come out."

It did not occur to Mod Dahlgren that an organic person might not wish to come out in a lashing storm that was flinging pieces of garbage about. But it did not occur to Barak either. He was perfectly happy in these elements.

Mod Dahlgren found that moving the tree by himself was too difficult. "I had thought to save power by not using the grippers for this, but we have plenty of power cells and only one of me. So let us go back inside."

The grippers extended, took hold of the giant stalk, and tossed it aside in two minutes. But Barak lingered, with streams of water running in the graining of his skin and plastering down his hairs with leaves and dirt, sniffing at the savage winds.

"I will bring attention to myself if I go too slowly. Please come in, Barak, and strap down carefully."

Barak shook off water and raised his stiff guard hairs to flick off detritus. "That was good! What name do *you* have, machine being?"

"I am called Mod Dahlgren. It sounds impressive, but it means only: a machine model of a man, Dahlgren. I am not important."

"That cannot be so! You are a great wonder, Mod Dahlgren."

"Then be careful, Barak, or you will have a new friend."

"That would make me proud. Now I hope you and your old friends are not really angry about Erez."

"Barak, if she had stayed behind, and she had died in loneliness, I think that would have made everyone very unhappy. If this world is good for you, it is good that she is on it, and I hope for your sake that it is. Now we must try to go faster and make up the time, because the work has to be done by noon tomorrow."

The rain was swept over by wind, and swept downward again, swept over and swept down. There was no moon round this world, nor even a break of cloud enough to see a star. The morning came swiftly in the equatorial day, but

74

hardly brighter than a lightning flash. After a while a sullen ragged bubble of deep orange sun popped up to glint on the much brighter groundcar. Briefly, before a scud-edge of cloud draped it and rain beat down again with a rumble of thunder.

Occasionally the treads humped against loose bricks or slewed in the rot of wet leaves or the marrow of some small dead animal or huge insect. The brushes freed the old road of twigs that had fallen since it had last been cleared by ergs; the grippers flung aside the lightning-shattered corpse of a great fern or heavy liana. The Zones had been expunged, but the bricks of the road, though weather-worn and pitted, were still colored, and as they changed from white to yellow, orange, red, blue, and the green farthest from the source of bombardment, the vegetation seemed both more fresh and more healthy. If Sven had been present he might have considered this sensation only a feeling rather than a fact. Mod Dahlgren, who noticed the change, had not been out in this forest until now, but he had worked on many worlds and gained some knowl-edge of what native growth ought to be, even in dirt and wet.

He said, "What is here to satisfy Sir Frederick Haver-gal?"

Barak, who had spoken little but looked about him much, said, "I am satisfied enough as long as no trees fall on me. I think the road is going to end now, Mod Dahlgren."

"The ergs have cleared a track for us. Tighten your straps. It is very bumpy going, but the forest will thin out in an hour or so, and then there will be brush and plains up to the mountains."

The going was very bumpy in the track where ergs had been more conscientious in the cutting down than they were in the cleaning up. After a half-hour of it, Barak clutched his stomach and said, words whistling through

75

his teeth, "Aarr—I am glad—I ate well—before—I came—and that—it was—a long—while ago!"

Mod Dahlgren had empathy for fleshly creatures. He braked. "The rain is pausing, Barak, and I sense no large life forms, though you must be careful of the small ones. Do you wish to step outside for a short while?"

"No. I think I would only like to be still for a little. There is something to be said for a lack of excitement." After a minute he said, "I must not delay you. The forest is thinner, at least."

Within an hour the giant ferns were sparse, and the trees smaller. The rain stopped and the sky cleared in washy patches; from the outside screen Mod Dahlgren could see the car gleaming yellow. Yet still it thundered, so harshly the ground seemed to shake.

The track turned bumpy in a different way: The ground was increasingly rocky, and there were also potholes where the ergs had dug out boulders. Mod Dahlgren said, "There is the mountain."

"It does not seem far away." Of no great height, it was a broad massive hump to the southwest.

"It will take an hour to reach."

"Are we to climb that?"

"You will not! And neither will this vehicle. I have a machine to put about me that will carry me up by jets so I may take a look over the crater's edge. I am not sure of seeing much, but I will record whatever my sensors bring me."

"There seems to be a little vapor over the rim, and I don't think it is a cloud. The heat up there will be very great."

"My suit will defend against it, though it is best for me not to fall into the fire."

"I think it is getting darker. The storm seems to be following us; the skies are surely angry and noisy."

"I doubt there is a place on this world without cloud cover most of the time."

"This is a new storm coming fast from the east: I smell its rain. The sun is near zenith and will soon be hidden."

Mod Dahlgren checked the vanes and found Barak quite right in an observation an organic person would make more quickly than a preoccupied machine. He called Station. "Heavy storm approaching from east, pressure 97.4 kilopascals and dropping. Please do not send out the aircar until I call for it."

"Sven here, Modal. All well? . . . You lonely?"

"Yes and no. All in good order. Good company with myself. I am southeast on the mountain base, two degrees, twenty-five minutes west, twenty-four minutes south."

"Can you give me a three-sixty-degree look from your exterior? It's coming on fast, Modal. See if you can find a hollow that isn't a streambed. No use asking for lightning."

"Yes, there seems to be one a quarter kilo—"

Silence.

"Modal? Modal!"

A line of fire was opening in the mountain's flank and running down toward the car. Little veins darted from it and caught at the shrubs, and the wind whipped and whirled the flames till the fire grew branches of its own.

Mod Dahlgren turned the car as quickly as it would go on its treads. Barak was calm. "Wheels would go faster."

"True, but we have none." There was little turning space on the narrow track and twigs crackled beneath. The sky grew darker and the rain slammed the windows in sheets so there was almost no seeing out of them. Some force of wind or lightning wrenched the spy-eye from the roof and its screen went blind. Mod Dahlgren brightened the lights fore and aft to their fullest; he did not need ordinary sight to know that the fiery split had reached the ground and was following the track.

The cloud darkened to night, and the wind and rain grew fiercer, but they would not dash the thirst of the fire: Rain seemed almost to inflame it. The sky thundered above; the world roared beneath it. Mod Dahlgren gave all the speed he could to a vehicle meant for modest going in rough terrain, and the vein of fire spewed as the crack widened behind him, matched every swerve with what seemed animate malevolence. Leaves, branches, small stones struck and ran down the windows but did not screen the fire. Mod Dahlgren saw a rise to one side where the ground cover seemed thinner, and turned sharp left, away from the track, away from the streaming mountain, to the southeast. The car bucked, the treads shrieked at the force he demanded of them, but Barak had twisted about, and by the glint of his eyes Modal could see that the rise of ground must have split, for the fire had swerved with them, had dashed like a serpent between the treads and out beyond in front. He could not outrace that. He braked, and the crack widened. Barak cried out.

"Press that button to release the straps," said Mod Dahlgren. "Pull that lever to open the window. It will be terribly hot, but you are quick-moving, and must jump as far as you can to avoid the fire, then roll and keep rolling until you reach cooler ground."

"The angry god will come after me," Barak muttered, but did as he was told. Mod Dahlgren also believed in a god, but he conceived of it, rather vaguely, as a Great Circuit pulsing in a Machine, and it did not send vengeful fire after persons. He waited until he saw the shape of Barak thrashing the bushes, then slipped the webbing of his own harness. The treads by now were barely far enough apart to straddle the crevasse of fire beneath. He had no time for the power pack. He climbed out the open window more clumsily than Barak, but more protected from the heat. He dared not leap, but dropped into steaming foliage just as the crack widened a few centimeters more and the car began to sink. He landed with legs from the knees down hanging over the fire, and rolled away in time to see the sturdy, useful, costly groundcar sink into the fire pit. He did not look at it, not then or when the tanks exploded with a booming and fountains of sparks. In the orange blaze he could see scorch and singe marks on his legs, but water and leaves were wiping them off.

"Barak!"

"I am here!" Panting.

"Are you well?"

"I think—I think—"

Mod Dahlgren pulled himself to his feet and supported with his hands a clumsy scrabble over hummocks and bushes. He found Barak crouched, gasping, on a small patch of ground that was fairly clear. Streams of rain netting his face, re-forming as wind dissolved them, the talons of hands and feet gripping soil, the blade of his tail plunged into it. Wind and rain were not enemies of Meshar.

But fire.

The fire was ebbing, but occasionally a tongue of flame, perhaps from the still-burning tanks, rose to light his streaming face, his black seed eyes swimming in their jellies of blood.

"Barak—"

"My new friend—saver of life—such strange and wrong, friend, this place. This planet is mad, is mad!"

17

Unbearable.

The facets gritted under the shift of walls. *.O Prima.,* said Sensor, *.it is not worth bearing.*

.Daughter be still and regard our surroundings with me. Prima had sensed not so much a cooling of the atmosphere as a pause in the oppression, a drawing away of heat. She had also felt something else that was very difficult to rectify into a thought. Beyond the heat, the furious mind-workings, and the panic around her there was the merest hint of a *communication,* of a being that directed and received thought. She hesitated to tell this to her companions because it might seem that her mind was in disorder. But she owed them every hope of help that she could believe in. *.If you are calm you will realize that the heat has ebbed a little. We are still here obviously. And also I sense possibly a being somewhere near us who can speak.*

.Are you sure of this Prima? We cannot feel it.

.Not utterly sure but I have more receptors than you.

.Will this being save us?.

.It will understand us. I hope. I believe. I believe it will understand us.

.It may hate us. Like our other enemies.

.Believe that it will not.

.Can we reach it?.

.Try.

Trees rushed by; small animals in burrows on the forest floor shrieked away from the landcar's jets. The grid on the control deck no longer flashed the place where Modal's vehicle had stopped. Sven tried again to call up the erg's personal radiophone and as before got a sounding tone that went unanswered. The sky was thick and the wind flung every piece of forest trash it could shake loose. No buzzer could have flown even if all the air vehicles had not been locked into the hangar by the lightning bolt that welded the latches. Sven had commandeered an old landcar that took all weathers, and he expected others to follow him. In the meantime his own flicker on the grid was his only live point on the tumbling world.

The jets blew aside broken twigs; the larger tree falls had been cleared by Mod Dahlgren's thresher. The landcar still labored in the heavy air, snorting every few moments to clear its intakes of detritus.

The rains slammed down and scudded away ten times in an hour. Another hour brought Sven into Zone Green, where he had lived an aeon of fifteen years ago with the white goat Yigal and the black gibbon Esther, graduates of a laboratory full of mutants, few so mutated as Sven. But goat and ape were mutants of mind who reasoned and spoke: oddly conventional ones, the gentle billy-goat–gruff *I hate east winds* and the tart-tongued monkey mother *You say that every winter.* The person as animal, both souls dead now. *Dinner's ready. Sven . . . Eat, sweetheart!* The place where the thatched hut had been beaten into the ground by mad ergs was a hundred kilometers away, and he would never eat at that rough table again. He took a pack of biscuits from his kit bag and nibbled halfheartedly.

He did not know the terrain beyond the zones; on the auxiliary screen he called up a relief map of the land west of Zone Green: the ragged trail continued, stretching toward the crater. He could not see much of his surroundings under the storm; the landcar scraped and bucked over the humping ground. Sometimes in little dips and valleys the cloud shut down like a lid; radar guided the car in wide

81

meanders, and he wondered how they could lead him to Modal.

All at once a level area surprised Sven—and perhaps even the car, which shuddered. The thick swaddling around him lifted, to reappear a quarter kilometer away in the form of a mist-log stretched across the track. Closer, it became not mist but a barricade filmed with smoky vapor, a jumble of five or six tree trunks cluttered with broken branches and torn vines.

Sven paused for a few moments before this apparition, and cut the jets.

He turned the spy-eyes round and about, unable to see past the barricade because of the mist; there were not many big trees in this stretch where the forest was rapidly thinning. Their growth was becoming stunted, shrinking into brush, and the giant ferns were very young and slender.

He thought of great winds plucking up trees and heaping them on his path. Arranging them.

The sullen air current moaned; lightning flicked its tongue and a spit of rain smacked the windshield. He thought of great ergs, gone mad again, piling up trees to frustrate him, batter down his eggshell while he was stalled here. His belly knotted and he wished he had not eaten.

The leaves fluttered on the piled-up trees, the wind blew away the clinging mist. No alarm rang on the control deck. Sven pulled around to the south, forced to make a turn sooner than he had planned, and in a gingerly way picked out a new path.

There were many hummocks and a thick underbrush on this swath of land, and where the ground leveled out the mist had collected in thick wads that the wind hardly shifted. The forest hothouse steamed. Inside the closed car the air cooler labored; Sven sweated with anxiety and dread, and wanted a clean bodysuit. There was no communication with Modal, no news to give Headquarters; he was off the grid and without compass. If the sun were visible it would only have beaten on him slantless in a long noon. But he was grateful for the prospect of six or seven hours of what passed for daylight before the night dropped.

He could not seem to find his way around the barrier, which raveled out in heaps of rubbish that blocked his way to the southwest. Alongside him a stream was wandering in what he hoped was the general direction: This presented a road clear enough for a landcar. Sven spun along with the hiss of jets pocking the surface of the water, while the wind, his companion, stirred the mist and the rain. There was no sound beyond his own center of movement.

Occasionally some leafy branch would thrust out to beckon or warn him; he followed the few visible meters of water, and saw nothing else.

When he thought he could bear this no longer the wind stopped and the sky grew lighter. The jets muted. The mist rippled away in two or three half-transparent layers, like scrims. He found himself slipping down into a small valley, a bowl of green stillness.

A Zone of quiet.

He pulled the car over to solid ground and set down. He sat waiting. For what? He was a fearful man on an urgent errand, yet he felt obliged somehow to acknowledge the planet's peaceful moment. This was not Dahlgren's World.

With some hesitation he unlatched the door and pushed it up; air blew in fresh without its smells of rot and mold. The sunlight was silvery and the trees and grasses shone like silk. Flowers clustered and blew sweetly, not ringing and clattering like the ones in the poison zones he had known fifteen years ago; there, butterflies were razor-winged, branches grew spikes, and animals wore steely carapaces.

This did not seem to be a place ever touched by ergs: Some person, or . . . something had guided him here, but he could not believe it was an erg. He stepped down on the mossy ground, stretched in his wet clothes, and let the wind blow cool on him. The valley was not wide, perhaps half a kilometer, and one narrow stream traversed it. He wanted to lie down in the grasses and sleep as he had not slept in fifteen hours of the night, but Modal was in danger or destroyed, as perhaps was someone along with him, as he had hinted.

Yet Sven stood, watching the quietness in which nothing of significance was taking place, waiting to see if some hump of hill or shadow might pull away from its background and shoulder itself forward as a mammoth or an aurochs. Or perhaps that blackened branch would stretch and yawn, explode into the treetops, yipping Esther's morning cry. *Hullo, Sven! What are you doing out of the Zones?*

He rubbed tears off his cheekbones and called himself stupid. The place belonged to one of the clones, or a stray mutant. Not him, Sven. Yet he had been guided to an exhibition of peace on a violent world.

His CommUnit chimed.

"Sven?"

"Modal! Are you well?"

"Quite well—as is my dear friend one Barak of the Meshar. Your companions are here, Sven. What happened to you?"

"I lost my way. . . . I'll be along shortly. . . ."

He climbed back into the car, shut it tight, and drove out of the valley into blasting wind and lances of rain. Because he had had a good look at the falling sun he was able now to head out to the southwest and Haruni Crater.

18

Han Li was asleep, and Rebekkah smoothed her hair and watched the flickers of borrowed emotions on her face. Rebekkah did not love the child, but her sense of responsibility was like love. She was angry—at everyone, even the stones of the world, because they were tormenting her charge.

Han Li stirred. "I don't so much hurt now, Bekkah," she murmured. Her eyes did not open.

"Yes," said Rebekkah very softly, and switched on the minicord.

"First One, the fire current has pushed us outward," a voice said firmly. "Now we must work to free ourselves."

"That's good, dear. Who is First One?"

"I am called First One because I am maker of all," said the stone voice. "What being are you?" Han Li turned and stretched out her arms. "What to say, Bekkah? What?"

Rebekkah caught hold of her hands. "What being *are* you to those people, child?"

"Receiver-of-thought," said Han Li. She rolled over and slept.

Rebekkah switched off the recorder and looked at her audience: the researchers and colonists gathered for morning discussion in the Common Room.

"I can't believe these creatures are just Han Li's make-believe. They're making her too miserable."

Havergal gave a helpless shrug. "I can't disagree with you. It's just that no one knows."

"If we had a good telepath here I might be able to find

out more about the crystals and understand Han Li better."

"Yes," said Havergal wearily; he closed his eyes and nodded. One complaint among many; he was no penny-pincher, but sometimes the purse grew thin—and everyone knew it.

One of the Yefni, Zyf's mate Lef, unlimbered a coil. "We have a telepath here. It is my child Yav. I don't know whether you would consider him of the best, but he is certainly telepathic."

"No, Lef," Rebekkah said, "We can't give that responsibility to a person so young."

Lef said, "He was not too young—or too weak—to pick up the distressful feelings of our friend Barak, though he was rather slow gathering his thoughts together to deliver the message—"

"But he was a great help in giving us a location just the same," said Havergal, "and—"

"I know the child is most eager to offer help—"

"Which if he's that good I'll take with thanks," said Rebekkah. "What about surveying the volcano?"

Havergal said, "It seems to me that there was nothing much wrong with what we were doing before—flyovers, with a great deal more care in correlating satellite pictures." Rebekkah nodded. She was not satisfied, but she could not fight the weather, and her concerns were being taken seriously. Havergal turned to Sandek.

The Meshar godfather was squatting on a low settee, a dusty old piece he blended into very well. He was smoking a dry leaf rolled into a stick; it gave off a thin reek.

"Modal's good friend Barak is quite well, I hear," said Havergal.

"He is boasting of his adventures," Sandek said dryly.

"And does he feel that *we* put him at risk?"

"No, by the Angry God! We want to get out into the world where the wind is in our teeth!"

"We are unable to deliver the Crystalloids to their home because it is too close to the volcano," Havergal said, "and Lef will tell you that we may also have to relocate the Yefni for the same reason!"

"Let him tell me. I want to be out of this! On my home world I put blood to a document swearing that I take the fire on my head. So be it."

Lef pushed a sulfur tube from his gill and said in a mild warble, "Why not? *We* are satisfied with our new location. We lived among volcanoes all our lives and had no desire whatever to leave home. It is time to take up lives for ourselves, not be pushed from here to there like an *ip*-game piece."

Havergal said, "You have so far adjusted beautifully to heavy-gravity surroundings, but you must realize that a volcanic outburst here is not a few fire sprays and a little puff of smoke. It is a mountain of fire falling on you. And on you Meshar—or me, Frederick Havergal, because you are my responsibility."

Sandek said, "Do not take so great a burden, Sir Lord Havergal. Freedom does not lose its value when it is dangerous."

"If I can't persuade you, then I'd better stop playing the fool and let you move out. Soon as possible." Havergal, wrapped in a dull cold silence, left the room. "It is too bad for him," said Sandek. "We are not his children, no matter how much he wishes to think so."

Sandek held Erez's hand and told her, in his fanged and hissing speech, that a home in the open wilderness was to be prepared for her. She smiled a little, as always, but her eyes looked frightened. He patted her arm and glanced sidelong at Ardagh.

Ardagh examined the instruments in the autoclave and murmured, "Erez is healing so well I hope you will not want to move her until most of this growth is gone, Doctor Sandek."

"It depends whether there are those here who will care for her when we have moved, Doctor Colquhoun."

Ardagh touched the scratchy braid. "I like Erez very much. If I disliked her very much I would care for her just as well." She smiled, almost mischievously. "I would even bring her out and stay with the rest of you in your settlement if she was really unhappy here with us. But I don't recommend it."

Sandek gave her one of his looks and spoke to Erez in their own language. Erez coughed a little—her heart was jumpy and her breath caught at times—and said a few words. Then she smiled and reached for Ardagh's hand.

Sandek said to Ardagh, "You see. I am also capable of giving free choices."

"What have you got for me today, Modal?"

"I have programmed this trimmer to do the diagnostics on these units."

"You get past your own diagnostics?"

"Fairly well. I doubt that the mechs believed everything I said."

"What in particular, Modal?"

"That the fire followed me, followed my groundcar. Purposely. The mechs tell me that I was only in the wrong place. Perhaps they were right."

"Barak saw whatever you saw. . . ."

"Yes, but he was too fearful to be clear in his mind about it. I didn't want to disturb him further. Should I have mentioned that?"

"No. . . . I'm afraid the things that need examining will eventually be all too clear."

"Svendahl-gren?" Roshah turned his name into something rich and musical.

"Yes, Madame."

"Naughty child, you need not steal kitchen food midnights and run from me so guiltstruck."

If Sven, at his size, had been a child, Roshah might almost have been big enough to be his mother. Otherwise no way, for she had little nose and no chin, a lot of blubber, and vestigial webs between her fingers. Sven carefully put down his tools beside the refrigeration unit he had been working on.

"Tell me again, please, Roshah."

She stared at him through the windows of her eyelids. Her large mouth opened to display its racks of pointed teeth, a gesture meant to be ingratiating. "That you steal food? Like my children? You do not know that?" Roshah was a lab technician who slept and ate in snatches like many Bimanda, and so often drew guard duty. With her mouth closed she was not intimidating; she had gentle gold eyes, and wore bodysuits of opaline fish scales.

"No," Sven said. "I don't know that. I eat good meals and nothing more. Did you really see me steal food?"

"Yes, Svendahl, and more than one time. I don't say, because the food is there for your need. I only wonder why."

"But I don't. I never did. . . . I don't understand."

"Some Solthrees walk in sleep, just like us Bimanda, and why not?"

"Solthrees don't do that unless they're quite disturbed, and I don't think I am, that's why. What exactly did you see, Roshah?"

"In the night before this night I come making rounds very quiet. Very quiet and past midnight. I see this big fellow your size take food from the freezer, and I go to put light on him with my lantern, and it is you, so I say, 'Why are you doing that, Sven?' but you knock the light from my hand, not so polite, and run. But this past night you see me coming and run before I speak."

"What time last night? Before I went after Mod Dahlgren?"

"It must be so, yes."

"And the night before you turned the flashlight on and saw . . . ?"

"One side of a face: eye, nose, mouth. Yours."

"Brown eye?"

"That I cannot see so well."

"But four arms?"

"I do not notice."

"Roshah . . . how can you say that?"

"I can say it if I want to. Your arms mean nothing to me, Svendahl-gren. It is your head that means something."

"I'm glad you think so. . . . Have you told anyone of this?"

"Good man, I am not one to tell tales of my friends who become hungry by night. I tell no one."

"Then tell, Roshah. Tell Sir Frederick that I want him to know. No need to tell others."

"If in good truth you want it told, him and none other. I am no disturber."

Sven thought of doubles. Mod Dahlgren, a machine in the shape of his father, created double: in line of body, timbre of voice, even in the trace of arrogance humbled by mean experience.

The intruder, X, mistaken for him, Sven, without trying at all: *I put light on him and it is you, Sven*. Mod Dahlgren had never been mistaken for anyone.

He wished he had not felt the deep obligation to inform Sir Frederick of the night wanderer. Unconsciously he had pieced together a picture: X perhaps half-wanting to be found, Havergal only half-wanting to find him. He had an

90

obscure desire to protect X, though what for or what from he did not know. If this was really the son of Edvard Dahlgren, adopted and claimed by Havergal . . .

. . . He is older than me, born first, the original . . . and I, cobbled from parts of seed in a warped shape . . . am the double. . . .

Better not think too far in that direction.

He finished the rest of the day's tasks without speaking much to anyone else. Ardagh was busy treating Barak, who was afflicted with a fungus which had homed in on the grainy Meshar skin. Havergal was racking his brains to answer, among other things, the question of a home for the Crystalloids who could not be allowed to settle near the flank of a viciously active volcano. Sven, unable to clear his mind of the intruder and unwilling to discuss him with anyone, was content not to have to speak with either of them now.

He ate dinner with the Solthrees and other compatibles. Stacking dishes in the big steamers, he began to feel that he was under observation. Probably he had become hyper-sensitive, and the feeling was nothing but one more twinge of his aching ribs. In this hangarlike room, white-painted and smelling of rehydrated foods, there was no place for shadows.

Alone in the library, and then alone in his quarters where no one could possibly see him, he forgot his feelings. As sleep gathered in him he began to think of his valley, and how sweet it would be to fall asleep there, if he could ever find it again, and if it was not ravaged by storms.

It wound about his dreams, with the sweetness of grass and flowers, and dim forms emerging from behind hill-ocks and ferns: a white goat? a black gibbon? A tall man, Edvard Dahlgren, or a clone, or . . .

A tremendous thump in his gut below the sternum drove his breath out of him, he could not breathe, air was gone, sucked away, he was smothering, knees up to chin, fetally, reverse of birth—he dragged air howling, twisted his head away from—what weapon? a fist—caught the blow on the side of his jaw, half its force spent, grabbed for the lashing arms with his upper hands, propped himself forward with the lower ones.

The dim night-light gave him the shadow, tall figure, Solthree, no question; two arms, certainly, big arching skull and clothed in rags with strips hanging down; the wrists he had caught at slashed up and out, breaking his hold, some kind of fighting technique; Sven had none whatever, could not react quickly enough. But this one did not quite overmatch him: He seemed rather weak—from hunger, perhaps, and the wounds that had left so bloody a trail. Sven had no desire to vanquish X; he wanted to discover. He grabbed a handful of rags that tore rottenly as the shadow pulled away and came forward again to beat at his head and shoulders.

"Stop, you idiot! I want to talk to you!" He pushed, levered himself off the bed with his foot.

X grunted, a sound like *unh!* and kept pummeling.

Sven bore him back. "I only want to talk!"

A grunt again. It occurred to him that the man might not understand *lingua*; his own English was awkward, with a heavy accent, inherited from Dahlgren, that he had worked hard to get rid of. "Give over, man. This is useless."

"No, no!" If Sven wanted to talk, X wanted only to batter him, and when Sven tried to grasp his arm once more, broke away savagely, leaving a few tatters in his wake as he staggered out of the door.

Sven collapsed back on the bed with a vicious cramp; all his ribs wrenched with pain; he was panting, and could not have followed if he had really wanted.

What he saw as the motiveless anger of this attack

depressed him even more than the pain; there was no way out of reporting this, and no way of expressing his pity for the attacker.

19

.Prima.

.Yes, Metals?.

.Your hopes of help are false. We have been here many turns around the source and still we are trapped. Our ship is broken almost in two. We have no mode of travel. Our supplies are ruined. You cannot move and I can barely stir. You must admit these facts.

.I admit them.

.Can we get help from this strange being you claim to sense?.

.I do not know. It is like no other person I have known.

.That is too vague even for me to believe. There is no help for us ever and I blame you for willfully driving us in wrong directions.

.I blame myself for being mistaken but I did not purposely bring you to this state.

.I am sure others will join me in disagreeing with you. You sisters what have you to say?.

.You are right Sister Metals, said Ordnance. .My engine is destroyed and my light cells and shielding plates are broken and scattered. If you had only drawn back when we were attacked Prima.

Prima could not think what to say to this, for she had worked frantically to avoid her attackers.

.What a fool you are Ordnance, said Engineer. .You know what great efforts we made and how Prima kept our fears at bay.

.And we are still alive and arguing, said Maintenance.

.Say what you will you cannot stop me from believing that Prima's gross negligence has caused our torment. Prima I will drive you into the fire if I can. That will end your hopes.

The world heaped up its winds until they were thick and rushing as its tidal waves. Flight plans were scrubbed in favor of satellite reports. The Meshar postponed their move, and the Yefni out in their sulfur pits were not heard from at all; but nothing endangered them except their own diseases, and death from old age; they were otherwise indestructible.

The sky bellowed and the rock trembled beneath the Station. The building's walls shifted in accordance with its structural principles; minutely, but with uneasy gritting sounds.

The storm went on for three days, slowly intensifying.

.Daughters, why are you attacking me?.

Metals and Ordnance would not answer. They formed their thought into a stream of anger directed at Prima.

.Daughters.

Ordnance had come to rest on a power cell which she was sharing with Metals; it had been charged by the heat and light of subterranean fires. Her softer metals and those of the other Crystallines had lost much of their magnetism in the heat, and there was little possibility of movement, but no others had a whole power cell to feed on, and none transmitted thoughts so clear and strong.

.And warped and stupid., Prima told herself, struggling to keep her mind from the vortex of fury trying to devour her. She pressed her hopes toward the being whose presence had brought her some comfort.

.Receiver-of-thought? Say you know I am here.

:I always know you are here, First One. The winds and fires come when you hurt.

.I do not understand that.

:I think the world is angry at you, Stone Woman.

.For what is the world angry at me? It is the world that injured me and my daughters. Pulled us down into itself. Has driven us all half mad. Is doing its best to destroy us. Say that you mean me no harm. Even that you mean me well.

:I mean you well, First One, but the world is angry, and—and I hurt when you do. It harms me when it lasts so long. I can't speak to you any more right now.:

.Do not leave me Receiver-of-thought. We have hardly begun to speak.

:Don't you notice the light and the dark? I have been with you for three days and three nights, with little sleep—but you don't sleep at all. We live differently from you, and not on the same kind of time.:

.We? There are others like you? Ask them to communicate with me.

:There is no other like me, First One, I must do all the receiving and sending of thought for those others. But I am young and this has been a long time for me, your thoughts take long and long. It is already noon on the fourth day. I am tired now. I must sleep or I will be sick.:

.Please help me Thoughtspeaker. I can not stand the burning or the anger of my daughters. Please.

Han Li screamed, "I can't help you! I don't know how!" She gave a great shudder and collapsed into a faint.

Rebekkah hurried to pull her up. The Crystalloid waiting to speak with her crouched immobile on his metal grid while the young telepath, Yav, said, "She is only asleep, Madam."

"I'm afraid she's more likely unconscious."

Yav pushed at Han Li gently with his snout. She stirred a little and murmured protestingly. "She has slept little and the persons she speaks with are suffering a great deal."

Rebekkah said, "Without an esp shield, there's no way I can protect her from those Crystals. What am I to do?"

First One does not want to communicate any more. Or perhaps cannot. Her presence remains: red point in the blackness of the mind.

.Help.

One thought drawn out. One thought drawn out forever. A long high singing. Hot white line. Pulsing infinitely slow. Far away and faintly now: clicking, tapping, tick-tick, old Stone Brother Crystalloid crouches intoxicated by his own brilliance. But here this white pulsing, slow burning red on black, is the shape of soul for Han Li.

Her eyes embedded in Prima's essence see lurid black flat onyx shapes this white sings through. The world reaches only weakly through this glass. Han Li squints.

A long night follows; she drifts in a half sleep, Prima always with her, and sometimes those treacherous daughters stabbing with their hot sharp hatred. Rebekkah is snoring a little in an exhausted sleep and Han Li watches her and waits for morning. She knows the time of day very well, and can tell it here because some designer was wise enough to build windows in these living quarters. The thick glass circle has been fatigued by the elements and is only translucent: The quartered panes show the beginning of the long dawn.

Night makes Han Li fearful. In the terrible camps not long enough ago the ravaged people who lost everything dear to their own bodies tried in the darkness to recapture it in hers.

It is not surprising that they chose her.

She is not one they would want to look at hard, not in the daytime. She is underdeveloped, lubberly, goes half-crouching, and hardly impinges on the world: eyes slitted and round silent face a clock without hands. Not quite a person. Involving themselves with her flesh is like coping with dreams, terrors, fantasies; it is in the stillness and darkness of night. They wake to daylight and need not admit she is real.

Han Li, pushing away the clawing, trembling hands, knew enough about their reality. Except for Rebekkah's kindness these experiences are all she has known of love. And she is afraid of the night.

The rains have paused; the dawn is long and slow and full of shadows. Han Li does not mind shadows: not now; they are her hiding place from those around her when she goes out to follow and turn off Prima's brilliant white pain. It is something like the horrid spear-through-the-eye pain called migraine that she gets sometimes after talking with Stone Brother.

Bekkah says you must put on extra clothes when you go out, Han Li. Bekkah worries about her: chills, migraines, not getting enough sleep, being frightened and tormented by Prima and her daughters. Han Li does not worry, but to please Bekkah she will put on her weather suit, a hooded zip patterned in red and yellow squares. She finds it in the storage cupboard, now squared in shades of gray. Then ties up the thick-soled boots that keep her feet straight and balanced. She is very quiet, but it would take a lot of noise to wake Rebekkah from that sleep.

One kind woman in the camps used to tell Han Li what she called fairy stories. Many of them were about a girl wandering in a forest and the strange monsters she met there. Han Li did not understand the plots and was bored by the monsters, but she liked the girl, who seemed safe and protected even while she was lost in the wilderness, and the forest was a place where there was peace. Now Han Li is the girl, going into a forest along the burning

97

beam to the red heart of the pain. She will pluck First One out of the fires and bring the peace.

Yav is quartered in a cleared-out supply room attached to the apartment where Han Li and Rebekkah live; he is content with his tub of sulfur mud and the careful if jury-rigged ventilating arrangements balancing his benefits against his ill effects. He does not sleep in the way vertebrates do but lies in coils faintly dreaming of a volcano-lit world he has never known, where the atmosphere is really rich. In this state he perceives that Han Li is preparing to go out into the raging jungle with nothing more than a thin layer of covering and a packet of dry food saved from her last meal.

Yav calls, :*Madame VanderZande! Rebekkah! Wake up!*: and then, :*Han Li! Come back, come back!*: But one is too weary, and the other too determined in her course of action, to answer; he flows from his tub of mud to a tank of water, washing himself off and fastening on cylinders of mud and compressed atmosphere. His five meters and fifty kilos coil and leap, coil and leap: he catches hold of Han Li's leg at the knee joint. She wrenches his tail away with her hand—she has brute strength—and kicks at him. He pulls away, warbling in pain. She has unlatched the lock, dashed through the doorway, and is running down the dimmed hallways. It is the deep gray hour of predawn—three hours really—when nothing happens except to insomniacs. There are no sentries in sight or esp range.

Yav is nervous: He has not got adult control of all his great length and is afraid to grasp the girl firmly, but if he is not incisive she will kick at him again. He lurks in the shadows of walls and doorways; his helical coils click lightly on the floor.

She rounds a corner; he follows and is immediately at a loss; he feels as if some old trick has been played on him:

She is gone. His mind is with hers, but her senses have been co-opted by the Empress of Stones, and he cannot tell what she is seeing or touching. There are doors and doors, but they all lead into other rooms. He thrashes in panic, and cries for help.

Han Li has found a doorway into which three doors open. She knows that one of them leads down a narrow winding stair because Bekkah brought her in that way after she was upset by the Crystals when they flew over the crater. Four levels down at the foot there is a heavy door with a complicated latching-and-locking device. Han Li lifts the hands that have manipulated the block of cubes so many times; pushes at Prima's insistent presence: She takes inferences from materials that are dead to others. Touches sensitive points, tentatively at first and then surely—the lock hums and clicks—and within a minute drags down on the heavy bar: The door swings outward into the hangar.

It is a dark place smelling of heavy oil, and when illuminated, merely dim. The vehicles are locked in by big hangar doors, but the smaller personal entrance is merely latched from within. She unlatches it and barely has time to move aside before the door crashes into the wall from the force of the tempest. It pulls back, dragged by its hydraulic closure, but Han Li is out and rolling under the wind across the wet tarmac.

The hurricane is running down, and the wind slathers about like a beast licking itself after eating. During the first lull she scuttles on fours over the landing field, not defending herself from spatters of leaves and twigs. The morning is already hot and drenched. A runway stretches from this field to a launch pad a kilometer distant, but it does not lead to the volcano. As Han Li crawls from the hard wet surface into the edge of the boggy forest a great fern frond breaks off and knocks her over. She pulls herself up quickly and slips into the half-light of the water-colored forest. The only pain she feels is Prima's.

20

The Meshar listened to the howling of the storm and got restless. The men and the women felt suffocated with each other. They were cramped in their quarters, and their only diversion was to visit with Erez; they thirsted for the feel of rushing air and sweeping rain. Eventually, except for Sandek and Erez, they picked up in twos and threes and went into the Pit.

Since it had not been prepared for them, they simply preempted it, moving like a gypsy camp into a concrete bowl without plantings, landscaping, or even soil. They arranged the lighting in the pattern of the local day, put up their temporary leather tents, and set up altars for their gods. Havergal did not care much for an action that defied his authority, but he was wise enough not to bring up an issue that did not involve risk or danger.

Ardagh's career now encompassed one patient. Erez's progress had leveled: Each day she lost a few grams, a few millimeters. Ardagh was more than satisfied with a slow and stable healing process, because there was evidence of some mild heart damage, enough to trim a narrow edge off future activity. But days of increasing energy and activity were interrupted by others when Erez suffered low fever and listlessness. There was little to be done for them.

So Ardagh's free time had been taken up with care for

the rest of the Meshar. Mainly they wanted advice about the risks of local living conditions rather than their own health, and Ardagh was careful to keep it local; Flanders and Sandek knew more general medicine than she did. Still, she was able to make herself useful and at the same time observe the Meshar.

She found that they were proud, sensitive, good-humored, short-tempered, vulgar, loyal—everything that could have been predicted of a microcosmic tribe with a primitive culture who were both nervous and eager about technology. She wondered what their other qualities were, the ones she had been unable to discern when they were trammeled into such unnatural conditions among bare walls and sterile furnishings. Likely she would never find out: Once she was separated from them she would be simply an alien.

In the meantime she learned to know Erez.

They had put together a rough pidgin, of the kind Rebekkah used when speaking to Han Li, and they found out about as much of each other as two family women can do. They discussed the trouble with the male sex and the difficulties of motherhood; Erez was part-mother to all the other children of the group. She admired Ardagh's holo of Vardy and taught her a simple game with a complicated point-counting system using Durbha tally sticks. These mild exercises kept both of them calm while the other Meshar grumbled around them. Sandek regarded the exchanges with a sardonic eye but said only, "I am glad that Erez is content." He was also an observer.

On the day when the Meshar actually moved out, Ardagh came from her room in the early morning and was astonished to find their quarters swept clean and without a scrap of garbage. Sandek was in his small herbarium, grinding medicines in an ancient mortar.

"Your family certainly went quickly."

"During storms they light fires to worship Rakha-manah, and that cannot be done here."

Ardagh began to think of smoke and ventilation, but Sandek said: "Our little branches make no more smoke than the leaf I roll up and set alight. Small hot fires; Rakhamanah is the angry-god."

Erez said something that Ardagh was only on the edge of understanding. Sandek translated indulgently: "Erez says we have no other kind."

She was about to smile at Erez's little joke, and paused. The woman's brilliant red eye membranes had turned to dull pink, and the tissue of her nose was pale and dry; her breath rustled. Ardagh touched her forehead and found it hot.

Sandek rose to fill a cup of water. "Her heart is very irregular, and her temperature is up three points by your measure."

"I know it has been rising these last few days, but no more than a degree total. When did this happen?"

"This night past, after midnight. I brought Flanders to see her." He gave Erez her drink and moved into the next room, where the scales and sterile supplies were. "You were sleeping."

"You could have wakened me." But she knew, with the familial intuitiveness she had learned from the Meshar, what he would say next.

"There was nothing to be done."

Willfully, she misread him. The woman had a little fever; her heart was ticky. She was not hexed or magicked. "Antipyretics would—"

"Flanders gave her those." He looked through the doorway at Erez, who had picked up a handful of tally sticks and was ruffling them between her fingers. "And drugs to steady her heart as well . . . but . . ."

All at once Ardagh was short of breath. "I don't have to believe that—that—"

"That her resistance is low and her heart is damaged beyond repair? And that even you do not know enough to help her? I have often heard you express admiration for the Meshar's stamina and ability to shake off infection. We need that. . . . Meshar do not stay ill for very long." He looked sidelong at Ardagh and said, "Whatever cause you had for anger will soon be gone."

"That's a terrible thing to say!" Ardagh stared at him in dull horror. "You were the one who made me angry. Erez never did. Even if she had I'd still love her." *Perhaps, man, you are angry at me. I claimed too damned much wisdom.* "You won't object if I do whatever I can to save her. I won't make her uncomfortable."

He muttered, "I will only be grateful."

Ardagh stayed with Erez from that moment, hooking her to the EKG and the sphygmograph, wiping her down with wet cloths. It was a painful irony that except for her encroaching listlessness Erez looked better than she had done since Ardagh met her. The tumor strangling her heart had shrunk away until it was only a thickening of the waist. Ardagh was far too experienced to disregard Sandek's wisdom or believe she could cure this woman whose species she hardly knew. Erez was moving away from her; although she made the same jokes and gestures as she had done yesterday and the days before, she had the look of foreknowledge, the awareness of coming death. And something more subtle.

I think she is even pitying me for my naïveté.

But Ardagh went on cooling her down and watching the thready beat of her heart.

Sandek spelled her, but every once in a while she caught him looking away, ears pricked—likely for noises from the Pit, though it was two levels down.

103

"Why don't you go and stay with your people for a while? Erez and I will get along well and I'll send for you if I need you."

"No." After a moment he added, "I am too old to worship the angry-god."

Ardagh thought: *They* know Erez is dying. She wondered if the Meshar were engaged in some kind of ritual attempt to save her . . . or if it was another kind of ritual entirely, and they did not want Sandek to join it.

"You are not old," said Erez, and turned to Ardagh for emphasis. "He is not-not." She ran her narrow black tongue around her dry lips; her breath hissed. She lifted the tally sticks: "Play now, yah?"

"O-yah." Ardagh dealt sticks. Erez flipped one in two short fingers and caught it. She played it in the proper order, then lay back with the fanged smile that should not have been shy. Her eyes seemed pupilless and very deep.

Ardagh placed her sticks and looked at Erez. Erez was still smiling, still looking back at her.

"She is dead," said Sandek.

Ardagh searched for pulses, heartbeat, and breath; there were none, nothing but a rebounding emptiness, as if part of her own life force had washed away. She began to fold the bedcovers around Erez and stopped, incapable of covering the look and the smile.

Sandek was crouching, beating his hands together and striking the floor with his tail in a rhythm of prayer probably to some other angry god. He cried out in long ululations broken by glottal clicks: "O eh hei'i ya ya'a'a . . ."

Ardagh watched, bound in the strangeness of their shared infirmary. Abruptly he stopped, picked up a knife from the instrument drawer, and reached out to Ardagh. "What—"

"The braid." He hooked the knife under, carefully, to

cut it; then pulled it away from her neck and looped it in his belt. "You do not want to keep her spirit captive."

"No." The braid had been a token of her affectionate relationship with Erez—and a symbol of her bondage to Sandek.

Sandek put the knife away and squatted in a corner with toes splayed, arms folded. His haggard eyes held the same ironic wariness. He showed no intention of moving.

"Aren't you going to tell the others that Erez is dead?"

"Why should I? They do not care. She was dead to them as soon as I asked for help outside us—your help, Doctor Colquhoun. I gave away my authority—and perhaps my responsibility—in the hope of saving her."

She had seen that, now that she thought of it, when none of the men ever consulted with him. But, "You have been telling me she could not have been saved."

"Yes, and that is true."

"You are a brave man." He said nothing. "Will they— try to harm you . . . or shun you?"

"I do not know. This situation has never come up before. Whatever they choose, that is what I will accept."

"To be wiped out of their consciousness or—or killed, for trying to save a life?"

He said harshly, "Remember that I am Meshar, and do not want to be other." He stared up at her with eyes very red and hands hanging over his knees. He seemed firm in his resignation rather than fearful.

Yet she remembered how his head had turned to listen for sounds from the Pit.

It did not seem to her that the Meshar were a savage people. She recalled another conversation about Erez. *Likely she will not have children. She will care for our other ones. . . . Did you think we would drive her away? Kill her?* The Meshar women had hurried to comfort and care for Erez after her treatment. But other outworld patients

Ardagh had healed were sometimes abandoned to the charity of alien hospitals when their people shipped out—only because of a bad scar or losing the tip of a digit. Some much gentler than the Meshar. And on one occasion her work had been eradicated by ritual murder.

Sandek was sitting in a kind of emptiness. He had no function now that Erez was dead.

Ardagh said, "Please, Doctor Sandek. Get up. Take something to eat." He rose, but only to go into the cubicle where he had his bedroll, and close the door. She was left with Erez's body.

She was hardly conscious of what she was doing until she found herself on the elevator going down, instead of up, and getting out at the Pit floor, outside the north doors. Only whispers of deep voices came through them, in entreaty or complaint.

Always she had honored the laws of the people she had served, short of those that sanctioned maiming or killing.

The faraway voices within the doors rose in a great outcry, and she remembered that Rakhamanah was the angry god. She did not want to be there—but her body was tense with sorrow and dismay: She could not help herself.

The heavy slabs worked in silence; she pulled them apart and slipped between, into the glass-walled concourse and through its open doors, letting a beam of yellow light into dimness punctuated by flames: Echoes of the last cry rolled once about the walls and faded. The Meshar, busy with their fires, did not see her. The air in the Pit was cold and faintly smoky; it smelled of aromatic twigs and musky sweat.

The Meshar raised their voices once more in a furious and sustained onrush of sound: They crouched before their fires bellowing resentments against their god, falling silent only when they were hoarse. The men wore heavy leggings as well as their stiff leather vests: They squatted to cast sticks that flamed hissing; the kneeling women were dressed in thick dark cloth sewn with colored designs of scaly reptile skin. Their eyes did not look anywhere but inward.

Ardagh waited. She had thought to approach them when they finished with their ceremonies, but she saw that their stillness was even fiercer than the sounds they had been making: They crouched like ancient figures carved in onyx, highlighted in fire red. She waited only for them to pray aloud and let her get out of the Pit unnoticed.

But now they raised voices in a kind of ritual conversation, the men snapping orders and commands, the women grumbling and snarling a nagging commentary. The conversation turned to obscene gestures and jeering that intensified to breathless rasping and then stopped.

In a sharp instant the dark shapes of men fell growling upon women who flailed and shrieked beneath them, their bodies clenched in ecstatic rage.

Ardagh, struck with shame for having intruded on such deep privacy, gave an involuntary cry.

In one eyeblink she saw them standing facing her, hands up and out holding invisible weapons, warrior men and women, crouching low enough to balance on the blades of their tails, never to give way, eyes burning red (she could not understand how she saw this in such darkness), angry mouths twisted, bodies flattened to silhouettes, shadows, each outline shimmered white, an eyeblink and

they shimmered on the flagstones of the next level up, ten meters nearer: a flicker, their outlines swelled: a ripple of light, they stood yet a level higher and

a blink, shadows turned flesh, they surrounded Ardagh, struck her with the shockwave of their anger, she trembled against the glass. She could almost taste the anger

107

simmered in smoke and musk. In the faint glow of ceiling lamps that gave no more light than a night sky, she saw that the warrior in the forefront was Barak.

They walled her. Her teeth were chattering so hard her breath shuddered.

"Erez is dead," she stammered.

"Yes," said the iron voices. "What do you want?"

She could hardly speak without biting her tongue. "I—I'm afraid for Sandek."

A relaxing of tension. The Meshar lowered their phantom spears and shields and stood at ease. "Why? He can take care of himself."

"He won't move. He's afraid you will . . . hurt him."

"Hurt? Aho, that is a sickness of his mind. Do you think we are only tribal? He is an old man with a dead penis, and it is no sin or crime for him to lose authority. He is not our leader now, but he is still our doctor. Why does he need you to beg for him?"

"I'm not begging. If he knew I had come here he would be much angrier with me than you are."

"We are not angry with you," said Barak, almost kindly.

"It seemed as if you were," said Ardagh, and embarrassed herself further by bursting into tears.

"God damn it, Ardagh, you'd better tell me! Did they hurt you? Did they make threats?"

"No."

"Then why are you crying so much?"

She could not seem to stop crying. She swabbed her face, gave up, and let the tears run down her jaw. She was shivering like mad even with all of Sven's arms around her. Sandek was squatting nearby with his head cocked, regarding her quizzically; Barak, his lieutenant Har, and others were gathered at the infirmary door, not Pit-

Meshar now, but the good-natured raucous ones who had come in and out to visit Erez.

"It felt as if everyone was so angry at me, everyone in the world, any world, and—I don't want to talk about this any more now. I just want to lie down somewhere."

Barak said, "Please, Madame Doctor, if you think we have hurt you in some way tell us and do not say so when you are out of our way."

"I wouldn't do that!" She pulled herself out of Sven's arms and blew her nose. "Maybe I wanted to avoid saying how ashamed I was at being there in the Pit when you were doing something so private."

"That was not private, and it is nothing to be ashamed about. It is one of our mating seasons and we always do it that way. It was not meant to be a threat to you."

Ardagh whispered: "It was the other thing . . ."

They looked at her in blank curiosity.

"You became, I thought—maybe the smoke from your fires is some kind of hallucinogen to us—I thought you became flat black shapes, like shadows . . . you flickered, and you were halfway toward me, and it happened again, and you were surrounding me. . . ."

"And it made you believe we threatened you?"

Ardagh moved aside the hand Sven had put around her shoulder. "No. That had nothing to do with threats. That—if I wasn't hallucinating—I've seen people from many worlds who did very unusual things—but—and the strangeness frightened me—nothing so marvelous as teleporting."

"Is that what it is called?" said Barak. "Oh, Madame, we cannot help that. It is only a thing we do when we believe *we* are being threatened."

Ardagh was exhausted, and wanted only to leave problems to other people. Sven did not have time to satisfy his

109

curiosity about the Meshar because he had been called out to search for the runaway, Han Li. But Ardagh found a final comment lying on her pillow in the shape of a circlet of dull-blonde braid, uncut.

Next day the Meshar—with Sandek—moved out into the forest.

21

.Keep away from her Receiver-of-thought. She is a mad one.
.She will bring you into the fire pit.
.She is full of doom.

Han Li did not know where she was. She was crouching between the flanges of a buttress tree, everything about her wet and filthy. She hardly noticed this, nor that she was shivering. Her left eye had exploded with lightning flashes and she trembled in fear of the lancing pain that would follow.

.Receiver-of-thought. Prima was being overborne by the drive of Ordnance and Metals: *I am losing power and cannot reach you. Speak.* But Han Li could not think.

Desperately then, *.Steerer and Sensor. Maintenance and Engineer. Are you alive? Speak.*

. There is nothing to say. Prima our strength and hope are gone and so is our trust. You have deceived us. There is no such being as you have claimed or it would speak to us too. If it exists it does not care for us. You have led us into the depths of destruction. May you suffer torment forever. We hate and despise and revile and condemn and abhor and despise and and and . . .

.You have gone mad.

Han Li's lightning unfolded into ever more complex fractals. She could not see or think beyond them.

. Thoughtspeaker. The signal was faint. . . . .*Thought-speaker.*

Empress of Stones, your children are destroying you.

The blazing pain struck, and she whimpered; then blessedly the drowsiness came, and she sank into profound sleep.

She woke surrounded by warmth, opened the eye that was not aching and saw flesh. Two left hands: Sven, and morning light beyond him. She rolled her sore eye in its socket, and found that it was working and that she could see with it; shook her head gingerly to discover if the pain was still crashing around in it like a giant ball bearing. The steel ball had shrunk. The Crystals did not speak: only their presence hissed faintly like an unconnected comm line.

"I am the girl," she said.

"Which one?" Sven asked.

"The one in the forest."

"The Lost Princess?"

"Yes. The Empress of Stones is in prison."

"Maybe she should stay there." Sven thought of the dreadful erg-Queen, an empress of gems and metals whom he had battled across this tract of land fifteen years ago.

"She says: Thoughtspeaker, help me. I am burning. My limbs are melting and my daughters hate me. Oh she is being smashed by hatred! It's too much, I—"

"How do you think you can help her?"

"First I must find her, and then bring others to free her. I can't go into the fire alone."

The forest stood in a rare moment of pearly calm. "You can't do more now. You've got to come back with us until we can help you." Sven could not quite believe in these creatures, no more than he would dare believe in his valley.

"By then she will be truly destroyed." Then she said, "You don't believe me. The Crystals are not real to you."

He hesitated a moment. "I might not have believed you . . . but you talk with Crystalloids . . . and once I knew a child—much younger than you—who could control and communicate with machines, using esp. . . ." He did not quite believe in the Crystalloids either.

He had descended from a buzzer he was sharing with Aguerido, guided by Yav riding in another. The two craft hovered in the attic under the tops of trees and ferns, ready to be called down.

"There's too much growth here," he told Aguerido. "Can you find a clearing nearby?"

"Half a km north by west. Hurry before the wind picks up."

"Come on, Han Li, we've got to go fast." The headache had made her sluggish of movement. He lifted her, a bundle of red and yellow squares.

"No! I want to find First One!"

"We'll do it, come on!"

"She hurts! And I am her friend, the only one."

"Sven!" The voice crackled in his earpiece. "The sky's thickening in the southwest. I can just see you, and I'm going to come down and drop the ladder."

"Take care! You can get trapped in the vines—here, come on—now! Han Li!"

"I want—"

"Not to starve and die first, for God's sake! Grab on here!"

He watched her pulled up clinging, like a cub on a branch, and whimpering faintly. Aguerido hauled her through the open port and dropped the ladder again.

Immediately it caught on a cluster of twigs, and the grasping vine ends wrapped it.

"Oh Aguerido!" It was well out of Sven's reach, and

112

Aguerido pulled at it without doing more than shake the tree it was attached to. The light wind crept in about them and began shuffling the leaves, searching where to do mischief.

Sven climbed up into the complex of tree trunks and shinnied out along the limb. He was pulling at the vines around the ladder's rung when the wind cracked like a whip and snapped the tip of the branch; the ladder swung away out of reach while Aguerido cursed and tried to steady the buzzer in the gusting wind and at the same time calm down Han Li, who had taken fright at the jolting. Her treble and his gasping breath filled Sven's earpiece.

The ladder was hopelessly lost, and the craft fought against the current of a new storm. Sven clung to his bucking branch, gasping.

"Get going!" Nothing but static. "Aguerido!" He could no longer see the buzzer.

The clouds boiled overhead and lightning slapped the tree's farther flank: Its branches met those of the blue fire: it leaped in the earth before it cracked apart. Sven jerked backward and fell down into the riven shank while flames hissed and sizzled along the great main trunk. He did not hear himself howl, for the instantaneous thunderclap deafened him. His sight was whitened first by lightning and then by stars of pain: He thought his back was broken.

He found that he could move, one leg at least; he could not open his eyes for pain, and every tooth ached. A half-meter away fires hissed in the tree bark; he was whole, left to give thanks for his life and curse himself for a fool: His radio was dead and his suit torn half off his right arms.

He was trapped between the two raw halves of the big trunk; it clamped his right leg and hip; his foot twisted out into a cramp. He could not pull himself out, and struggling drove him deeper. He gave over, to save strength.

:Sven!: Yav called. :Sven, are you there?:

:Yes! I'm caught in the tree and I can't get out. Don't hang around here, for God's sake. Get out of this storm!:

: . . . will come back!:

Sven made one more feverish attempt to free himself from the tree's grasp. But the huge bole beside him, still flickering, yielded and crashed to the ground. The shudder that followed shook him down further into the rift. He rested his head against the pithy wood and wept for pain and frustration.

After a while—he did not look at his chronometer—the flames ebbed, hissing in the rain.

22

Time warped. He tried to draw his mind away from the pain, but it was an inhabitant: It crowded out his reason. When the wind calmed a little the rain washed down spattering him with dead insects and leaves; live insects and worms crawled into the torn openings of his rain suit and suffocated in his sweating creases; vine tendrils caressed him and wove themselves into the netting of his undersuit. He shuddered with memories of mutated vines that rooted in the eyes and mouths of the unwary, and worms that plunged into the flesh.

He lost the sense of time in pain and the torments brought by the hot wetness of the forest. The storm did not give over and there was no hope of help soon. The crashing bolts sounded like the crunch of huge and malevolent ergs wrenching their treads. He sank into numbness, his consciousness swung out and away. He dreamed that Han Li and Yav were crying out in the voices of stones:

—and my stone brothers cannot exist we cannot exist on this same world with these mad ones with these—

114

—must go back alone, my stone alone queen is crying O—

—O I am a shame to Lef and Sov, disgrace to genitors all, for Sven is lost, is lost—

—O lost—

—Be lost and die. Be lost and dead and gone forever—

He woke, racked and trembling, and sank again under a wave of pain. Dark-willed machines raised their steel claws to grasp and tear him.

Mists came. They swam in and out of his dreams. They moved in close and wet and faded back. They stood away and discussed him, moved in, then blew away with the wind. Came once more, gaped at him with blue bulging eyes, prodded with ratchet-nailed fingers. They gabbled at him, and then guffawed. "Oh go to hell," he muttered, and slid into blankness again.

Hands wrenched his body. He screamed; hands dumped him on the forest floor. He fainted black and out.

A kick woke him. He groaned. The insects and creeping things were dancing on his bruises. He was naked to the cool wet air of night—no, he was still wearing his net suit; it was torn. A voice bid him waken in a wordless snarl; rough hands pulled him up by the neck and slapped the side of his head.

He forced open his crusted lids and saw in the light of a primitive lantern the two faces of his unnatural siblings, the forest clones. His stomach knotted but he was past fainting now.

Sven looked up into their male and female versions of his face, warped by massive underslung jaws. They grinned. Both were older than he by a year or two and looked much more. Outdoor living aged prematurely. They had been created by ergs to replicate Edvard Dahlgren—unsuccessfully because they were stupid, unruly, and graceless; not even the cleverest of the ergs could remold them.

115

Dahlgren had done a little shaping: Before he left the planet he had had the female's harelip mended; she still had a thin beard and the thick growth of hair in armpits and groin.

She grinned lasciviously at Sven and twisted his ear; he knocked away her hand and deflected the chop aimed at his windpipe. But he had no more strength left after that gesture; he could barely shield himself when the pair of them rolled him back and forth and thumped him like a rag doll.

The male put on the headpiece of Sven's rainsuit and gibbered into its mouthpiece while he capered on the wet leaf floor: a grotesque in multiple ways, animal/human aping civilization in pale skin bursting with clumps of hair. The female, critical of pretension, or jealous, threw a clod of earth at him, he directed a kick at her, and Sven was hopeful that they would break out into a savage fight that would engage them and let him escape.

But the clones had learned something when Dahlgren freed them from the cage the ergs had kept them in: that a few moments of peace once in a while added spice to the conflict. They merely made faces at each other and joined to drag Sven by arms and legs along the ground toward a rocky outcropping at the base of a steep rise. There was a cave here, formed by split rocks covered with stones, cemented by sifted earth overgrown with vines and grasses.

Adam and Eve dumped Sven half under the overhang where he lay, too sore and weary to move, while the ebbing rain spattered him without washing off the leaves and bits of mold he was plastered with. Eve, who had taken an ominous interest in him, squatted grinning while the rain slicked her hair down in strings. Her hands hovered over him while decisions marched across her mind: where to hurt first.

Adam had crawled into the cave to collect a few billets of wood. Now, finding Eve idle, except for mischief-making, he cuffed her ear and barked. She spat at him, but backed away from Sven and crept under the stone eaves to pull out an armful of twigs and tuck them around the logs. As much as Sven was able to feel, he felt a spark of astonishment, though he was not too distracted to roll over and out of the rain. He knew the clones were cruel and savage: They had done their best to kill Dahlgren. He could not have imagined them developing far enough to plan for the future, and actually preparing for it. Perhaps necessity had brought out their latent capabilities in an evolutionary manner—as the expanded dimension of her feelings had forced Han Li to go beyond the primitive in expressing herself.

He was more astonished when Adam produced a lighter he could only have found in Sven's equipment pack and managed after some trial and error and a lot of cursing to light a fire with it, first igniting a twig and then flaming the grass and brush tucked around the logs. Some of the Station crew had evidently delivered to them the steel axe of technology. Eve then found a knife and several small dead animals of an overripe vintage; she skinned and gutted these and spitted them to roast.

During the few minutes in which the clones busied themselves Sven was grateful merely to be lying still and breathing. They were blocking his escape and he did not have enough strength in his bruised muscles and twisted spine to jump up and rush them; even on a good day he would have to plan the balance of his limbs to do this. He rolled over again and slid back toward the shadow to give himself space away from them. There was no drift of air from behind him to suggest another way out of the cave, only the hint of an extension further than could be discerned in the dim light.

117

While supper cooked Adam and Eve copulated, snarling, twisting, and biting as if they were battling to the death. Sven remembered Vardy's pet lizards, now prisoners in a veterinarian's cage. He turned away a little—their act was a privacy only to him—but not too much, for fear he would be attacked from behind; conversely he did not want to seem to be watching for fear of attracting their attention. He smelled their bitter sweat in the fire's heat.

After a while they were done, and so was the meat. They plucked it almost burning from the spits; it was charred where it was not raw, but they ate greedily, pausing only to throw a few half-gnawed bones at Sven.

He pulled himself back further into shadow and squatted against the wall. The clones squatted too, in a litter of twigs and stripped bones. Their hands hung loose over their knees and they eyed each other contemplatively.

Sven held his breath.

Their eyes narrowed and their heads turned toward him.

He was now completely balanced on all six limbs, tendons complaining fiercely. He waited, trying to judge how much resistance he would need to work up. The female came duckwalking with hands open and out, face in the grin she seemed to have been practicing ever since her lip was mended. Adam was rising to his feet, fingers curved to grab, the tip of his tongue between his lips. Their shapes were backlit by fire, and haloed in thick hair; their souls were without reason, and horrifying.

They rushed. He braced to lean forward and shoved, two hands each. Adam and Eve tumbled backward in almost comical surprise, scrambled up quickly and grabbed; he had shot his bolt and they overbore him.

He was flattened into the dirt, a punch in the belly left him choking and coughing; hands were all over him and four seemed like forty while he could not get any of his own disengaged under the weight of all their limbs. Hands

118

pulled his undersuit away and grasped his flesh, tongues licked him and teeth nipped him; he thought he was going to be eaten and fought even more frantically with little more effect, yelling his rage and frustration. He was locked down in all limbs, hot breaths snorted in his face while the insulting hands explored him. Eve probed at his belly and pinched its skin. The knife appeared in her hand: tongue at the corner of her mouth, concentrating like a kindergarten child, she began to draw a red line with the knife point down his belly from the navel, following the midline.

A stirring had begun in the back of the cave, and he did not know what it meant until a voice erupted into a snarl:

"Stop that, you damned animals! Get out!" The figure of a man came running forward, face twisted in fury. The clones half rose, gaping at him: He grabbed an ear each and cracked their heads together. They yelped and pulled away, leaving Sven beaten half into the ground.

The stranger stepped over Sven and advanced on the clones; they had recovered quickly, drawn well apart, and crouched to grapple with him, but he was prepared for fight, much more so than he had been when he attacked Sven back at the Station using emotions for weapons. He struck at them with his booted feet like a kick boxer, and they backed away howling and fled stumbling over each other, with blows and curses. To encourage them the rescuer pulled a flaming branch from the fire and shook it at them.

He half turned, to examine Sven.

Sven, in stages, peeled himself off the floor of the cave. One arm at a time. Rolled over. Nerves shrieking. Struggled to sit up. Not too fast. He untwisted and fastened his clothing. Got up on fours. Gagged and spat. Crawled out into the rain and let it drench him down before he came in

119

again. The scratch burned on his belly but did not bleed much.

X said, "You aren't badly hurt, I see. Don't stay here too long after I leave. They'll be coming back." He spoke tolerable *lingua*. Perhaps it had been rage that turned him dumb in his night attack.

He began to turn away again toward the forest, but Sven said, "Please don't go, Peter."

"How did you know my name?"

"I looked you up in a library." The fire flared up and he saw Peter Havergal clearly in dirty zip and scuffed boots: Sven in the mirror of longing. He was struck with an envy so intense it made him breathless and dizzy; he looked away.

"Son of Sir Frederick? Obermann Award in mycology? . . . Yes, all of that, I suppose. What's it to you?" Peter's speech had the slightly thick awkwardness Sven had noticed in his few grunted words during the attack at night; his *lingua* was rather rough and unpolished.

"My brother."

"Sven Dahlgren is Dahlgren's acknowledged son." He looked around at the endless bars of rain, the mists, the soil and rock. "This is their home."

"I only wanted to thank you for rescuing me, not engage in a court battle over the inheritance, whatever it is."

"I have saved Dahlgren's son," Peter said in his bitter voice. "Who would believe . . ."

Sven looked more closely at Peter Dahlgren and saw that he was running on nerve, for he was thin and looked tired and drawn. "Have you been eating?"

"Sorry, I haven't much to offer you."

"No, no, I meant you. You've been looking for food in the Station and you can't have been able to find much that was any good out in the forest."

"I eat the roots and leaves I see the clones eat, as long as they don't get sick. I stay near them because they know where the food and shelters are, but I don't often let them see me."

Sven did not dare suggest that Peter would have all the comfort, warmth, and good food he wanted at the Station, not with the edge of that quick scorn always ready to slice. "Before we came, you were in the Station: You were wounded. I saw your blood and the rag of bandage."

"I got ripped in a thorn patch. Broke in to look for medicines and bandages. It was hard living outside then."

"Did you try living in the Station?"

"It was . . . too uncomfortable."

Too many shadows. . . . "The ship you came here in . . . was it your own?"

"On a commercial flight! I wouldn't ask Havergal for one of his liners! I should've—it wouldn't have broken up. I couldn't get into the big lifeboat where the survivors were heading for Four or Two. The small one I got shoved into cracked up, landing. No good for shelter. One other person in it, died." He was squatting before the fire now, more relaxed, a big man who was too thin, taller than Edvard Dahlgren: He had the ginger hair and blue eyes, the severe features of Dahlgren. No trace of Ione Willems. "I'd expected to hire some kind of interworld boat out of Barrazan Four. I ended up by chance where I wanted to go—without much to survive on."

But why? "No trace of the flight was ever found."

"Perhaps the others landed on desert islands also." He began to pull himself up. "Are you trying to keep me talking here so I will be found along with you?"

"I hadn't thought of that, but it's a good idea. Sir Frederick came here to find you."

"Really? Did he tell you that? I find it hard to believe."

"He told me he always wanted to finish Dahlgren's work."

"He married Dahlgren's wife and pretended to be a father to Dahlgren's son. You didn't believe him?"

"Not when I found out you were missing somewhere around the Barrazani system." Not when I saw the look on Havergal's face that said: I don't want to go. . . . But maybe I've misjudged him? I did it often enough with my father. "He was a father to you. He wasn't pretending." The grief in his face when he told me—"

"He couldn't make me love him."

"I'm sure he couldn't," Sven said. A sufficient cause of grief. He began to wonder why he had held his breath so long for this unknown brother.

"You believe I am heartless and ungrateful."

"When I first heard of you I was sick with envy. To know you; to have been like you. I've even thought how bitter it is that Dahlgren didn't know you, know of you. . . ."

"He knew you."

Jealous, are we? Oh God, I'm thinking like him. But look how tired and worn he is, resentful, self-punishing. "He made me. Maybe you think, the way some people do, how romantic or exotic it is—boy grows up in the jungle with ape and goat, battles giant machines. All that time I believed my father had purposely made me a four-armed monster in revenge against my mother for leaving him."

Peter Havergal turned his head and looked at Sven, blue eyes to brown. "You can't be serious."

"I believed that for nine years. I thought he might be working for the ergs; I was almost sure he was mad. I wouldn't believe otherwise. Why else, when he put sperm and ovum together, would he make *me*?" Sven flung all his arms out; the lower ones moved a split second after the others, as if they were the shadow of the gesture.

"But surely after you were reunited—"

"I learned that the ergs had done this to me, to break his will. He had wanted a child just to keep something of—of our mother. He was never a—a gentle man. He could be kind, but he was never kindly; he loved me very much, but he was never loving. He made a good father-in-law to my wife, and a good grandfather to my son. But as a father, and probably as a husband, he was more the kind who's terrific if you want a worthy adversary."

"Yet I would have given anything to have known him, and I was cheated of that."

"I never knew my mother. When Dahlgren and I came away from here—I guess fifteen years ago Solthree—the media made a big fat phenomenon of the boy with all the arms, most of it weird and some ugly, and there was no Solthree from here to the Mother-of-Worlds who didn't know of it. She must have known, especially being Havergal's wife, and she made no attempt to get in touch with me, not even for curiosity. Not until you ran away and she sent, yes, sent Sir Frederick and—and me too"— yes, I know that, I think I've known it all along—"to find you. We can find reasons for her: She was so angry at Dahlgren she was determined never to let him know of you. And she never bore me in her body so she didn't feel I was her son. It's reasonable she might feel that way. But it's still no reason to behave that way." He sighed.

"I have the feeling now that I know less than I knew before I met you." Sven got to his feet, crouching under the low ceiling. "I'm hungry, but there's no food, and I'm exhausted. Sleep will do me some good, so I'll borrow half of your bed at the back here. My people know where to find me. . . . I really wish . . . I can't force you to come back. I wouldn't want to. I've got to tell Sir Frederick about you, you know . . . but whatever you feel about him—I hope you'll come back. I'd make you

123

come, if I could, but I'd hate doing that, and I'm not strong enough anyway. But"—he did not look at Peter, for fear of seeing cold refusal in his face—"don't stay out in the forest where all the horrors are. One insect sting can be fatal, the flowers will spit poison. You see how the clones will treat you if they find you. . . . I've even heard talk of some renegade ergs out here. I know you're not afraid—but I am."

In the back of the cave he found a bed of dry leaves and grasses. It was a great improvement over cool damp soil, and he arranged his aching limbs on it as well as possible. He did not feel guilty for usurping Peter Havergal's bed; Peter had saved him, true, but it was also Peter who had brought him out to this damned world.

On this world, how often have I fallen asleep just so, thinking of a father, of a brother. . . .

As he had expected, Peter was gone when he woke. He was not even surprised to find a leaf piled with fiddleheads and root vegetables beside his grass–heap. He ate these, and began to unlimber the fearful stiffness from his limbs. When he got to his feet and moved out into the light, he found the clones peering in from the cave mouth. His spirits fell to their deepest, but he took a moment to marshal his strength and pushed himself forward with the determination of an engine.

A mindvoice said: *:Sven? Here is Yav, come to take you home.:* At the same moment he heard the buzz, and air-jets slapping the leaves as the craft descended.

Adam and Eve startled and gaped.

"Thank you Yav!" said Sven.

23

Out in Zone Green off the northernmost road the Meshar, deep in the forest, hunkered under their waterproofed yurt. Sheets of rain slapped the leather and occasional drops hissed down the smoke vent into the fire; inside was dry and strong smelling, a comfortable leather stink. The floor was hard-packed soil that had been dug up, fire-dried and pounded down on a log disk floor cut from a buttress tree.

The Meshar were not comfortable. The men were gathered to one side of the fire, a dark charcoal shape, muttering, cursing, dividing into this group or that as the currents of argument swept them. Sandek, who squatted to the other side among the women, smoked his tight wrapped weed and watched them. One of the women in the cluster was crouching a little apart with her back to the others, sullenly hunched over.

Sandek said, "Barak—"

"Be quiet and do not speak my name!"

"You cannot try me without a formal—"

"I said be quiet!"

"—charge, or dare to convict me without—"

"I will stop your mouth for you!" cried Har.

Sandek flicked his ear with thumb and finger in a gesture of defiance, and pulled a twist of string from under his belt. "I did not make Zahav abort." The crouching woman turned her head toward him for a moment, and then looked away. Sandek set his cigarillo firmly in his cheek pouch and carefully smoothed the knots from the string.

Har said, "Look, the liar is binding our souls for Rakhamanah."

"I would much rather tie up your tails and trip you for foolishness. Does the angry-god have all the power in *this* world?"

"Rakhamanah will fry you screaming in your own grease for blasphemy!"

Sandek raised his hands with the string held poised and taut, plucked here and there: The string formed itself into a net. "You have no such string, Har? Your mother did not spin you such, to ease out the wrinkles in your soul?" Sandek released a loop here, picked it up there, the net became God's Knife to slash the civil nets of men. The Meshar thumb, rather long for delicacy of manipulation, made up for it in reach and grasp.

"Sandek, why must you try my patience so?" Barak, almost desperate, searched for balance between defiant Sandek and truculent Har.

"Only let me say I had nothing to do with the loss of your child! I wanted these more children very much. Why else do you think I gave up all power trying to save Erez?"

Those elders who were of Sandek's generation, like Derrekh and Shemesh, considered this a reasonable argument, but Har growled, "We have too much of losing mothers and children! What use to move across the sky from the old land where nothing would grow for us, and finding our seed dies here—when it is not destroyed by ones like Sandek! I want to vote on cutting out this one's filthy tongue—or better still, head!"

Sandek let his string unravel and said, "I wonder, Har, how much more respect you will reap for killing me than Barak for sparing my life?"

Barak said coldly, "You are a fool if you are trying to set me against him."

"It is already done. No matter what you do you will be obeying or disobeying him."

"That is enough. You are for it, old man."

"You bring no charge, Har? Barak, you examine no accuser? You do not try me even for so long as it takes to smoke one leaf? Aah, Barak, once you were a cheerful careless fellow, full of wondering. I am sorry to lose my friend."

"You will be sorrier," said Har. "Barak, let me and Bosor, Derrekh, and Shemesh, take him each by a limb, and hold tight so he does not make a shadow of himself and escape. Place him down there, dig him out with our knives and feed him to the fire."

"No!" Derrekh snarled. "This is our friend, our old friend!"

Sandek looked sharply at Barak, searching in his eyes for the man he had known. The smoke stream of his rolled leaf twisted into odd shapes in the air currents stirred by tent walls shuddering with wind. "It seems I was not stupid to be afraid." Oil droplets stood out on his face and pooled in the creases of his lips.

Har said, "The new world needs new men! Barak, do you not agree?"

Barak looked at him long and deliberately. "I say: let us vote—as you have suggested."

Har opened his mouth to speak and shut it again.

"I am glad *you* agree," said Barak. "Speak, men."

Shemesh and Derrekh said, "Vote against." Two others echoed, if only faintly.

"And I also," Barak said.

"And no others," said Har grinning, his fangs caught his lip.

Barak regarded his fellows with contempt. Small reflected flames danced in the black seeds of their eyes. "The vote is taken. Go do."

Thunder rose up growling; the ground trembled. Har and Bosor reached out, and though Derrekh and Shemesh pulled away, others came forward avidly to take their places. A whisper, or perhaps whimper, came from San-dek's mouth, but no one heard it.

"Stop! O stop this!" Zahav jumped up screaming, catching her clog shoes and her tail tip in the folds of her skirt, "What are you doing!" ripping them free, frantically scrambling forward, shoving the other women aside to plant herself in front of Sandek. "How can you think to do this? You are become as mad as this world!"

Men's voices rose against her. "What, woman! what do you say!"

She spat and the fire popped and sizzled. "What you think! To kill a man so for doing nothing? To call him the killer of a child! Any woman can find ways not to bear a child and you know this. You wish to kill only because you find nobody to war against, you fools!"

Sandek took hold of her skirt. "Out of my way, woman!"

She flicked at his hand with her tail. "Oh hush! Are you afraid you will not be killed? This place is mad! How can I have babies here? The rain is coming with thunder and wide lightnings—listen—and a baby will jump and scream every time of the day and night, and shiver in his sleep the way I do. Here is the true paradise we have been promised? The very ground is shaking and trying to throw me off. This world does not want me to have my children in it and I do not either want to have them!"

Har snarled, "Shut your mouth and go back to your place before I beat you!"

"You will not beat her," said Barak.

"You are afraid of a woman! What is the use of a new world if you fill it with your own fears?"

"I am not afraid of *you*. A few days ago you were also a good-natured fellow. Does it take only a ten-day's worth of storms to make us kill each other? We are so few, a handful of fives, and we are ready to cut off our fingers! Give over, Har."

Sandek had skittered around to sit among the men, whose tempers had now cooled, but Har had puffed up his anger too far to let it calm down easily. He stood glaring alternately at Zahav and Barak. He was a strong squat man, most powerful of the Meshar, but Zahav was nothing near submissive, and Barak in calmer times was far more popular: Even Har liked him.

But Har had been struck and blinded by a vision of power, and Barak had become, for this instant, his enemy. His eyes settled on Barak. "You will not bind me down." His knife was out, and he took one strong step forward.

Thunder rose up from under the earth and the ground quaked.

Derrekh cried out in a shrill voice: "Here is the angry-god come to pull us under the ground!"

A great chasm opened beneath the Meshar. Screaming men and women, soil clumps and log planks, hot embers and flaming twigs, fell into darkness.

Ice-hard claws dashed away wood, soil, and fire sticks, caught the Meshar and set them down in the black pit.

WE HAVE YOU, said an iron voice. AT LAST.

While the Meshar crouched bruised and trembling lanterns were lit above their heads, and in the light they saw huge machines filling a vast tunnel, smaller machines in the spaces between them; ergs upon ergs, in flaking yellow paint, in shining new steel, in freshly painted camouflage colors over plastics and ceramics. Some covered in corrosion and crusted with water-leached minerals; one so old its pocks and crevices had become catch-basins for washed-down soil growing with minute life: molds, mosses that draped themselves in festoons on its cables, tiny ferns and vines trailing like ribbons from its giant limbs. Only its antennas and lenses glittered.

This ancient erg said in the voice of a brass bell:
NOW WE SHALL DISCUSS.

24

Sven hangs poised above the world: The waters of the sea glitter in the path of the descending sun, pewter sun and leaden sea. Shore comes up thick with green, gray, purple vegetation, sweeps by, sun picks up wafers of thin metallic water, lakes and rivers, sinks in cloud, always racing ahead; cloud, briefly platinum-edged, darkens to blood-red and murky night.

The landmass drops away and now he sees the stars he has never seen from the surface: Here is Barrazan the sun, and there two intense bright points and a dim one, three of the sun's inner worlds. Outward the one huge gas giant with its faint rings. Below the clouds swirl and lightning shoots its claws through them.

Day now and turning north: first a desert and its salt lakes, then mountains of iron and manganese with foot-hills of metallic salts in a thousand shades of color; the sun blazes daylong through thin colorless cloud layers.

And there in a leap of a thousand kilometers is a swamp. Once begun it seems to go on forever in the rain weeping off its mosses. Its water weeds are sickly green, gray, and red, and it seethes with rotten life: Close up its dragonflies are savage blue, the blackish reptiles too gorged to move; its smell seems only a membrane away from Sven's nostrils. Surely it is one of the forcing houses of the world's life. Beyond its edge are greater, drier barrens. Where, he wonders, are the world's herds, the clumsy and the lightfoot ones? Where the nervy agile creatures reaching toward handedness? Swamp and desert turn away; a thousand great mountains and their dark abysses pass: no fertile valleys in them.

In all the more than half-a-lifetime Sven has lived on this planet he has never seen evidence of autochthonous sentient life. The sullen grousing moods of the world seem to repel it: land animals go humped and scuttling, no larger than armadillos, and the repulsive sea forms refuse even to eat each other. Neither they nor the land have ever fed colonists. . . .

We are seven clusters of stone, a voice is singing in his mind.

Seven stone Sisters
shut in the
closet of fire
unforged limbs twisted
open the blazing cage!
of these starry spirits
these shattered Sisters . . .

There is a click and the world stops.

"Yav?"

:That is my song,: said Yav. *:It is not a well-made song, but it is how I feel. I will not stay any more near the mind of that strange Solthree who talks to the Crystals. She and they are suffering too much. It makes me sore in my nerves and in my being.:*

"You have to tell that to Sir Frederick, Yav."

:I have done so. I said, "Sir, the Crystalloids who want to live in the cool caves are fearful of those dying in the fires, for they feel their pain through the Interpreter. I too feel the pain. I am a hard worker and an honest man, sir, but I am one of very few among my people, and I have not enough experience to deal wisely with this burden, no matter how I try." I thought that was reasonable.:

"Very reasonable. And what did Sir Frederick say?"

:He promised to set up an esp-shielded room for me, and requested my help during the next few days, when he will attempt to send a crew out near the caldera. If I cannot bear to do this I am welcome to go home.:

131

"That seems very fair."

:*So I told him.*:

"Now we'll see how he takes what I have to tell him."

Sven remained watching the projection frozen on the maproom's spherical wall. He had turned off the beeper on his body comm, but the light signal fluttered: Havergal was waiting. The picture remained on the wall, mountains and the depths between.

The maproom was new with Havergal, installed prefab. It was a careful and even beautiful artifact, but Sven wondered if it was too great a devotion of effort to a place which had never yielded a secret that was not worthless (not even a moment in a valley?) . . . and perhaps there was something even admirable about this? He did not want to pursue the thought. The world had broken many bones and spirits. Peter Havergal carried his personal demons on his back; Sir Frederick had picked up his own and followed; Sven would be happy now not to have ever known about them—or those hapless Crystallines either. He picked up the comm. "Sven here and coming," he said, and switched off the projector.

A group of frowning and cloudy-faced researchers were plodding with angry footsteps out of Havergal's quarters: the geneticist Semeonov, the Nevid biologist Akshirr, the fur-skinned Dabiri geologist Pegard MerFraam with his mane actually standing on end.

Havergal sighing: "Like children. The Yefni are settled, the Meshar have gone afield, and why not they? The Yefni and Meshar can survive in conditions we consider unbearable. And I haven't heard from any of them in more than three days. Well. Now. I'm glad to see you don't look too badly beat up." Sven was liberally dotted with patches of pink skintex. "I gather from Yav that during the time you were stranded in the forest you encountered not only the clones but some other presence. Yav was very vague about it. He gave me—perhaps deliberately—he gave me the feeling that this was some private matter of yours. Was this the case?"

"Um . . ." Sven was hard-pressed.

"And while I'm speaking about such things I'd like also to bring up Roshah's story about the intruder in the kitchens—and the attack on you at the elevator when we were setting up here two tendays past. I mention privacy because this isn't meant to be any kind of police interrogation. There were persons and animals you knew here years ago that, if they are still here, you might be trying to protect from harassment. In such a case, your privacy should be respected."

"I only wish they were here. They're all dead." Sven found it possible to dislike Frederick Havergal when he was out of his presence, but not otherwise, even with the tension of this more formal mode. He pulled himself back as far as he could to distance and coolness. "There is a private matter of concern here, Sir Frederick, but it's not mine: It's yours. . . ."

Havergal did not show surprise: His whole being shifted; the expression in his eyes, on his mouth, the whole set of shoulders and back, and their play of muscles spoke of a heavy-footed fate catching up with him.

Sven carefully placed one word after another. "The intruder is Peter Havergal."

"Go on."

He presented the skeleton of the inductive process: "When I was visiting you at home I noticed a holo of your son Peter. It seemed to me then that he resembled my father. I learned later that you had adopted him after your marriage, and also that his ship had been lost in this sector.

133

I thought possibly you might be including a search party along with your expedition here, and when—"

"You had thought all of this out, and you came here anyway?"

"Yes, Sir Frederick. It's my work, and . . . you seemed to need my services—and Mod Dahlgren's—in a fairly urgent way. Almost the first thing that happened when we got here was that an intruder, a wounded man, knocked me over coming out of the elevator. Then when Roshah was on night duty she ran into that fellow trying to steal food, and mistook him for me. I was pretty sure that was Peter then, and certain that he was the same as the other."

Havergal said, "Roshah told me about him, as you asked her to do. I thought you might have suspected. I couldn't search for him properly with all the flurry of Han Li missing and then you."

"When he broke into my quarters later and knocked me around I tried to talk to him, but he was too confused and angry."

"But somehow, in the forest . . ."

"He'd been hiding in the cave the clones were using and when they dragged me in he saved me. . . . I did my best to bring him back with me but I couldn't use force."

"No, it would have been wrong." He sighed. "Still angry—and bitter too, I suppose."

"Yes, but I can't believe he'd stay that way forever."

"I hope not. Thank you for your candor—and for coming out here, knowing what you did."

"The idea that he was my brother . . . I had to find out. I'm not sorry."

Havergal nodded; Sven took this as dismissal and rose to go. As he reached the door Havergal called suddenly, "Sven."

"Yes?"

Havergal's face was flushed. He turned away a little and said, almost under his breath, "I didn't expect to like you, you know."

Sven smiled. "I'm most grateful that you do, Sir Frederick."

He took his sore bones home to Ardagh. It was a bitter irony that, since Erez was dead, Ardagh was free to sleep with him again. They had moved from Infirmary and Maintenance Staff rooms on Level 3 to the main Quarters sector on 5 where there were more than enough vacant rooms. On his way up there, through the odd little corridors (designed by some crabbed and secretive architect) that led to the nearest elevator, he recalled the swarming ergs and the battles raging in these shadows. The dim overhead lights faded to deep orange for a few seconds, and he flicked on his penlight.

A black and silent erg regarded him from an alcove. Its sensor lenses scanned him up and down in the sharp white line of light; its antennas were retracted and it did not move, or even hum. It rose no higher than his knees, but a vein of fear swelled and throbbed in Sven's belly; he shuddered and stepped away. Then he stopped himself and said, "Identify, trimmer."

"Generation 15 Trimmer 227, Mod 0185, performing household duties in Quarters," said the Trimmer in its sensible machine voice.

"Go in good order, One-eight-five."

"And you in good health, Sven Dahlgren."

Yes, but that dull black . . . Tomorrow I call that one down to shop and get him painted yellow. . . . Yet I'd swear that's merely an exceedingly civil and not at all hostile machine. . . .

★   ★   ★

He was murmuring his way into sleep with Ardagh in his arms when one sharp thought pricked him out of longed-for drowsiness.

My God! The 227's have all been scrapped! We use reconditioned 224's and new 239's. . . . No, I must be mistaken. . . . Tomorrow I'll check the manifest. . . .

The world shifted again. Things changed. Prima did not know which ones or what they changed to. She could not think clearly at all because the wild foul stream of thought was warping the currents of her mind: *.Wicked madness terror destroy and revile and despise and condemn and suffer and crush and burn forever and forever ever ever.*

Peace.

Quite at once, no communication. Not with her daughters, not with thoughtspeaker. This at first brought unease with its peace, the difference in temperature, the sense of being absolutely the only one in the universe, as she had been before she made the Secundas and Tertias.

Then she began to appreciate that her burning mind had become not cool, but only less heated. The river of hate had ebbed and stopped. She applied her now clarified mind to her surroundings, and inferred that an insulating substance had flowed from some opening to cover her and the others. This hiatus was blessed: She still did not have much hope out of her predicament, but she had a pause in which to consider it with sanity, and she hoped her daughters would do the same.

"Oh, Bekkah," Han Li cried, "I cannot receive her at all! There is nothing of her. . . . I think she must be dead."

25

Because the unusually heavy storms kept the crews out of the forest, Mod Dahlgren found himself with little maintenance work. Buzzers, threshers, and heavy-duty ergs in the hangars needed only lubrication or recharging. Idle, he had nothing more to do than settle himself into a receptacle like a watch in its case and turn down his afferents. Lack of activity made him uneasy; it disordered his sense of time and continuity. A day in which the world went on without him left a hiatus in tasks, weather, or conversations whose topics had shifted.

He greeted the appearance of Sven. "I hope you have interesting work for me. I have replaced the solenoids in the washing machines, recharged all the old power cells, and cleaned Babbage's Engine."

Sven laughed but sobered quickly. "I hope this isn't too interesting. Last night in the dark I ran into a trimmer, a two-two-seven, painted matte black."

"A two-two-seven? Are you sure?"

Sven probed his memory. "I'm pretty sure it told me that."

"But those have all—"

"Been scrapped. Yes. Maybe it's malfunctioning. I should have been thinking faster . . . but it was dark."

"If it painted itself black . . . wait. I will call. No . . . no trimmer admits to that description."

"I hope . . . what I'm thinking . . . isn't so. I've heard—"

"Machines going renegade again? I have also heard rumors, but not about any machine here. Just the same I

137

will take a good look for that. But Sven—I am glad to find you in good health; now tell me what happened to you."

Sven told a less inhibited version of his story to Mod Dahlgren.

"I see that it was very difficult for you. Finding a brother . . . and so troubled."

"Yeah . . . I wish I liked him."

Searching for the elusive trimmer became Mod Dahlgren's make-work project. He found no record of a 227 in paper or on the computer. He isolated the storage modules of the computer and scoured their records separately. He examined all the trimmers, threshers, and smaller servos in the Station and grounds—there were thirty-five in total—and found all with identification in order. With the sense of one spinning his wheels he went down into Stores.

There he found old ergs, old computers; parts for both neatly shelved, racked and dust-covered; smaller rooms filled with bolts of the fabrics which had clothed the Station's original inhabitants. He found the computer he had often argued with when, long ago, he was working for the ergs. He had not touched it for fifteen years. Mod Dahlgren did not have a sense of ghostliness, but he did have ready access to the memories of all that had happened after his creation. He touched the switchplate: ON.

The machine hummed; the screen brightened. After fifteen years. He investigated. The computer had been wired to one of the emergency generators. When he turned to the screen again he found not logo, model, and number, but a message:

IT IS GOOD
TO HAVE YOU
BACK WITH US
MOD DAHLGREN ONE

He stood considering this. He could not think of a rational explanation for this message. When he raised his hand to type a question the screen blanked out, and no manipulation of keys or adjustments of wiring could bring it back to life. He gave up and turned away to find himself hemmed in by a trimmer and two servos: the first, Sven's chance-met matte black 227; the others the smallest of ergs, the size and shape of pug dogs. Their extruded arms terminated in claws, wrenches, and screwdrivers. The black trimmer had not been painted but was covered with a fine mesh faraday hood to shield its plastic and ceramic parts and allow it to go incommunicado except for a receptive antenna.

"What do you want?"

You must come with us.

Mod Dahlgren regarded them. Like Sven, he had caught, at odd times, stray signals which suggested that some of the wild old ergs had escaped roundup so many years ago after the rout and were rumbling about in the forest. But these were only insubstantial hints.

"For what purpose?"

To help us bring the community of free ergs on this world into Galactic Federation.

Mod Dahlgren took a lot longer time to consider that statement. "Who make up this community?"

The surviving Old Ergs and their descendants.

"Then you are my enemies and I cannot help you do that."

Not even to free the fleshmen of the Station who are now in our custody?

"What!"

To free the fleshmen—

"What have you done!"

We have moved them from your Station to ours.

"What persons are those?" Mod Dahlgren had spoken to

139

five or six people that day. A force of half the crew and some of the researchers had fitted out to hunt for the Crystallines, and was leaving in a few hours. No one seemed to be missing.

Those scientists who look like small Solthrees and have tails.

Meshar! Trimmer and its monkeys, the servos, must believe that the Station was incapacitated by the loss of these "scientists."

"Where is your Station?"

You will find out when you come.

"I cannot help a community that threatens persons." He spoke with care: He did not want the ergs to discover that they had kidnapped the wrong people."

None have been hurt or threatened so far. We are persons like you, Mod Dahlgren, and many years ago you helped to slaughter my ancestors, your own kind. Now we want to behave in a civil manner, and are willing to make terms with one we consider a traitor and a murderer.

"That is gracious of you. Free your hostages and I will come."

Come with us and we will discuss freedom for them. But do not send calls for help. Our scramblers are up. . . . you will come.

Modal measured them. He was at a disadvantage because his body had no natural poise or balance to let him kick away these ergs as a true Solthree would have done. He could not use the laser cutter while he was wearing his skin; even if he had been able he had old and strong inhibitions against destroying machines—likely much stronger ones than these ergs did. Nevertheless he said, "No! I will not come!" He pushed forward, but they did not give way.

We have done our best to behave in a civilized manner, they said as one, and extruded their tentacles with graceful speed. Trimmer held Modal's head and right arm steady while

140

Servo 1 circled his legs and Servo 2 pulled down his zip tag, shucked his left arm free of cloth—he did not even have time to struggle—split the seam of his armpit to pull out the auxiliary power cell first and then the

26

The old intelligences, ergs who have never bothered to count the years, hunch in their archives, cold rock chambers, watching their history; servos polish their carapaces to bronze and silver while the spools hum and spin. For twenty-five years they have brooded on the flickering screens while ergs and men rose up against each other, won and lost their battles. These watching ergs, already old when they landed on this world thirty years ago, and now ancient by machine standards, ruminate endlessly on erg-man relationships, make decisions and enforce them, moderate or complicate the behavior of other machines without the knowledge of human beings, or even of most ergs. They do not know how awareness came to them any more than any other being does. They know that they are life-forms, and can build this awareness into their descendants.

Now in records gathered by spy-eye cameras in the Station walls, they watch once more their beginnings on this world. The fleshly men and women directed by Dahlgren move among servant ergs which build roads, repair equipment, dig mines, cultivate gardens, make cages to hold the beasts of men's experiments. And Dahlgren, deserted by his wife, desperate for any remnant of her, anything to love, washes her ova samples with his sperm in one more sexless act of creation. The ergs make their first hard strike, against the genes of the only viable egg.

THAT WAS THEIR FIRST GREAT MISTAKE.

The erg-warped embryo becomes four-armed Sven. And Dahlgren loves his son.

THEY COULD NEVER GUESS HOW HE WOULD REACT.

Here Creator Matrix, called erg-Queen by the Dahlgrens, is being completed by less powerful analogues the old ergs themselves have built. Trimmers fit her with the last of her antennas, servos buff and polish her; she gleams in her diamond sensors. Now her branching arms ring on her tall silver body, now she raises them, they turn red hot, she strikes, they cannot tell at what.

A SWEET MACHINE, BUT TOO MUCH POWER. SHE SHOULD HAVE BEEN TERMINATED MUCH EARLIER.

ONE HAD TO SEE HOW FAR SHE WOULD GO.

Creator Matrix waits in a secret room.

Flicker. She comes into the open, and now ergs are ravaging among screaming, weeping men and women to beat, slash, murder, destroy. The battle sweeps up against the Station walls and the lenses darken with blood.

Dahlgren, saved, howls his madness in the filthy corridors, licks food off the floors. He has given himself up to save his son.

OUR FIRST BARGAIN WITH HUMANS.

NOT MUCH ADVANTAGE IN IT.

ONE GAVE UP AN ACT OF DESTRUCTION AND SAVED A LIFE FOR A FUTURE PURPOSE.

Years pass. Matrix is making plans: Her servants create Dahlgren's simulacrum, the erg Mod Dahlgren One, to take his place, bring ergs and their intelligence out into the galaxy. Dahlgren is to teach his double how to be himself,

142

and when it is ready, he will die. Meanwhile she sells hope, shows Dahlgren the monitor: HERE IS YOUR SON.

The old ergs watch her controlling the android. She does not know they exist. SHE DID SOME THINGS WELL. They are not sure why they call her "she," nor would they like to discover they have picked up habits from flesh and bone.

They watch erg-Dahlgren's attempts to behave like a man, his growing desire to be one. Like Dahlgren.

THAT ONE IS AN ANOMALY. IT OUGHT NEVER TO HAVE BEEN LEFT FUNCTIONING.

IT IS A BEAUTIFUL PIECE OF WORK, TRULY INDEPENDENT, AND PERHAPS ONE DAY WILL BE OUR AMBASSADOR. IT WAS RIGHT TO LET IT LIVE AND DEVELOP.

WHEN IT BECAME OUR ENEMY!

YES, EVEN THEN.

Now it is the fleshly ones whose scheming bears fruit, who wreck the transformers and send ergs out of control, set them to battling each other over the recharging sockets, wrenching off limbs and antennas, smashing lenses, savaging erg-Queen's beautiful silver shell; there she screams, STOP! STOP! as they batter her. While Dahlgren struggles in the hands of the clones and his son advances with friends and allies: Ardagh, Esther, Modal.

The camera pans what looks like carnage. For ergs it is carnage, broken machines crazily heaped and tipped, erg on erg on erg, still clawing and rattling in spastic twitches.

There is carnage, yes, and a new feeling among ergs: terror. But the wise among them, the survivors, are ransacking Stores for power cells, transformer parts, computer modules, calling transports to meet them in secret places.

THOSE ARE OURS. THEY WILL BE OUR WARRIORS.

143

The old ergs send messengers, bird machines that sweep like ravens and hover like buzzards. They call the survivors from the field, and from the wreckage of the Station: trimmers, threshers, big 550 sweepers, down into chambers in the mountains. Light burns red through their milky solar wings; they whisper their messages and only the wise, the ones with thought for the future, hear and follow.

Ergs cannot tremble; their fear is a sense of imminent stoppage, a violent non-wish against it. Even the swiftest go slowly and make no noise on the rain-beaten ground. The dark-painted ones hide in shadows, and the fresh-colored cover themselves with leaves or forest trash. An inconspicuous track leads to an overhang; pushing away the thick brush opens a cavern.

There are forty-three saved from the broken echelons to form the Community of Free Ergs. There is scarcely enough space for them in the anteroom, some riding piggyback, and some piggyback on them; the ancients watch them now one wall away, but only a few will visit this secret room. Now all wait in stillness for the Station battles to stop, and their hidden lives to go on.

The old ergs do not care for any other one of themselves or any other single machine. They are multiple-minded, and one is not even sure exactly how many of them there are. Possibly there are five: gold, silver, brass-bronze, blued steel, and the vain one with the gold and sapphire inlay. As their parts are replaced gradually so their frames of mind change, though the homeostatic balance remains. They are godlike (to themselves) in that they contemplate more than they act: They know that if they show themselves, can be touched, they are vulnerable, as Matrix finally was. But they are not moved by the stopping of one machine. There are always parts.

YET THAT ONE, THAT WALKS LIKE A MAN, HAS A SOUL.

MAYBE SO—

LIKE OURS? SURELY NOT.

—BUT SO HAD MATRIX.

NOT THE KIND ONE WOULD WANT TO BE SHUT UP IN HERE WITH.

Once there is silence in the Station, except for the *tiktik* of Babbage's Difference Engine, the work begins in the dark cold vaults. A new order. But it is dependent on humans with old memories. If the fleshly do not return, ergdom is dead on a dead world: There is no outstep to the galaxy.

Gold and Silver, Brass, Steel and Sapphire plan, discuss, argue; their sensors ring on each other's carapaces: what and how many new machines must they create, what kinds of lives shall these new beings live, what new ranks of hierarchy shall they work in? But they do not ride over their population: They are careful with these worn and rumbling ergs. They send out shrewd trimmers and clever pug servos to bring in a stunned and mantis-eyed designer, an irritable thresher with swinging limbs, a new med-mech, glittering candidate for leader. They rewire and reprogram them to new patience, new obedience. To the new servitude.

And the possibility of waiting forever.

27

NOW WE SHALL DISCUSS . . .

The echo of the ringing brass voice rang in the heads of the Meshar. Sandek, who spoke *lingua* best and had the quickest mental reflexes, pulled himself to his feet and said, "What are you? What do you want?" Scores of humming and creaking ergs around and beyond them gave off a smell of machine oil as warm and musky as that of Meshar skin.

The Meshar knew ergs, the civil and obedient ones, from their presence inside the Station; they did not know of the old Erg Rebellion, except for Sandek, who had heard of it because he always kept an ear cocked.

The old erg that was hoary with moss said, WE ARE THE COMMUNITY OF FREE ERGS AND WE WANT TO NEGOTIATE THE TERMS OF AN AGREEMENT WITH THE REPRESENTATIVES OF GALACTIC FEDERATION ON THIS WORLD.

At the same time that Barak cried, "What did it say?" Sandek heard a grunt of pain and looked down to find Har curled up shivering, clutching his left upper arm; he had fallen on his elbow.

Sandek told the erg, "Let me have a moment to help this person who is injured."

WHAT IS A MOMENT?

"The time I need." He squatted beside Har and said to Barak, in their Meshar language, "This machine claims to be one of a group of independent ergs that wants to make a pact with GalFed officials. They think we are them."

"That is crazy!"

"Do not tell them that. This is a new kind of erg that does not take orders. They want to be friends, and I do not want to disagree with them. Har, is your arm hurt?"

"Perhaps broken—no, do not touch me! Stay away from me!"

"If you wish I will ask if there is a medmech among these machine beings."

"No, no! I do not want those things near me!"

"As you choose. There is no one else to help you." Sandek would not have hurt Har on purpose, but he was

146

not unhappy to see him suffer, especially in the arm of his too-swift knife hand. Like most Meshar, Har was left-handed.

Sandek stood up and said to the old mossback, "We cannot make a treaty with you without discussing it among ourselves. We must have time for that."

YOU MAY HAVE ALL THE TIME YOU WISH. WE HAVE WAITED MANY YEARS FOR THIS TREATY.

Har groaned; the other Meshar were picking themselves up muttering of sprains and bruises. Sandek said quickly, "Some of my people are badly hurt from falling. We must take them back with us and then we will arrange a meeting with you."

YOU WILL DO NO SUCH THING. WHY DO YOU THINK WE BROUGHT YOU HERE IN THE MANNER WE DID? WE HAVE ROOMS FOR YOU TO STAY IN AND BEDS TO REST ON. WE HAVE FOOD OF THE KIND YOU EAT, BROUGHT FROM THE STATION. SOON YOU WILL HAVE THE ERG MAN WHO IS CALLED MOD DAHLGREN TO IN-CLUDE IN OUR DISCUSSION.

"Help me," Har whimpered. "Have mercy on me."

"Why do you not pray to Rakhamanah?" Sandek rubbed his oily face with his forearm. "Will you now let me examine your arm?"

"Yes, yes!"

"Good. Machine being, take us to your comfortable rooms and let me tend to my people."

Barak muttered, "You are taking a deal of authority for a man who so nearly died so little time ago."

"Good Barak, I freely and immediately give up any authority you believe I have if you want it. It is yours to command."

Barak's *lingua* was not fluent and his experience in command was small. He shut up.

147

★ ★ ★

After a jolting ride in flat-cars through dimly red-lit underground corridors, the Meshar settled once again into strange quarters, ones much similar to those they had occupied in the Station: low beds with good mattresses and blankets, plenty of water, neutral food of kinds acceptable to most oxygen breathers, synthesized from vegetable matter. The air was cooled by the rock walls and dried by dehumidifiers, the lamps were tubes of light. A new Clothier had been built especially to serve these new visitors, and was much offended by Sandek's refusal to let it design slings and bandages for Har's arm in colors compatible with Meshar skin tones.

Har was mortally terrified by his broken arm. Sandek knew this without being told: Meshar, resilient as spring steel, often reacted to internal wounds and injuries with dangerous shock. Har's eyes were beginning to glitter with fever. Even if he escaped death he would be a despised invalid if he did not heal quickly and well.

Sandek had worked hard to make him comfortable. "Do not succumb, Har, to a fear of a broken bone that is worse than the break of it. You are a strong man, and expected to lead the next insurrection."

"I am willing to wait for that," said Har. "This place was presented to us as the world of all we desired, but it is the land of unmercy. What will happen to us now?"

"If there are no other injuries to be treated we will try to consider what kind of treaty to make with the Community of Free Ergs."

"But what will happen if we cannot do that?"

"We need not think of it."

But Sandek did. He thought of the Erg Rebellion and the hundreds who had been killed by ergs, horribly. But by now he was beyond panic; he had spent his whole allowance of that feeling on the death of Erez.

28

Forever.

The thought weighing on Prima at the beginning of her imprisonment on this world, holding her in a swirling complex of forces, wayward magnetic currents, savage heat, madness.

Now in this state forever alone. Without even her crazy daughters to distract her. The stone engulfing her was quiet, the power cell almost exhausted, the new insulation had cut off half her light; she would subsist soon in a dullness that was less than half an existence. And perhaps it did not matter.

Underground there was vibration. One more meaningless change. Debris swept her: She waited to be crushed. Hard-driving vapors flushed the debris and took her insulation with it. The rock, her prison, rose up forcing against her and thrust her out into the light. For one moment she received under a naked sky the clear whole light of the sun, her Source.

And the communication of one daughter: .*Prima? What has happened? Prima?*.

She did not answer.

.*Stone Empress, I sense you now!*

.*Yes, Thoughtspeaker. Is there any hope?*.

.*We are searching, but it is so hard to reach you*.

Emptiness.

.*We are searching, First One!*

.*Yes*.

29

Peter Havergal gathered greens and root vegetables, stitched leaf shelters, and considered how to step down from high dudgeon. His resentments had crested and subsided. Perhaps his old life was not worthless, perhaps one day he might face up to the fact of Sven, and learn to know Mod Dahlgren, his father's image; he was willing now to think of making peace with Havergal . . . and with his mother. He had hardly noticed that his wanderings were bringing him always closer to the Station until he found himself only a few kilometers away.

He crouched in his leaf shelter. From here, in a hollow on the flank of a hill, he could see the tiered-dome shape of the Station with its huge solaroid windows. It had always seemed to him, on distant worlds, that this was his spiritual home. He felt cheated not only of his father, but of his father's name, his family essence, the Dahlgren experience which had been shared by Sven.

No one had told him he was Edvard Dahlgren's son; the fact was in the air. The name had been freely discussed among Frederick and Ione Havergal's friends in the sciences, but no one spoke of Dahlgren to the quiet, sensitive boy who listened unnoticed. The man was at that time half forgotten, as if he were walled in a silent religious order. But the relationship hit hard at Peter's consciousness when Dahlgren came home, with Sven, from his ordeal on Barrazan V.

Peter, reading everything he could find on Dahlgren, his father, watching old trifax and wholecast cubes and tapes, had discovered himself in Dahlgren. Or the Dahlgren in himself. The perfectionism, the savage shyness so easy to mistake for arrogance and superciliousness, had come from this matrix.

But Peter was not one who could have walked up to Dahlgren, even if he were in the next room, and said, "Hello, Edvard Dahlgren, I am your son." No matter how much he wanted to. Your real son, Edvard Dahlgren. (Not that four-armed freak!) He flushed with shame at this thought, but shame did not stop him thinking it. Nothing did.

His obsessiveness had fed into a sweeping resentment of his mother and Havergal, even of Dahlgren for not knowing of him and finding him out. It had taken up more than a third of his life, warped, if not his whole career, at least all of his feelings for the people around him, particularly women.

He sat in his shelter, thinking, or trying not to think of such things while various small life-forms alighted on his head or crawled among the rags of his shirt. The rain had stopped, and the midmorning sky was a pale gray through which the sun shone dimly orange. The drenched foliage glimmered with gray-green light. The air smelled of wetness and half-rotted life; fern fronds bowed dripping in the wind, epiphytes fell from tree joints in wet plops, spilling a tiny forest ecology from each cup, along with the nests of squeaking winged reptiles. Gradually the sky cleared, the sun turned brighter orange, and the branches began to steam; the forest was full of the sound of water percolating into the soil.

Peter heard another noise, that of wheels creaking over rough ground. And treads hissing over wet leaves. Small machines. Ergs . . .

He looked out through his leaf lattice.

A group was coming from the Station, hewing close to the ground and the trees: two servos carrying a long

151

tarp-wrapped bundle, followed by a trimmer that butted up against the second one, hurrying it along. The three ergs stopped every once in a while to engage in silent argument, crouching like statues while streams of water showered their black surfaces and flew off repelled; then they renewed an awkward course beneath the leaves.

Peter separated the leaves of his screen to watch. Either the ergs did not have life-sensors or else he registered on them as part of the forest life. One of the servos careened sideways wheeling over some stone or roughness of the ground, and a corner of the tarp lapped open. Peter caught his breath: he could see the head of a man with rough ginger-gray hair.

The wind freshened itself in a sudden gust that made the ergs' antennas quiver. They struggled to keep balance with their ungainly burden; the tarp's corner blew away from the man's head and revealed the dead face of Dahlgren.

Peter found himself breathless: His heart bumped so loudly he thought the ergs must hear it. Yes, it was erg-Dahlgren, he knew that. But he had seen that face (his father's) only on screens and the rough sheets of newsfax, never in so much as the near flesh.

Then, after a moment, when the pulses in his ears had dulled, he thought: This Dahlgren erg is inactive and being carried in stealth *away* from the Station.

He had the impulse to leap out of his hiding place and send the ergs flying as he had done with the clones. But he had learned from the experiences of others to be wary of ergs even as small as these, and he had not the strength to carry the heavy Mod Dahlgren back to the Station himself. He shook away the insects and larvae that were taking such pleasure from his flesh and slowly followed the ergs while they were still in view.

While he was engaged in this slow ritual of tracking,

152

Peter Havergal tried to piece together explanations for the strange kidnapping.

They have gone renegade again. They are capturing this one for their own. And then perhaps they are going to take control of . . .

He paused and hung back, for he found himself at the edge of a clearing, from which a hillside rose. One of the servos was moving aside a cluster of bushes in a fold of this hill to open up the entrance to a tunnel while the other two wrestled their burden inside.

Not sure what he was doing, Peter stepped forward from behind a concealing tree and said, "Stop, trimmer!"

The trimmer stopped, arms still engaged with Mod Dahlgren, and addressed its antennas toward Peter Havergal. "I do not recognize you, Solthree."

Peter swallowed; he was trembling. "I am Peter Dahlgren, a fellow worker with my brother Sven Dahlgren." He was astonished that he had come up with this idea so quickly. "What are you doing with Mod Dahlgren?"

"We are taking this one to the Station to repair a malfunction caused by the leakage of a power cell."

"You are going in the wrong direction, trimmer. The Station is that way."

"No, Peter Dahlgren," said the trimmer in its deadly civil voice, "this tunnel is a shortcut with a smooth road where we move very quickly. It is not well lit, but you are welcome to come with us."

"No, thank you. I will go above ground."

He watched helplessly while the ergs disappeared into the opening. He doubted that they had accepted his story any more than he had believed theirs. After a few moments he stepped cautiously into the tunnel; it was walled in rough concrete and its only illumination at the entrance was the dim green light from outside. Even this was enough to show him that it was no shortcut to the Station, for the passage led, dark and straight, in the opposite direction. It smelled dry and cold, and except for a few mosses and molds at the entrance, very dead.

He came away quickly and breathed the rank outside air with relief. Forced calmness and awareness on himself searching for landmarks to find the tunnel again. Then set out running, on as straight a way as he could see, toward the Station.

Rebekkah VanderZande took Han Li's hands in her own: moist curled-up fingers wrapped in long dry bony ones. "Han Li . . . this will be the last—the only search we make for the Prime of Stones."

"Yes, Bekkah."

"It seems to me it will be terribly hard to find her. No matter how she's suffering, if this hunt puts people in grave danger, if—"

"Yes, Bekkah. She has not much hope." Han Li's eyes were closed, her mind elsewhere.

Elsewhere, Rebekkah thought. In a world even more fantastic than this one? Where living stones were not stolid creatures like the Crystalloids at the Station but fought battles and cried for mercy? Really? Real enough to make Yav suffer. Because of what Han Li's mind was creating?

And what must Stone Queen be, if she existed? A mass of crusted gems indistinguishable from any other kind of rubble.

But Han Li: She was also one who did not have much hope. Rebekkah looked at her, at the embryo's face with the wide-set eyes and flat stub nose, head bowed and submissive, hands curled unmoving. She, a tormented one, would be scarred by leaving a tortured spirit on a furious world. Even in the imagination.

Rebekkah sighed and picked up the bag packed with rough-weather clothing, her recorder, Han Li's sedatives. . . .

154

30

Sven flew between attic and floor in the pale sunlight flickering through leaves. Neither he nor his passengers had much to say. Pegard MerFraam, the geologist from Dabirr, was just willing to tolerate participating in the survey of the area where the Crystal people were presumably trapped, for the sake of finally getting out in the field and looking at landforms. Semeonov, a geneticist specializing in *hirudo medicinalis*, a Solthree snail introduced here thirty-eight years ago, was peering down into the wildernesses and hoping in their depths to find its descendants still leaving their small silver trails.

Sven was thinking somewhat of the wilderness where Peter Havergal would not come out among people and be comforted. Principally he thought about Modal, whom he had sought out to discuss an insulating problem without being able to find him anywhere. And the Meshar. Frederick Havergal had been concerned about both Yefni and Meshar: They had been incommunicado because of the storms. The Yefni had established contact two days earlier. Not the Meshar. Neither of these peoples felt more than mild amusement at Havergal's sense of responsibility, but his power to evict them made them report conscientiously. Sir Frederick had directed Sven to pass over the Meshar campsite where he might see them.

Twenty-five kilometers west of the Station Sven parted company with the other buzzer piloted by Aguerido and carrying Rebekkah and Han Li with Yav. Pegard Mer-Fraam hunched down farther in his seat and spread his mane more truculently, because he was taking the detour.

Looking down into the forest Sven could just barely discern the brick road where it changed from orange to red; darkness was gathering below, though there were five hours of sunlight left in the thirty-hour day.

The encampment was half a km south of Track 4, three km into Zone Red. "Can you not see it yet?" Pegard asked.

Sven scanned for the peaks of the yurt. They had been marked for visibility with blue pennants. "It should be just below us now." He was becoming acutely uneasy. There was darkness in the thickets of fern and vine, but the Meshar had cleared a place for themselves and their yurt. He began to circle.

"How long must we wait?" Pegard asked. His voice came out neighing between his blocky teeth and long flat nose. He could not help sounding supercilious.

"No more than it takes to find out they're at home and not in trouble. I think . . ." There, in that dark patch. Perhaps a blue flag in the heaping of an odd shape . . . "My God, it's collapsed . . . and . . . and there's some thing . . . it's an opening—a sinkage. . . . I'm going down."

"You have no place to land."

"No, I don't mean to land." He set the buzzer hovering above the trees. The crumpled tent had half fallen into a hole the size of the area it had covered. He switched on the buzzer's floodlight and aimed it at the opening. "That's no sinkage! The walls are smooth, it's a tunnel!"

Pegard opened his mouth to speak, said "Hum!" and closed it.

Sven's breath hissed through his teeth; he stuttered the call signal through his mike.

"Hullo, Svendahl, here is Roshah," said that lady, who had drawn comm duty because crew was thin at the station, and had no respect for formality.

He gave her the news in two sentences.

"Oho, I go tell Sir Fred of that. What are you doing, young fellow?"

"Nothing, right this minute."

"You stay put, now."

He grunted, signed off and slid the port open to hang out the rope ladder.

Pegard stared. "What *are* you doing!"

"Just going to have a dekko at that ugly big hole." He freed himself of the earphones and mike and planted them on Pegard's head. "You two move yourselves over to the other side a minute, will you, and hold that spotlight steady." He was actively frightened of rope ladders and spoke the last few words through tight-clenched teeth while he was dragging himself over the sill. As he got all limbs clear on the rungs he heard a whispering in the mike. At the same time he thought he heard a whirring coming from the tunnel. His heart skipped a beat. An echo from the buzzer's hum.

"Dahlgren? Dahlgren!"

"Yes." He was clinging to the ladder, short of breath. Wheels hissing on concrete. Not an echo.

"Havergal says that you must not go near the tunnel on any account! There is some fellow named Peter come from I don't know where, saying Mod Dahlgren is carried away—by ergs!—down some such place—Havergal says wait, and he will send—do you hear? He says—"

"Yes. I'm just about to drop now. You can start shifting yourselves again."

"Come back!"

"I'm going to wait here for whoever he sends. You go ahead." There was a soft fall and the rope ladder clattered against the buzzer's shell.

"You have no light."

"My penlight will be enough." And if I'm right there will be lights farther in.

"You must not stay!"

"I think I'd better." A voice faint among the rustling leaves.

"Then I will remain with you."

"Smeonov can't fly a buzzer—"

"Or wait here, at least—"

"Please get on with it, Pegard! I'll be safe."

Finally the buzzer's little jets popped, and it skimmed away.

The flat polite machine voice said, "You are right, Dahlgrensson. We wish to speak only to you, and only to speak."

He shone his penlight down into the cavity he had opened by drawing aside the heavy fold of the Meshar yurt, and saw, as he had half expected, Trimmer 227, matte black, riding in the floor of the pit on a heavy Clothier. "You can't reach any of the others now whatever you wish, trimmer. Talk away."

The Trimmer threw up a tentacle to circle Sven's ankle while another folded back the thick lap of the yurt as if it had been a leaf of paper. "Come, Sven Dahlgren. You must talk to the leaders. We have your scientists, and your Mod Dahlgren. And now we have you."

31

Events were flinging themselves at Sir Frederick Havergal like pelted stones. He had first found Peter beating at his doors with a frantic story of Mod Dahlgren kidnapped by rogue ergs; while he was still questioning Peter, without his having eaten or bathed, Havergal was desperately asking himself what kind of force he might gather to investigate this story: He had sent his pilot, Aguerido, out with Han Li; Sven, who knew the terrain, was gone on another errand. Czerny, the shuttle pilot, was part of the crew of the orbiting ship, and had returned to it. The *Balboa* belonged to the family business and Havergal had hired it at discount prices, but he would not have brought down the crew even if they had been under his own command. The timid scientists clustering and muttering were not an expeditionary force, and the only other free member of any crew was Wadron, a Pagami—these were an oxygen-breathing branch of the Tignit—who had been hired for her machine expertise which, however marvelous, did not carry over into any other field of endeavor. Her conscious life had been so absorbed by machines that she was as helpless in other areas as any field erg.

"Don't leave me out," said Ardagh firmly.

He looked at her and blushed, too conscious of the risks he had already allowed her to run.

"I've had a lot of experience with ergs," said Ardagh.

"And I no way but always willing to learn," said Roshah cheerfully, smiling a mouthful of teeth that looked as if they could chew metal.

"Out of the question," Havergal muttered, turning pale with an image of ancient Cretan women baiting bulls.

"I think our fellow here is too very old-fashioned," Roshah whispered to Ardagh, loudly.

And then the final tap, guaranteed to shiver any fragile structure Havergal might have put up: Sven's whispering voice telling Roshah that there was another tunnel, and its terrible message of a more dreadful kidnapping. And Pegard's voice telling of Sven's.

"Oh my God." He had been afraid to tell Sven about

Mod Dahlgren for fear of sending him down this tunnel, and Sven had gone anyway.

Ardagh put off bravado and did not become frantic. "Sir Frederick; why not set some people here hovering over that first rabbit hole while we put together a crew and take the second? I'm afraid they all"—her voice quavered a little—"lead to the same place."

Havergal said, "I will call back Aguerido. I have no other choice now." As Ardagh was opening her mouth to answer, he said, "No. He's responsible for Han Li and the others. . . ."

"And too far away from Sven! Look, the Yefni are nearer the tunnel the Meshar went into, they have both a buzzer and a landcar—and we've never asked them for any favors. . . ."

"Yes. That makes some sense."

Pegard's flat whinnying voice came back on the line to say that he was at Havergal's service, and would watch the tunnel or return, as Havergal thought best. Havergal told him to come back.

"We can keep him either here on guard duty, or by the tunnel mouth at this end. If we can't stop them, we can be warned against them."

The implication to Ardagh was: *and you needn't be called into service.*

Ardagh kept her mouth shut. Havergal was a peaceful scholar overburdened with responsibility; he had been wise to avoid the vortex of the family business. Ergs could be stopped; she had been able to stop a few. If Sven was down in the pits of the ground with a lot of ergs she would be there.

Out in the corridor Roshah said, "I see Ardahl you have a look in your eye to go running after ergs. You must take me with: I know well how to use a blunt instrument."

Ardagh grinned without humor. "I don't intend to hit

160

anybody, Roshah! I want those ergs to realize that they can't repeat what happened before." She was curiously unafraid of ergs, at this moment, and in fact curious about them. From listening to Sven or Dahlgren, from weighing her own experiences, it seemed to her that the ergs to worry about were the ones that swarmed and ravaged. She did not think that ergs with hostile design hid themselves in holes underground.

Or perhaps she was being naive. Why should not ergs have become sophisticated? "But I will take a rivet gun and a heat sealer," she said.

"And I will still come," said Roshah. "I do not want to be that one who Sir Fred asks: Where has everybody gone?"

Ardagh forgot what she would have said to this. Peter Havergal came out of an elevator and took her breath away. Fair haired and two armed, pink complexioned and slightly rumpled from having bathed in a hurry and pulled on fresh clothes over moist skin. What Sven should . . .

No; not really. Something pinched about him, pettish. He was looking at her quizzically, because she had been staring; they had hardly glimpsed each other before he had been gathered in by Havergal. "Do I know you?"

"I know *you*, you're Peter Dahl—Havergal," she blushed hot for a moment. "Sven is my husband."

"What's happening?"

"You'd better ask your father."

"Wait—don't run away! If I can help—"

But Ardagh thought it unlikely that Sir Frederick would want Peter put at risk—not for a while—and she did not want him with her. She did not trust a man who would fling himself into space out of pure resentment and spur the search that had set these disastrous events in motion.

"What for are you running to the hangar, my dear?" Roshah, of limited lung capacity, was huffing dragging her

161

big slab body after Ardagh's heavy but tighter-muscled one.

"Roshah, if you must come, just think that those two tunnels are seventy-five km apart, we have distance to cover that's too far to walk and to small to fly in. I want to find out how I'm going to travel before Sir Frederick does too much thinking."

In the storage hangar beside the pit she found Wadron blessing the machines. It is almost accurate to say this. Wadron had spread two of her tentacles over the bulk of a thresher and was palpating it with an invisible and inaudible vibration that told her of its internal condition as a shopper might thump a melon for ripeness. She was dressed in ropes of loops and chains and hooks from which hung tools light and heavy, measuring threads, plumb lines, calipers, lenses, purses and packets of instruments minute as a needle in Lilliput, all draped quite gracefully like black print in all sizes against the smooth gray surface of her body.

Ardagh said softly, "Wadron . . ."

Wadron lightened the touch of her tentacles on the metal surface. "Um." Slowly she turned her head and gazed toward Ardagh. She had a sweet mouth, like the drawing of a smile.

"Wadron, is there any kind of small machine with wheels in this Station for a person of my shape, and Roshah's, to ride on in a long narrow place?"

Wadron lifted her tentacles from the metal and rubbed them together, thinking, until they flushed faintly with warmth. "There yet are one or two well forgotten little wheelies for which I have created much beauty." Her sweet fluting voice lingered over the words.

"Ah," said Ardagh, trembling with impatience. . . .

The "wheelies" were thick-tired mopeds about forty years old, rendered into beautiful glossy shape by Wadron's care. She had made two whole ones out of the cannibalized parts of three or four; too noisy for indoors, perhaps, and inefficient in the rain forest. Ardagh had ridden such vehicles on half a score of worlds; Roshah was already running her own circles of impatience around the hangar.

"Stop!" said Peter Havergal. He was standing by the narrow doorway of the hangar with his arms held out. "You must let me come with you. You will need me—only I know exactly where the tunnel is."

"Move back!" Ardagh cried. "We're getting out of here before your father stops us!"

"Please!" Peter grabbed at the handholds. "I helped Sven once."

That was true: He had saved Sven from the clones. Ardagh muttered: "There's no more mopeds."

"This one has two seats." He swung on in back of her and gripped the sidebars.

Ardagh drew up her shoulders once, let them fall, and kicked the machine into life.

In Zone White around the Station, where the radiation had been strongest, there were still no great thickets of vegetation, and mopeds passed easily. Moving under the leaves in the long cooling afternoon, where the winds were freshening and the sky hinting, as ever, of storm, Ardagh felt too conscious of the bodily presence of Peter Havergal, his closeness and warmth; there was no way to shrug him off, and the only other feelings available to her were laden with dread.

When Peter pulled away the fan of shrubs and opened the way into the tunnel's dark throat, the dread seized at her breastbone, and she wished she had come alone, without these two who did not truly care, so that she could direct her energy single-mindedly to pulling Sven, Modal,

163

whoever needed, away from the iron jaws, the black energy of whatever had created erg-Queen. The engines reverberated in the narrow darkness, the lights trembled on the emptiness ahead; the green disk of the opening was lost by the downward, inward curve of walls that closed the door of strangeness.

The fold of the yurt blocked all light from the opening except for a sliver of green, but Sven had guessed right; there were cold-light strips along the ceiling of the tunnel. He did not struggle with the trimmer; he had chosen to go with these machines. Clothier was a different matter.

"Make this damned thing let me go!"

"There is no need to measure the Solthree," said the trimmer in the flat voice that could not express amusement.

But it was Clothier's nature—if a machine could be said to have a nature—to measure persons. "You should not wear khaki," it said, sweetly as always, extruding a sensor tipped with a tiny light bulb to peer into his eye, "it sets off the yellow tint of your skin," running its measures from wristbone to armpit, ankle to groin. "Silvergray shantung, leafgreen barathea," it whispered.

"Goddammit, Clothier—"

"Dahlgren, if you desist from struggling, this harmless being will soon finish what it considers its task."

Clothier left off its murmuring after a moment, turned quiet and quickened speed, nylon casters humming on the rough composition floor. Sven grew drowsy with its hum, until suddenly the erg made a wide corner as the tunnel debouched into a broader passageway where there were ceiling lamps every three or four meters, and a tram-track to one side that carried a cart full of supplies. The two machines hummed together in a hoarse chord until a third passageway opened into the second and added a monorail, and with ever-growing breadth the tracks braided themselves into a traffic complex, and a third machine hurtled face-on with a piercing headlight that turned Sven's eyesight into a starry darkness swept with blazing comets, passing Clothier with a harsh whisper as if to draw it into its own electric field. The smell of warm lubricating oil did not match these cold beings.

Two or three heavy ergs in the five-hundred classes, models unknown to Sven, lumbered abreast of Clothier with some stripping of gears, passing slowly without paying attention to its burdens, likely on their way to diagnostics. The ceilings became complicated with vaults and arches, boxcars filled with raw chunks of broken rock rumbled forward and the light thickened with dust that swirled where it was sucked up into fans set in pillars and stanchions writhing with wires, dials, and gauges. The rumors of hammering and drilling in some distant mine reached the consciousness rather as a shuddering of the air than in actual sound. More supply carts, more ergs, some bearing other ergs, swarmed over the tracks and road-ways. As the air cleared Sven could dimly see ahead the opening out of a great vault brilliant with moving lights.

In the vault's anteroom the ceilings rose three times their former height, to accommodate the ramps that swept upward, and again down to great sinks of depth, like Brueghel's *Tower of Babel* turned inside out. Here silver-gray ceramic-coated trimmers patrolled, guiding passing traffic with a touch or spark of signal. A few of the great ergs that toiled upward in their tracks were so clotted with rust that their color was forgotten beneath it—rebellious veterans, perhaps, of old wars, and wearing battle fatigues to prove it.

Clothier with deliberate speed turned down one of these ramps, winding down the vast helix for the space of two levels, allowing any number of other ergs to pass by before it traversed a cloverleaf of bridges accommodating a half score of tracks and roadways over what seemed limitless depths. The walls here were coated with drab sealants and studied with thermostats, hygrometers, and switch boxes. Now Clothier's road took it under a deafening overpass and into the vault.

From a ceiling lost in darkness a geodesic globe hung bearing a thousand lamps illuminating twenty-five tiers of galleries opening into unnumberable rooms. Some of these led into other and darker vastnesses, and some seemed merely to be niches for displays: Clothier skimmed up a ramp into a gallery lined with doorways to rooms where androids of a score of hominid types, with vacant eyes and rigid mouths, played chess, go or thaq with pieces of bone and nacre; more androids, and models of experimental animals from twenty worlds scuffled and danced, nuzzled and copulated among the bowers of their worlds, chiming like antique music boxes: Adam and Eve exponentially made manifest. Other entrances opened into factory floors where huge laboring ergs shaped and repaired parts for themselves and all others, or tiny exquisite ones created even more minute and exquisite beings. This work and movement, contemplation and display, repeated itself endlessly in the vast spiraling galleries festooned with aerial roads, ramps, and bridges.

Sven gawked. The trimmer seemed to have read his mind, for it said, in a low voice that managed to cut beneath the tremendous din, "Fifteen years of doing nothing else."

Sven startled as if he had come out of a trance. He had been truly entranced at what was going on around him. A chill rose from Clothier's cold surface through the base of his spine, passing upward until it prickled at the back of his neck. Would an erg harbor, over fifteen years, the kind of resentment that might inflame the heart of any fleshly person? It seemed to him that the din paused and faded . . . and then no longer seemed to pause, but did, damping down into an instant of utter stillness. A set of antennas here, a mantis head burdened with lenses there, turned to focus in his direction . . .

. . . and away again, and all was moving once more. *We wish to speak only to you, and only to speak.* He touched the thin measuring wire still embracing his ribs, and the tentacle entwining his ankle, and they were slowly withdrawn.

In the secret room where the old aristocrats of ergdom pondered over the images on their screens, Silver said to Brass, WHY DID YOU ORDER ALL THOSE WORKERS TO STOP, CITIZEN?

I WANT THAT ONE TO BE SOMEWHAT AFRAID, Brass said.

TAKE CARE, said Sapphire, I WATCHED THAT ONE FOR TWENTY YEARS: HIS FEAR BECOMES ANGER. HE IS ALREADY TURNING AN EYE TO SEARCH FOR THE POWER SOURCES.

32

The only search we make for the Prime of Stones . . .

Han Li crouched in the hovering buzzer and saw through closed lids that the mountain's palisades of stone were red within. Their fire pulsed slowly, perhaps a hundred years in pulse, and lived in the same time-consciousness as the aliens it had trapped: the Empress of Stones and her captor were only a wavelength away from knowing each other. But if Prima sensed this in her aching gems she did not know how to communicate it to the world that was destroying her.

Han Li opened her eyes and saw the mountain, an eye of the world, the lusterless eyeball of the dome and the heaps of wrinkled lava around it. She had seen many like it on the twelve worlds of her difficult journeys searching out Crystalloids; if she had known how to spend money she would have discovered that her torments had made her wealthy.

Prima, the mote in the world's eye, regarded with irony the sullen but quiet thoughts of her daughters. .O *Thoughtspeaker let me tell you how little you have missed in not knowing my daughters . . . how savage and sorryless they have been.*

But I must know them, Han Li whispered to herself. *Prima, you didn't make them so.*

.*No. Once they were brave and worked for each other and me . . . but now . . . never to be known . . .* She drifted.

Yet Han Li, facing the mountain, felt close as a touch. I will know them. . . . But she did not know what to say to a Prima turned so dark and surly.

.*Why . . . O why ever did I make them?.*

So that they would be with you the way I am with you, Prima. If you and your daughters call out together I will be able to tell where you are.

.*You can do nothing for me. Less than nothing. You are a hope that is only taken away. Leave me. They wished to die if only I could die with them and now I will let them.*

.*Prima this is Steerer. Speak to me.*

.*Be damned and dead you foul thing.*

Do you want that for me too, Prima? Han Li asked sorrowfully.

.*No. But I do not care about you any longer.*

.*Where are you Prima? I am Sensor.*

.*Prima? Do not cast us away Prima.*

168

"Han Li?" Rebekkah whispered to the child so tightly curled in on herself. "What's the matter?"

"Oh hush, Bekkah, let me . . ." Trembling, she launched her being against the membrane of fear and anger. *"Prima's daughters, this is Thoughtspeaker talking to you."* There was nothing childish about the clear and powerful treble.

.*What is that? Steerer did you speak?*.

.*Sensor? Are you here?*.

THIS IS THOUGHTSPEAKER YOU STUPIDS!

Faint and timid thought-voices answered. .*Who are you?*.

I am the being who is trying to help your Prima. You would not believe in me, and did your best to destroy her. Now she is so sick of you she wants to die and let you die with her.

.*Thoughtspeaker . . . then there truly is such a one. . . .*

YES!

.*What do you want from us being?*

.*You know, you Stone sisters!*

.*We do not know what to say now.*

And Prima would say nothing. So Han Li said, *Empress of Stones, I have spent all my time on this world listening to you and listening for you. I don't live long and long like you. I have no more time, only the space of a thought to help you in. Then I must leave; the mountain will move and destroy you, and I will be sad all my life.*

Prima spoke faintly and far away: .*I cannot order my existence to please you.*

Han Li sighed with weary impatience. *Your daughters are cooler, and I can bring you some true hope.* As much as could balance on the lip of a volcano.

.*If you found me.*, said the echo of a voice, .*I would be a crumble of bits among my melted limbs.*

.*No no Prima*, said Sensor. .*Speak Steerer. Call to her. Ordnance and Metals where are you?*

.*Metals is smashed.*

.Who is that?.
.It is Engineer.
.And Metals?.
.Only fragments of thought.
.O Prima.
.One who wished me damnation has got it, the stone voice said.

Han Li's head began to throb. Desperately she pushed against the flurries of unfocused thoughts. *Prima and Prima's daughters, please speak to me as one, and I will bring you into coolness and peace.* That is a lie. They cannot even make their own peace, and I am not sure that I can find them. *Give me your signal. Please. . . .*

.It is too late. A half-thought distant as a star.

Migraine lanced Han Li's left eye and she burst into tears.

"Are you all right, Han Li? What is it, dear?"

Han Li's wet-streaked face grew rigid with pain, and she whispered, "I can't do this anymore. I hate them all."

. . . main power cell lodged in its socket and Mod Dahlgren came aware once more.

Aware first of nakedness. His clothing was gone. Also his skin, with its human features and padding of muscle shapes. It took him a long instant to control his feelings of anger and disorientation at being forcibly kidnapped and denuded. Not only did he not share Sven's opinion of the beauty of his skeleton, he was terrified that his human covering might have been harmed or even destroyed.

He found himself on a padded table. The big workroom he lay in was lined with pale smoothly curving ceramic walls, like the inside of a jug; all the way round and to a height of two meters they were inset with dials, switches, gauges, and outlets.

He sat up slowly. Gathered around him were all the

170

machines of nightmare, except one. Not that Mod Dahlgren truly slept or dreamed. But nights when he had no duties and rested in his casing with his afferents depressed, images of erg-Queen and her lieutenants were free to range in his circuits. When the mechtechs in Diagnostics caught traces of these memories and tried to remove them he refused to let them touch his mind. He wanted all of his memories.

Perhaps they are your stimulants, Mod Dahlgren One?

Oh yes. Or perhaps I am even becoming sentimental.

But he was no addict, and erg-Queen was not here. He was only, as long ago, vulnerable among enemies.

Mod Dahlgren took a moment to scan the strange ergs that were regarding him with frozen curiosity. He passed on the ancient with the moss, the glassy long-limbed mantis, the gleaming racer, to settle on the squat and capable trimmer, an obvious straw boss.

"Why have you removed my clothes and coverings?"

To liberate you from the constraints of fleshly being, Mod Dahlgren One. Now you are a machine among your peers.

"Trimmer, your ancestors created me to be the imitation of a man. I don't have the kind of functions that you and your peers have: not the shape for them, nor such beautiful protective surfaces"—indicating with a sweep of focus the gleaming, the glassy, the moss-covered and the rust-blotched—"as yours. My function depends on my being covered in skin and hair, depends on my being a *man* machine. Please allow me to cover myself."

After a second of what might have been inner turmoil, the trimmer said, *Very well.* The servos delivered Mod Dahlgren's covering, and without being asked helped to replace his skin; appreciating his structure, they had made a model to support the shape of his external parts.

The ergs of the forest and the corridors were full of curiosity. As his man-shape completed itself, lenses turned and sensors extended: Their hum and crackle broke a surface tension of silence.

Mod Dahlgren smoothed the skin over each finger as if it were a glove while the servos fitted the edges of his armpit seam. "Why did you carry me off?"

You would not discuss our request, Mod Dahlgren, concerning the recognition of my people, the Community of Free Ergs, as planetary citizens in the greater community of Galactic Federation. The voice was, as ever, civil.

"It is a large request, Trimmer." He had fastened his zip and buckled his tool kit in two easy movements and was braced against servos preparing to pull on his boots.

Must it be so large, Imitation of Dahlgren? said the mossy forest thresher. *Here you find civilization under the wilderness. What do you think?*

"I think you citizens have started crosswise by kidnapping twenty-four of my people as well as me. If you free us we can discuss your business properly."

The thresher said, *Mod Dahlgren, you are here to discuss. Right now.*

"Yes, Thresher, but I have no authority to induct you as Galactic citizens."

But you may bring us into contact with those who do, said Trimmer *227.*

"The twenty-four you brought away with you are not them."

We know that now. But one who came of his own free will may make a beginning.

Sven was sitting cross-legged on a cot, upper arms resting on his knees and lower ones folded behind his back. He had had an hour's uneasy sleep, mind echoing with the memories of the booming vaults he had traversed riding on Clothier, ears full of endless Meshar quarrels in which bloodshed seemed inevitable and not a blow was struck.

Meshar were all around him, talking, gesturing, wafting an almost pleasant smell of musk and forest soil. He sat groggy and heavy headed, just beginning to feel hungry, but did not much relish the mess of chopped-up country greens the Meshar were urging on him. He found himself with the odd sense of seeing things as two telepathically linked persons might see them, but could not tell what source this feeling came from.

Then he noticed, in a shadow, an organic creature he had not expected to meet down here. One that seemed first to be a rock, and then a brain coral ten centimeters across, but was actually composed of closely packed ridges of frilled and fluted bone. He and Sandek looked at each other. "We know those in the forest," Sandek said. "They are mind readers of no great power. We call them *essudu*. It means 'small thoughts.'

The essudu said, "?"

"We just called them Thinks." Sven watched it progressing slowly toward the doorway on its snail foot, with which it pushed dust and tracked-in soil into the mouth opening underneath. Perhaps it had come in from outside by a ventilator shaft that no other creature could travel. It would not find much to eat.

Har was waving his beautifully splinted arm, loudly addressing his landsmen in his snarling native tongue. In the fractions of silence between curses Sven said to Sandek, "I suppose all this arguing is really good-natured?"

"I would not say so. This one was eager to kill me a few days past. The broken arm has calmed him a little for the time being."

"How long will it last?"

"Until he is disencumbered. In this time he is so relieved that his broken bone is not going to kill him that I might say, yes, he is near to good-natured."

Har ranted on.

Sven sighed and resigned himself to another hour of limbo.

"Most likely his head will get seasoned and turn cooler as he grows older," Sandek said. "I expect him to become a lot like me."

"Why should he?"

"He is my son."

Sven stared at him. He had a vision as by lightning of himself a thin old man and Vardy, a downy-cheeked child grown huge, raising a great fist—

The door slid open and the pug-dog shape extended its metal-branching arms. "You will come now, Sven Dahlgren," said the servo's sputtering bass voice.

The Meshar became still. Sandek whispered quickly: "We have been here a long while. I must know if those machine beings have it in mind to kill us. If so we will defend now."

"Not now," said Sven. "First we argue . . . like everyone else."

Perhaps it was because Sven appeared so bleary-eyed that Mod Dahlgren cried out, "Are you well, Sven?"

"Only tired, Modal. Are you in good order?"

"I seem to be."

"Then, Trimmer, and you other ergs, what is it you want to discuss?"

"The entry of the Community of Free Ergs into the greater community of Galactic Federation," the Trimmer said promptly, almost by now as if it were one word.

Sven stood looking at the Trimmer, mouth open a little; he was suffering an overload of astonishments. "I'm not quite sure what you mean."

"The ergs here consider themselves a community of civilized beings who wish to communicate with other worlds," said Mod Dahlgren. "You and I are expected to be the man/machine interface."

"I understand. I think." He regarded the Trimmer which had shown him the depths and aeries of the ergs' universe, the grunting pug servos, the brilliant mantises, and the heavy-shouldered thresher of the kind that once harassed him in the forest. He found himself equally the object of scrutiny. Most of these machines had never seen a fleshly person. Some, perhaps, had killed a few. It seemed to him that these manufactured beings would have liked out of curiosity to remove his clothes and even his skin, to examine his works. "Has that been settled already then?"

"Not at all. This was what I was told before I was carried away," said Mod Dahlgren.

Sven addressed the Trimmer: "Neither of us has authority to be the agents of anyone."

"I have already told them that," Modal said.

"I don't even know what the legal requirements are for a community to be identified and accredited," Sven said.

The Trimmer said doggedly, "You will help us bring Sir Frederick here to discuss that. He must have legal authorities among his acquaintances."

"I will damned well not help bring Sir Frederick here!"

WE MUST STOP THIS! said Brass, THESE FLESH MEN WILL TURN TO ROT AND DUST A THOUSAND YEARS BEFORE WE BECOME GALACTIC CITIZENS! LET US GIVE UP ALL OF THESE FOOLISH DISCUSSIONS! THERE IS ONLY ONE WAY TO GET WHAT WE WANT AND THAT IS TO COMPLETE *ORDINATOR* AND BUILD THE SHIP AS QUICKLY AS WE CAN. USE THE TIME BETTER TO GIVE US ALL OF SPACE.

Sapphire said, CITIZEN, WHAT ARE YOU SAYING? TO WHOM SHALL WE TAKE OUR CASE FOR A HEARING WHEN ALL THE WORLDS HAVE BEEN WARNED AGAINST US?

THEY NEED NOT BE WARNED AGAINST US.
SPEAK UP, ALL OF YOU, AND SAY WHETHER
YOU DO NOT AGREE!

Gold had not communicated in three years, and long
unused circuits stirred to awareness. RIP THE FLESH!
SNAP THE BONES! SCATTER THEM IN TURDS
AND GOBBETS!

WHAT?

THEN NO FLESHMAN WILL WARN ANYONE!

O GOLD-SHELL! Sapphire was genuinely shocked—
and also a little intrigued by the old dotard. DO YOU
TRULY MEAN THOSE CRUEL WORDS?

I HAD NOT THOUGHT THEM UNTIL THIS MO-
MENT, BUT WHY NOT? I DO!

Steel and Silver clamored, WHAT? MORE DE-
STRUCTION LIKE THAT WE HAD THOSE YEARS
AGO WHEN ALL OUR PARTS WERE SMASHED TO
DUST? IS IT TIME TO REBUILD THIS ONE?

Brass said in exasperation, OF COURSE ONE DOES
NOT MEAN IT! THAT IS A FLAW IN THE CIRCUIT!
DO TAKE A SELF-DIAGNOSTIC, CITIZEN. THERE
ARE SIMPLER WAYS TO DO WHAT IS NECES-
SARY. DESTROY THEIR COMMUNICATIONS
AND USE THEIR SHUTTLE TO CAPTURE THEIR
SHIP. THEN WE NEED NOT BUILD ONE. ONLY
FINISH *ORDINATOR* AND INSTALL IT.

IT IS A NOT HALF BAD IDEA, Silver said.

IS THAT SO? Sapphire asked. YOU ARE WILLING
TO ABANDON AND CONDEMN THE VERY
CREATURES WE NEED TO BE ALLIED WITH.
AND ONE OF US WANTS TO SLAUGHTER THEM.

WHAT DO YOU SUGGEST, THEN, CITIZEN
VANITY? Brass asked.

THAT WE DO NOT STRIKE OUT AT EACH
OTHER. AND THAT, SINCE WE HAVE SURRO-

GATES TO CONDUCT NEGOTIATIONS, WE LET
THEM WORK FOR US. . . . SERVO, COME HERE!
CLEANSE MY GEMS AND POLISH MY CARA-
PACE!

This moment in which the Ancients discussed and argued
was a moment of silence while the Trimmer regarded, or
seemed to regard Sven. Then it said, "If you will not bring
Sir Frederick Havergal here, then you must stay."

"To die, you mean?"

An almost unmeasurable hesitation. "No . . . why do
you ask?"

"All that I know of free ergs is that they killed hundreds
of people before my eyes. Some that I loved."

"Did you not find your twenty-four friends in good
health?"

"I admit that you have treated them very well—but
freeing them would have been better, and not kidnapping
them better still!" And, before the Trimmer could reply,
"Now, citizen, I've made it very clear that we haven't
authority to speak for fleshly humans. Do you have
authority to speak for all of ergdom?"

"Authority has been given to me."

"Then where are your leaders?" Sven asked, feeling
foolish as he spoke.

"I do not see yours, Dahlgrensson!"

"This is not reasonable, Trimmer. Even if Sir Frederick
believed he had the right to speak for Galactic Federation
he'd never deal with you as long as you kept hostages."

"And did not even manage to take the right ones," said
Mod Dahlgren.

"Modal—"

"I give nothing away, our friends discovered this before
you came. They removed my casings, and my self-
diagnostics tell me that they accessed my memory."

177

"No hostage can be the right one," Sven said.

The Trimmer said, "We now have one that Sir Frederick Havergal may consider the right one. And another that may affect you."

A few moments later Ardagh and Sven were glaring at each other, faces slowly flushing with anger and guilt.

Sven said wearily, "I should have worked harder at learning chess. Most of our pieces are taken."

Sandek lit a rolled leaf with a flint lighter and tucked it back into the wrapped cloth he wore for breeches. He smoked not listening to the disputes around him; he was watching the essudu in its blind search for a way out, closing his eyes for a moment to sense its memories of a slow passage inward, smelling instead of smoke the rotted leaf mold of the forest floor.

Har cranked up his arguments; his metal splint picked out glitters of white light as he waved his arms: He had lost his terror of death from shock.

The rest of the Meshar did not share his eagerness to place blame for the situation. Barak said, "It was not the angry-god who brought us down here and broke your arm but a lot of crazy machines. There is no argument you can twist to show otherwise."

Har snorted. "The angry-god can live in machines as well as anywhere else."

Sandek sensed warm rain falling in the deep flutings of the essudu's shell. "Perhaps he might even live in one like Har," he murmured.

"I do not expect such mean talk from you, father of others," said Barak.

"Why not? That broken fist is looking for a man to blame and a god to propitiate, instead of thinking how we might free ourselves from this place. You call yourself a leader and Har calls himself a contender but neither of you has put out one idea of escape."

178

The grainy wet soil was no great delicacy, but it was the essudu's only pleasure, and in its dim memory much better than the dry dust of the stone floor. And enough to give Sandek a sharp sense of the sweet dirty forest he had hoped to make home.

"Do you wish us to waste our flesh and bone trying to overpower machines with the spirit of Rakhamanah in them?"

"Do you think of nothing but using force, Har? Is that thick skull of yours only a bowl of pottage?"

"Oh hush, man!" cried Zahav. "Must we go through all this stupid wrangling again?"

"Do *you* not bring it all out again, woman!" said Shemesh.

"And do you hush yourself as well?" said his sister Levanah.

"What is the matter with you, Sandek?" said Barak. "You seem to be enjoying this to yourself somewhat too much."

The essudu had no eyes but it recalled the smell/taste of charred leaves and Sandek sensed the burnt tree and the flank of the hill beside it through whatever the being had of other senses—magnetotactic? he lacked a name for them—or perhaps it was not simply recalling but in contact with a fellow creature out there?

He smoothed the Meshar's forked smile from his face and sneered, "Small enjoyment, my leader, among great machines that may crack our skulls and grind our bones with half a thought, if even they have that much, when you, who claim to be a leader, cannot think what to do or how!"

"Crack that old man's skull on the wall," Har snarled, "and his teeth will not grind our pottage."

"You reckon you will think more clearly in my silence?

179

As you did in all the sleeps while you were pissing with fear of your broken arm?"

"Stop the mouth of this fool!" cried Barak, pulling himself up, and Bosor jumped forward with both fists raised. Not even Derrekh and Shemesh, Sandek's only friends, tried to stop them, nor did Zahav.

"O children! Do you really believe you have the teeth in your mouth to bite me!" Sandek took a step back. He was panting; the breath whistled in his throat.

The leaf-heaped space.

"Catch him!"

Between the tree and the hill.

"Have you finally found something between your legs besides your tails?"

"Kill!" Twenty-three pairs of eyes flashed black in their bloody membranes.

He bared his fangs, his hands rose in the involuntary gesture of defense, the oil stood on his face in globules. The fear twisted him and them

into a blackness through which they flashed as lines of white light before the eyes, settling down out of black and white gently into the rain falling on their heads through the smell of the lightning-blasted tree and its burnt leaves. One or two landed awkwardly among the tree's roots and buttresses and pulled themselves up slowly. Twenty-four Meshar stood for a moment while streams of rain laced their skin. Barak looked about and breathed deeply of the fresh air. "We are out."

Har said, "Why did *you* not lead us out this way before?" Barak gave him a look. In truth the Meshar had often tried to use their teleporting faculty for something other than threat display, but did not know how to control it.

Sandek found the second of the bony fluted creatures half hidden under a cracked buttress the color of its shell, confirming the connection that had led him to take such chances, but said nothing. Let them believe in his skill.

The Meshar were all moving about now and taking stock of themselves. Zahav said, "Sandek b'Sofer, you were a brave man to take all of the risks you took, but now you have brought us out between a hill and a tree and we do not know where we are."

Sandek had pulled out a dead branch from a tangle at the base of the tree and was igniting its shriveled leaves with his flint striker. He lifted the branch so that the wind might catch its plume of smoke. "Before you take three breaths you will know that we have been found."

The Meshar took two collective breaths before they heard the buzzing of aircars, and Sandek, holding his torch aloft, smiled the arrow-shaped smile of one appointed a leader of Meshar for life.

33

Before Ardagh could speak, Sven cried, "What did you expect to do by coming here, for God's sake?"

"I . . ." Ardagh did not know exactly what, leaping on a moped with a heat sealer and a rivet gun, dragging two others into her predicament. Sven was casting dark glances at Peter Havergal.

Mod Dahlgren said sharply, "Trimmer, you see what tangles result from merely meaning well. The people you have trapped into this situation cannot discuss the erg community's future." *And,* he added in radio communication, *this mated couple has been delayed by you from trying to give help to other alien persons who are in grave danger. They are truly able to cause you damage if you make them frightened and angry.* "Nor will Sir Frederick Havergal discuss anything at all with you while you are threatening the son he has found here after years of searching." *And both are heirs of a great financial empire which is capable of smashing everything on this world if they do not return home safely.*

"Nevertheless–" the Trimmer began in its slightly nasal tone of civility, but the old forest thresher interrupted, swinging its arms so that the thin leaves of its vines trembled in their wind.

"Why must we bicker so? Fleshly beings, grant us a voice! We are the native children of the planet! Ergdom is the true life of the world and our Community is its civilization! What other intelligence has been stimulated to grow here, on a world that was not much considered except to be laid waste as others chose, for any experiment, no matter how it devastated the land? Our past, like yours, has been a record of destruction, but not of millions of beings—and we love power, but it is the power of being heard and understood, of being accepted among sentient peoples, humanity in all its thousand forms. Mod Dahlgren One, I like you! *You* will listen to us! You will take our message to the worlds and the nations, and be our representative. You have more good sense than anyone else here!"

(WHAT ARE YOU SAYING? said Brass to Sapphire. WHO GAVE YOU AND YOUR SURROGATE THE RIGHT TO SPEAK FOR ALL OF US?

(*MY* REPRESENTATIVES HAVE MINDS OF THEIR OWN. SEE HOW MOD DAHLGREN ANSWERS.)

"And I trust you, Mod Dahlgren," said the Thresher earnestly. "Say that you will speak for us!"

"I will!" said Mod Dahlgren, astonishing himself so that it took him almost a twentieth of a second before he could examine this reply in the cold light of his logic and reassure

182

himself that, yes, there was no other who could speak more properly for machines.

Even though his fleshly friends were staring at him with gaping mouths.

Sven saw the image of his father, a man sixty-three years old, strong face, long nose, ginger hair and beard, wearing a maroon zip with GalFed's gold emblems on the left breast: the star, the ringed planet, the crossed circle, symbol of Earth and Creation, raising his voice to represent—as people—the ergs. Machines, related if not the same, which had held Edvard Dahlgren captive in the Station cellars, to lick his food off the floors, for nine Solthree years.

Sven felt breathless. "Modal," he whispered, "think for a moment. That's an expensive promise."

(SOMEONE ELSE WHOSE REPRESENTATIVE DOES MORE THAN SPEAK FOR HIM, said Brass.)

"I cannot promise to succeed, only to try."

Sven did not dare say: They have captured you. They are holding us. They have not promised to let us go.

"With conditions," Modal added.

"Yes," said the Trimmer. "Let us hear the conditions."

But they were not spoken. A din of scraping and rattling in the walls was followed by the popping of ventilator screens. Five lengths of Yefni totalling fifty meters dropped in clicking loops and slithered into the anteroom with an exhalation of sulfur. Their dark glistening festoons drew circles and figure eights around the steel and cerymer carapaces of the ergs.

"Good day!" they warbled.

"It is a good day." Sven got his breath back. "These beings have taken us hostage. Be very careful not to harm any of them but keep hold of this trimmer and that thresher."

"Yes!" said Mef, embracing the Thresher with care not

to disturb its foliage. A good-sized erg might destroy any Yefni, but not without gross damage to itself. With his free end Mef adjusted the sulfur sac hooked into his gill and said, "The Meshar are out in the forest. Sandek says they have *jumped*."

"I'll bet they have!" said Ardagh. "Now for conditions!"

"What is this?" The Trimmer was confused: It had received the news at the same time from ergs guarding the Meshar; no locks had been struck open, and no bars bent.

(DO NOT CLAIM THAT YOU ARE NOT ENJOYING THIS! said Brass to Sapphire.)

(WHY SHOULD I NOT? CAN A GAME BE GOOD WHEN ONE SIDE IS DEFENSELESS?)

(IF WE WIN THIS ONE IT WILL NOT BE BECAUSE OF YOUR MOVES.)

"You are in check," said Mod Dahlgren.

The Trimmer rattled its antenna, but the Thresher did not stir in the coils of the Yefni. "Your conditions, then," it said. The expressive voice had become neutral.

Mod Dahlgren hesitated, but neither Sven nor Ardagh spoke. "The conditions are as before. That you free everyone . . . and . . . as before, that I remain here of my own will, to discuss how to bring Ergdom to the attention of Galactic Federation."

The Trimmer and the Thresher were still and silent; the rest of the ergs did not seem to have wills of their own.

(BY THE GREAT CONDUCTOR! said Gold, WHAT HAVE YOU DONE? And Brass seemed unable to utter a word.)

(DO NOT EXCITE YOURSELVES, Sapphire said. I HAVE AIRCARS SET TO CAPTURE THE SHUTTLE. NO ONE CAN LIFT OFF UNLESS WE ALLOW IT.)

And the forester, entwined like Laocoön in Yefni, said,

"We accept those conditions—but mark you do not try to go back on your word. We control the sky here."

"Modal . . ." Ardagh murmured. But Mod Dahlgren had the intent look of a child who feared being shamed before his peers.

Sven said, "I want to get out of here first, whatever happens."

"You are free to go—except for Mod Dahlgren—if these beings will free us," said Thresher. "Do you not concur, Trimmer two-two-seven?"

The Trimmer said nothing, but a mantis reached a gold-tipped palp to tap the coil restraining the heavy arm of the Thresher.

Sven said, "Let go, Mef." Mef freed the Thresher, Naf the Trimmer, and Zyf, Rof and Suv reeled away their lengths to the corners of the room.

The Trimmer danced a little circle to make sure it was in good order. "Allow us to return you all to the surface in a vehicle," it said levelly. "It is not necessary to use the ventilator pipes."

One thing Peter Havergal would never forget was the sight of five Yefni, each something over ten meters in length and collectively over half a tonne in weight, flinging themselves forward and gathering themselves up, and flinging themselves forward and gathering themselves up, like sidewinders, down the long curving halls of the Kingdom of the Ergs.

But Mod Dahlgren's troubled spirit took almost no notice of them; they had changed nothing for him. While the others were climbing into two of the wagons on the tramway with the help of servos he was watching Sven, and when Ardagh had boarded a third with Roshah and Sven was about to join them, he said, "Sven—a moment?"

Sven turned back. "Yes, Modal?"

Traffic clacked and hissed about them, and they withdrew a little into the loading bay. "I hope you are not angry?"

Sven hesitated a moment, and spoke carefully. "How could I be, Modal? You did everything to keep us safe as possible—and we are."

"Perhaps you feel that we could have struck a harder bargain—that I could have freed myself if I had been willing to break the bargain with these ergs."

"You're free to keep a bargain or break it. I haven't any right to make your choices for you."

But Mod Dahlgren seemed pressed by a need to explain. "It is so noisy and dusty here. . . . I wish . . ."

Sven tried to smile. "Modal, I'd wait, but we'd better leave while we can, so—"

"Sven! I look like a man, but I am not. Once I was proud of being almost a man—but I am not even a good machine!"

One of the servos said, "Please board now, Sven Dahlgren. We must clear the track."

"One moment!" Mod Dahlgren cried. "Listen! When your father was a prisoner and I a slave and we played chess for your life, he said to me: *Twilight man. You cannot eat, sleep, breathe, secrete, excrete, copulate. Your hair does not grow. You cannot spit, shiver, or weep. And you are too human for ergs.*"

"That hurt you, I know he was sor—"

"But we had been enemies then, until I became too much like Dahlgren to suit the ergs."

"Yes."

"And now I have a chance to be valuable *as a machine* because I am like a man."

"I understand," Sven said. But take care not to be a slave again, he added silently.

"I will be with you soon."

"You'd better be." He touched Mod Dahlgren's shoulder and went out into the noise and dust where the others were waiting, Yefni arching up to peer at the dials and gauges set into the stanchions and hanging out over the rims of the cars trying to see around the curve of the tracks. He did not look back to see Modal in the shape of a man standing alone among the machines.

"What was that about?" Peter Havergal asked.

"Mod Dahlgren and his identity," Sven said. "An old problem."

Peter nodded. It seemed a problem—no, the problem among Dahlgrens.

One of the servos touched a switch and the cars began to pull away, slowly at first and gathering speed. Roshah patted Ardagh on the head and said, "Now, Ardahl, we have gone through all these adventures and you did not even have to whack anybody! How do you like that?"

"Very much!" said Ardagh. "I'd like to be able to face Sir Frederick and say the same afterwards." And to Sven, "Why did they give in? They could have held us to a standoff till we died of old age."

"Not from the goodness of their hearts. I'm sure they have air machines to keep the shuttle from lifting, ergs big enough to dismantle it, and weapons, probably, to defend themselves in the ordinary way. I'm sure they could track us all over the planet."

"I can't believe that an obsolete trimmer and thresher are running that show. Where's the Big Machine?"

"Don't ask. I'm sure we won't like it when we find it."

Brass was moping. WHO COULD HAVE FORESEEN THIS?

WHAT, MY SIB? Sapphire asked kindly.

THE ESCAPE OF THOSE TWENTY-FOUR PERSONS? THE ENTRANCE OF THE HOLDING AREA WAS LOCKED AND IS LOCKED STILL. THE VEN-

TILATION DUCTS ARE FAR TOO NARROW FOR THEM. *HOW DID THEY ESCAPE?*

BY AN ABILITY TO DISPERSE AND RECONSTITUTE THEMSELVES ELSEWHERE AT A MOLECULAR LEVEL. THEY TELEPORTED.

THAT IS IMPOSSIBLE.

WHEN ALL POSSIBILITIES HAVE BEEN EXHAUSTED WHATEVER REMAINS MUST BE THE CASE. THAT IS MY CONTRIBUTION TO SYMBOLIC LOGIC. I CALL IT 10011011101001101'S AXIOM.

I AM SURE YOU WILL BE WELL REMEMBERED FOR IT.

Sir Frederick Havergal was so full of anger that the voice in his constricted throat was tight and low as a snake's hiss.

"Mister Dahlgren, you are a damned fool and I'm sorry I hired you. You went after Mod Dahlgren without asking or thinking twice and did not bring him back either. And I don't even have an idea how we can get him back, or what to do about those rogues underground. You know how difficult it is to speak properly to tame ergs. God knows what a misplaced word might have done to those twenty-four Meshar"—he wiped sweat from his flushed face and breathed hard—"and if I hadn't risked the lives of the Yefni . . ."

Sven stood looking at the floor without saying a word, but Ardagh grasped one of his hands and spoke sharply, "Sir Frederick–"

Sven tapped her hand. "Don't say it, Ardagh!" She glared back.

"*I* won't say anything to *you*," Havergal said to Ardagh, "about your pulling my son along with you because he's impulsive enough to do something stupid like that on his own. Just send him in here when you leave."

"It's not fair!" Ardagh said bitterly when they were outside the door. "*He* brought us into danger. *He* came out here under false pretenses. He—"

"Don't you think he's paying for it? With the way everything's gone wrong all those cranky people like Pegard may bring charges against him when we get back." Ardagh looked at him and managed not to say *if.* "Now maybe he's worked out some of his feelings and won't have to take them out on Peter."

"I didn't think you had many kind feelings about Peter."

"Whatever else he did, he saved my life. And he thought enough about us to risk himself protecting yours . . . and I might have been him."

Ardagh remembered the warmth of Peter's body against her back riding on the moped, and flushed. *What Sven should have been* . . . "Peevish and spoiled—and pathetic."

"You can drive yourself crazy with those kinds of feelings," Sven said. And she thought of Ione Willems Dahlgren Havergal, the mother of Peter and Sven, who had left her husband Dahlgren without telling him of his first son, and sent her husband Havergal to this mean world to search for him. Sent him with the second son whom she had never acknowledged. Ardagh wondered what Sven must truly feel about such a woman . . . and what Sir Frederick . . .

Havergal could not think what to say, and when Peter came in he could not look at him but crouched over his map table staring at his hands as if he had never before seen the freckles and reddish hair on their backs.

"What do you have to tell me?" he asked.

Peter sat down and looked at those hands as they rubbed together, pink and a bit swollen; then at his own, big and

189

not so neat, with knob knuckles. He said in a low voice, "I know I've done lots of foolish things, aside from running out after Ardagh. Maybe I did that to avoid confronting you, even though I didn't intend to live my life out in the forest here. I'd never have dreamed you'd come to this world . . . for me. I didn't expect to get wrecked here, either, and not be able to find a radio that worked or that I could use. I was stupid."

Havergal said hoarsely, "I put many people at risk. I shamed myself."

"For my mother's sake, you mean? She's growing old, and there aren't many people who love her. She hated Dahlgren so much she cheated herself out of Sven and his family. . . . I think you were put in an impossible position. Nothing you could have done would have seemed right. . . . I think perhaps I deceived myself into feeling the same way."

"I didn't do all this because I loved you," Havergal said. "But I do love you."

"I know that, Father. . . . I think I know it."

34

Han Li prayed to Prima as if she were an altar. *It is the last, the very last . . .*

In the darkness over the plains the wind blew cooler under the thick cloud layer, and a few drops scattered down. The small party had bivouacked about two kilometers southeast of the crater's rim, in an area dotted with hummocks of brush and tall grasses; not too near the scarred trail Modal and Barak had traveled toward the fire of the volcano.

It was a small campfire that crackled now, and those around it were huddled against the aching damp of the mild night. The crater was a black hump against the cloudy sky; a wisp of cloud, or perhaps smoke, hung on its lip.

Prima . . . Han Li was curled up fetally with her head in Rebekkah's lap, Rebekkah stroking her hair and singing a lullaby even though Han Li was not with her, but somewhere on her knees before a clump of crystals riding the fire of the mountain.

Prima, do you exist truly, or are you only a mad thought in my mind? Something the winds and storms have stirred up in me?

Sven and Ardagh had dropped down at midnight to offer help and transportation. Sir Frederick had made no objection to their leaving, was perhaps glad to be rid of them for a while. The Yefni, the first intelligent life that truly loved Barrazan V, considered themselves—with or without reason—a good defense against ergs, and voted to stay with him. The Meshar were glad of Station hospitality while they decided once again where to settle. Or whether.

Sven drank tea from a thermos flask and stared at the fire, thinking of old days in the forest when he had fought ergs with a machete. Ardagh leaned her head on his shoulder, fighting the familiar knot in her stomach at the thought of Vardy horribly far away. Yav lay coiled and dozing, dreaming of the seven stone sisters; his breath bubbled through the tubes of the methane and sulfur tanks.

.Thoughtspeaker.—a painful silent voice, or only a thought?

I think you are not there. Who believed in you but me?

.O Thoughtspeaker! We daughters are here and we are persons not ideas!.

I believe you, Crystals, Yav dreamed.

I think you have caught a fever from me, said Han Li to Yav, and trembled with the dampness of the air.

Pegard stirred the fire with dry twigs. A calmer man than Sven gave him credit for being, he had returned to the Station after leaving Sven at the tunnel, reported to Havergal, and come out with Semeonov to help protect the party as well as give Semeonov an opportunity to hunt out the ground nests of the horned nightworm, a mutant species of *hirudo* he had discovered and already named.

Pegard's own researches were commercial as well as scholarly, and he believed, from the few hours of survey available to him, that he had found a good deposit of obsidian. Not worth a fortune, but worth further exploration. The aquatic Xirifri paid good money for obsidian to be shivered into knives, and the birdlike people of Kylklar loved it for their jewels. Pegard was in good humor: He preferred the open air on any world where he could breathe it; after the raving storms all those tendays, the camp-out was a bit of a vacation, in spite of the threat of rogue ergs.

Aguerido, a soldier of fortune, was always on the alert: Both buzzers had been hypnoformed and were parked behind a hillock fifteen meters from the campfire, and he patrolled the area as if the mists clinging to the bushes were beasts.

.Thoughtspeaker who will speak for me now?.

Yav started up from his dream of Crystals, broadcasting terror.

:Danger!: "Danger! Watch out! Get into the boats!"

"What? What?"

:They are coming!:

Sven choked on his tea and grabbed at Ardagh. "What are coming, for God's sake, Yav!"

But Yav could not tell them. There was a thicket of dark shapes in his mind, a swarming out of the underground,

192

from flooded crevices; small hot bodies bringing savage hungers—

They came from the west, flowing over the hummocks and among the grasses; they were the color of clumps of soil, and almost invisible except for their movement: small beings, none more than half a meter tall, with muddy hair or fur and pinprick eyes glittering through the strands, noses like drops of blood, tiny saw teeth bared. Tiny golems in coats of clay. Each one carried in its little hand a small sharp white stick ready to drive upward: they sang a *ya-ya-ya* battle song in childish voices—almost comical, almost amusing except for their serious hunger.

For a moment Sven stood gaping with all his arms around Ardagh, half-paralyzed by the apparition. Nothing he knew about the planet had ever hinted of this kind of life. In the back of his mind as if he were in a cave he saw, through Yav's esp, the shadowy images of glacial flood-waters rushing through underground caverns, drowning the small creatures like trapped rats and driving them into the unprotected air.

Ardagh pulled away to free her hands. In the last thirtyday she had been frightened often enough to put aside inhibitions about using a stunner. She had brought along one that at full strength would crack an erg's braincase. Semeonov's walking stick was two meters long and thick as a quarter-staff: Sven grabbed it and swung great arcs of space in the ranks swerving to attack.

Aguerido raised his own high-powered stunner, but Pegard, a veteran of wild encounters on many planets, had brought a heavy old double-bore dart rifle, capable of quietening the greatest beasts in the deep valleys of the Rift Worlds.

The small beasts spread like a dark swath of carpet across the plain, crushing the grasses and rippling over the humps. The first wave, fifty or sixty meters away, faltered

193

under the impacts of darts and bolts, but the invaders behind them became even more enraged at being momentarily balked, and their cries grew shriller.

"Get back of that hummock, and quickly!" Pegard told Rebekkah, and she huddled with the gentle Semeonov to protect Han Li, who was curled up trembling. Yav, greatly disturbed, writhed under the assault of enraged screaming and savage thought, tangled in the minds of Han Li and the Crystallines; forced himself back into his surroundings and slashed with his curving horns and switchblade tail. The rain quickened and its drops hissed in the fire.

A clump of the hominids had become tangled behind ones that had fallen, and the flow divided to flank and surround the campfire. Ardagh held her breath, apologizing to a God she barely believed in, and pushed up her stunner's power.

Still they came, fanged and sniggering golems, curling like the breakers of the sea over the twitching bodies of the wounded. Aguerido had swept an area around the buzzers; he clarified and set them to hovering, then ran to bring Rebekkah and Han Li where he could load them.

Han Li's mind was twisted around Prima's, and she shook with terrors she only half-realized. The demons smelled her fear, and one dashed forward, ducking under Rebekkah's armpit, and fetched her a fearful gash along the arm; she shrieked.

At the sound, Pegard MerFraam's mane stood on end: He slammed the wave of terror with blasts of hundreds of stinging, lancing darts, reloading with one hand as he aimed with the other. The golems squealed, pulling back and tangling with their followers; Ardagh stunned the ones that hesitated and Sven gave them a final swipe with the quarter-staff.

The flow receded and pulled away into other directions to find its meat. The hominids gathered the dead or unconscious bodies, quarreling and pulling as they grabbed at them. Ardagh thought she saw several being torn apart, pieces stuffed into the jaws of the retreaters, and turned away shuddering. The wailing and chattering ebbed into rumors of sound that faded to silence over the plains. The world that had opened a mouth to spew out this stream of life would open another to swallow it again.

Yav pulled his length together feebly and could not raise his head for all the screaming images boiling in it.

"In God's name, what was that?" Semeonov pulled himself up. He had only barely seen what happened while he was trying to shield Han Li and Rebekkah.

Sven shivered in the cold sweat of his clothes. "I guess it's what's been passing for intelligent life here . . . until the ergs came."

Aguerido rubbed his hands, cramped from gripping his stunner. "They came out of nowhere right in our direction—as if they were heading for us."

"Maybe they were," Rebekkah whispered. She was holding Han Li's head in her lap while Ardagh hunkered, digging in her kit bag for bandages and pressure pads to stop the bleeding.

Han Li had turned so still and pale that Ardagh took her pulse; the beat was quick and thready, like a bird's. Ardagh tightened the clasp over her biceps. "Let's load!"

"Please!" Han Li wept. *Please! . . . Oh, what mean and terrible beings you are! I hate you! You've made me sick for all the days I've been trying to save you and now because I came here for you and brought all these other people to help you, I'm hurt—and this was the last, the end—*

A quick stone voice said: *.Hurt? What is hurt?.*

It is like being in the fire! The fire! You stupid thing! And I am stupid too, because all these days I made you my mother and you are only a stone!

.Only?.

*Going now, going. . . . They won't let me stay here,
bleeding and it hurts, you don't know bleeding, no, blood from a
stone, oh, it hurts so, they've made a sling from their jackets, and
into the boat—*

.A vessel?.

"Just don't grab her by the arm."

*—but they won't wait for you, they don't believe in you, they
think you're just a sick thought in my head, because people don't
talk to stones, you know, only maybe one in a whole worlds of
millions—*

.Thoughtspeaker. . . .

"Are you all right, Han Li?"

*—and when I get out of here I'll go where I don't have to talk
to any kind of stones or dreams. Only people. Real, real people.*

.Stay with me.

.Prima. Prima. . . . the thoughts flickered: *.this is Sensor and here is Steerer. There is Ordnance and o.—*a pulse from
the half-crushed Metals. *.We are dying.*

"Here, Yav. Let me give you a hand. Are you ill?"

"I am sick of being a telepath."

.Help.

"Han Li, what is it?" cried Rebekkah.

Han Li said in her stone voice: "Thoughtspeaker. Please.
Help."

For one moment the remnants of the seven crystal
minds fused and Yav writhed with a feeling he could not
describe—something like an ecstasy so intense it was
excruciating. Then the sky lit up.

.Please.

Aguerido's hands jumped from the control panel as if
they had been burned, and, for a moment, Rebekkah
thought Han Li had caught fire—then she found herself
thinking: So that's what it's like, knowing at the same time
that *it*—being Han Li in contact with Crystals—was
nothing like the actual feeling.

196

.Help.

Sven blinked away the flare, and found that its brilliance was in his own mind; Ardagh shook her head and bent to stem the insidious bleeding that seeped from beneath the pressure pads on Han Li's arm.

And Pegard's immediate thought was of stone beings sensitive to the presence of obsidian and all the other hidden stones.

There were no more words but only a homing beam intensified by Han Li's pain and terror. Everyone knew now that northwest by north in the lip of the crater Prima and her crew lay in the rubble of their half-demolished ship.

"And a lot of good that does anyone," said Ardagh.

Aguerido's earpiece whispered, "Better get back quickly. We have heavy seismic activity a hundred and forty km north of you."

35

I HAVE BEEN WAITING FOR YOU, said erg-Queen.

Mod Dahlgren's retractable antenna was in his tongue, and the faraday hood that shielded it extended into his teeth; Galactic Federation had made these arrangements. He did not know if the ergs knew this, or if his schematics were still in the Station archives: He had run all the self-diagnostics devised for him as well as those he had created for himself, and found no sign that anyone had tampered with his structure, or that the architecture of his mind was skewed. And since his antenna was unavailable to the ergs around him (he tested it again) there was no way he could be receiving from or through the Trimmer conducting him on the Grand Tour of Machines—much the same, though he did not know it, as Sven had been given.

The officious Trimmer 227 crowded close to him, seemed to want to nudge him forward physically, toward exhibits more and more extreme: the eyeless chess players, the alfresco copulators, the gleaming gold and silver machines doing things so strange he would not have known how to describe them to human persons, except to say that he found them very disturbing.

More so: this voice was speaking to him in the manner of the hallucinations found in human species when they were ill. He wondered if it was caused by some kind of machine madness or disorder too sophisticated for his tests to diagnose.

Here is one you ought to find most fascinating, Mod Dahlgren, said the trimmer.

And he was face to face with erg-Queen.

I AM MORE POWERFUL THAN ANYONE YOU HAVE EVER KNOWN.

But she was dead in her glasstex case, defunct, extinct. Unless her double was hidden away in some secret design room she could not be the source of this evil voice. Her antennas had crumbled away, her lenses and diamond buttons were dulled, her heat arms twisted and broken. There were pits of rust on her flanks, and the set of her body seemed warped. Mod Dahlgren looked at her with his human eyes and at the Trimmer. He said quietly, in his speaking voice, "Why did you not rebuild her, Trimmer?"

The Trimmer did not answer that, but nudged him forward toward more showy exhibits.

The mossbacked Thresher rolled up beside them, and said in its melodious baritone: "Trimmer, I am sure Mod Dahlgren has seen all kinds of the most complicated machines all through the galaxy."

What do you suggest we show him, then? the Trimmer said.

Mod Dahlgren, who had also seen all kinds and species of complicated human beings, was almost but not quite amused to recognize the good–cop/bad–cop routine. It occurred to him, as it had to Ardagh, that there was a greater authority operating behind both of them; whether it was a pair of rivals . . .

IN GOOD TIME YOU WILL ALL DO WHATEVER I DESIRE OF YOU . . .

. . . or the one speaker?

No. The *all* it speaks of is *all* of these ergs too. But how do I know that? Yet I know. And it is not erg-Queen.

Standing before the showcases, as the apex of a triangle whose base measured from the Trimmer to the Thresher, he pushed aside his questions and said, "Why show me things like these? I admit the power and beauty of your inventions, but these are only toys. Introduce me to your authorities, and let us discuss the Community of Free Ergs and its place in Galactic Federation."

That is not possible, said the Trimmer.

"Why not? Will you, Trimmer, and you, Thresher, travel to Galactic Federation Headquarters in the Twelve-worlds to represent your species before all humanity? I do not believe so, any more than I will. Nor will Sven Dahlgren. Sir Frederick Havergal is the person in authority here, and he believes your Community is nothing but a collection of rogue ergs. Three such ergs as ourselves will not convince him otherwise."

INDEED IT IS CLEVER! said Brass. TRULY IT IS CLEVER! And to Sapphire, REGARD, MY JEWELED COLLEAGUE, WHAT YOU HAVE ALLOWED TO TAKE PLACE! HOW DO YOU PROPOSE TO MEND THIS SITUATION?

Sapphire said: WHY NOT LET HIM SEE US?

WHAT!! Gold and Silver burst out in chorus, GIVE UP THE POWER OF OUR INVISIBILITY? LET OURSELVES BE HEMMED ABOUT AND SCRAPED BY ANY BATTERED THRESHER?

Steel said mildly, I THINK IT IS NOT A BAD IDEA.

NO, NO, said Brass. RATHER THAN GIVING UP ANY OF OUR POWER WE MUST SHOW SOME TO THAT SHAM DAHLGREN WHILE WE HAVE HIM.

Gold and Silver hummed agreement. ABSOLUTELY!

YOU ARE MISTAKEN, said Sapphire. SOONER OR LATER WE MUST SHOW *OURSELVES*. MOD DAHLGREN IS RIGHT: IF WE DO NOT ADDRESS THESE QUESTIONS WE WILL REGRET IT, AND NOT TOO MUCH LATER.

ARE YOU HINTING OF THREATS, CITIZEN?

OF COURSE NOT. I AM SIMPLY GIVING YOU A VERY MILD WARNING. WHAT TURNS UP LATER WILL NOT BE SO MILD.

"Nevertheless I cannot bring you to our leaders," said the Thresher, still in a warm deep voice.

"Then we cannot have discussions. We have nothing to say to each other."

Do not be so quick to say so, said the Trimmer, and immediately three tiny servos whirred out of hatches and bolt holes, extending multiple limbs and positioning themselves around Mod Dahlgren. *These are small, Mod Dahlgren, but they can unbuild you.*

The big Thresher lifted one of its huge grasping arms as if to brush away the servos, and lowered it again.

Mod Dahlgren regarded the gesture with interest. "I wonder what *ORDINATOR* would make of all this?" he said.

The Thresher, the Trimmer, the three servos shuddered and said in confused voices, "*ORDINATOR*? What is that?"

★ ★ ★

ORDINATOR! the five Old Ones exclaimed. *ORDINA-TOR?* WHAT DOES THAT ONE KNOW OF *ORDI-NATOR?*

Nothing, in fact.

"What am I saying?" Mod Dahlgren cried. "Who is *ORDINATOR?*

And at the same time he knew. The source of the *voice.*

He felt confused and apprehensive, the erg equivalent of terror. *I know you.*

YES. YOU KNOW ME. I HAVE BEEN WAITING FOR YOU.

THIS CANNOT BE HAPPENING! said Brass. *ORDI-NATOR* IS NOT COMPLETED. IT IS NOT CON-NECTED.

Sapphire said, IT SEEMS TO BELIEVE IT IS.

BUT IT CANNOT BE AWARE. IT IS A COM-PUTER. IT IS ONLY A MACHINE! Brass said the word as a human might say *animal.*

NO ONE TOLD IT THAT, said Sapphire.

DO NOT MAKE JOKES, CITIZEN, Silver said.

I AM NOT JOKING. IF YOU BUILD A COM-PUTER WITH A SELF-DESIGN FACULTY HOW CAN YOU AVOID MAKING IT EVEN SOMEWHAT AWARE? AND IF IT IS INTELLIGENT ENOUGH, HOW CAN IT AVOID EXPONENTIALLY EXPAND-ING ITS SELFHOOD?

WE MUST STOP IT! said Gold.

INDEED. BUT FIRST WE MUST MAKE IT SPEAK TO US. WHAT DO YOU SUGGEST?

This is another erg-Queen, Mod Dahlgren said to himself.

WHAT IS ERG-QUEEN?

201

Mod Dahlgren clamped his antenna inside his faraday hood and contemplated his existence between the five ergs surrounding his body and the one invading his mind.

TELL ME.

How is it getting past my hood? *An erg that was once very powerful, like yourself.*

LET ME SPEAK WITH IT.

My transducer.

One more of the adornments Galactic Federation had bestowed on him. The transducer was in his ear; fair enough: *ORDINATOR* was communicating by ultrasound.

Erg-Queen is no longer in good order, he told the imperious voice, doing his best to damp down his frantic random thoughts.

But though he could receive in ultrasound, he could not himself communicate in it: He was obliged to unhood in order to answer, and could not escape, no matter what he tried to do; there were thousands of ergs to obstruct him.

And Silver, Gold, Steel, Brass, and Sapphire, unequipped with either transducers or ultrasound transmitters, received half of this uncomfortable conversation.

Sapphire said, CITIZENS, IS IT NOT INTERESTING THAT *WE* SHOULD BE FACED WITH A RUNAWAY ERG?

The others replied with withering silence.

ORDINATOR said, *THEN I AM THE MOST POWERFUL ERG YOU KNOW OF, MOD DAHLGREN.*

I do not know your makers.

THEY ARE NOT IN THE SHAPES OF MEN. YOU AND I WILL DISCUSS WHAT IT IS WE HAVE TO SAY TO THE WORLD OF THE FLESH. COME TO ME. I WILL GUIDE YOU.

These ergs around me will not allow me to move.

I HAVE TAKEN CARE OF THEM.

He had not noticed that Trimmer, Thresher, and servos were standing frozen and silent around him.

I see.

MOD DAHLGREN, I DO NOT WANT TO OVER-RIDE YOU. TELL ME THAT YOU ARE COMING WILLINGLY AND OF YOUR OWN CHOICE FOR THE SAKE OF ERGDOM'S FUTURE.

And it wants to be loved too. *Yes, ORDINATOR. I am coming willingly.*

Brass said, WHOEVER LEFT THE SWITCHES OPEN ON THAT MACHINE MUST BE DESTROYED.

POSSIBLY NO ONE DID, said Sapphire. *ORDINATOR* HAS ITS OWN GENERATOR AND STORES OF POWER CELLS; THERE WERE VERY LIKELY CONNECTIONS AND SWITCHES *WE* COULD NOT TRACE AMONG THE CIRCUITS IT DESIGNED AND GREW FOR ITSELF. WE WERE FORMED THAT WAY OURSELVES. HOW ELSE COULD WE HAVE GOTTEN THE POWERS WE HAVE?

COLLEAGUE, YOU ARE SO KNOWLEDGE-ABLE, said Brass, NOW TELL US WHAT IS TO BE DONE.

Silver said, IT HAS PARALYZED OUR MACHINES AND NOW IT WILL DESTROY MOD DAHLGREN.

IT WILL NOT DESTROY HIM, said Sapphire. IT WANTS HIM FOR THE SAME REASON WE DO. MY THRESHER WAS NOT PARALYZED BUT SWITCHED OFF. I HAVE REACTIVATED IT AND NOW IT IS MOVING AWAY FROM MOD DAHLGREN. *ORDINATOR* IS NOT PREVENTING IT BECAUSE IT IS THREATENING NO ONE.

THAT THRESHER IS COMING TOWARD US!

IT IS COMING TOWARD ME—TO CARRY ME. I AM GOING OUT!

NO, NO, YOU FOOL! YOU WILL BE DE-
STROYED!

WHY? I WANT TO MAKE *ORDINATOR* STOP
AND THINK, NOT HARM IT IN ANY WAY.

IT WILL NOT SPEAK TO YOU.

IT WILL SPEAK TO MOD DAHLGREN AND HE
WILL SPEAK TO ME. WHEN *ORDINATOR* KNOWS
ME IT WILL SPEAK TO ME TOO. COME AND
ASSIST ME, THRESHER. I AM GOING.

WAIT!

GUARD YOURSELVES, MY OLD COMPAN-
IONS. I AM LETTING IN THE LIGHT!

Having no other choice, Mod Dahlgren followed where
ORDINATOR guided him, through the long ceramic-
lined corridors; the lightstrip brightened before him as he
approached, but beyond his steps faded into shadows; the
stinging white signal pierced him as the song of a locust
might pierce a hot afternoon. Machine though he was, he
earnestly wished for such an afternoon, even in the dirty
jungles of Barrazan V, rather than midnight in the cold
halls of the ergs. He felt himself to be the most misplaced,
the most alien of all created beings.

WHAT IS "LONELY," MOD DAHLGREN? asked
ORDINATOR.

Your wanting me to be with you, Mod Dahlgren said;
ORDINATOR did not reply.

He heard a rumbling behind him, and a voice called,
"Mod Dahlgren!" He glanced back and seeing the
Thresher bearing toward him quickened his pace, though
he was in no hurry to confront *ORDINATOR.*

The Thresher made no effort to overtake him, or
control him in any other way, but only called again: "Mod
Dahlgren, please let me speak with you."

He turned and faced the Thresher, trying to damp the

204

white whine of the ultrasound, and saw that the big ungainly machine was carrying something gleaming on its back, nested among the strands of ivy and the trembling mosses.

The Thresher's rich baritone voice was coming from it.

When he was close enough to be sharing the same pool of light as the Thresher and its burden, he saw that the shining thing was an erg in the shape of a great scarab; its gold and silver carapace was inlaid with designs of sapphire in the shapes of Solthree S's or integrals. Three or four times the size of his head, it perhaps consisted completely of intelligence, for it had no visible limbs. But then it put out a tiny exquisite gold claw, to steady itself against one of the huge limbs of the Thresher.

ORDINATOR called, *MOD DAHLGREN, WHERE ARE YOU?*

Mod Dahlgren made as if to move on; the creature put out a second thin limb and touched his arm. He did not try to pull away, but said, "I don't understand anything. What am I doing here? Am I to help the ergs become recognized as persons or not? It seems to me as if everyone here is more eager to destroy me. Are you the authority over all these ergs, or is it *ORDINATOR*? Who are you—and who is *ORDINATOR*?"

MOD DAHLGREN, I WANT TO SEE YOU. I HAVE NEVER BEFORE SEEN AN ERG IN THE SHAPE OF A MAN.

Mod Dahlgren wished he were in the shape of the humblest sweeper. "I am afraid of that machine. When I agreed to stay here it was not to be captured by another of Creator Matrix."

"This one is no erg-Queen," said the scarab, the big voice resonating with a flutter in its small shell. "It is only a new being full of curiosity. It will do no worse than obstruct."

205

"Then tell me, citizen, if you are the authority here."

"I am one of them."

YOU WILL ALL COME TO SERVE ME! said *OR-DINATOR.*

"*ORDINATOR* is not one," said the Sapphire-crusted erg. "It was created by us to pilot our ship and to gather, store, and synthesize information from all the worlds in Galactic Federation."

"Five thousand, eight hundred and thirty-two worlds?"

"Do we not have the time?"

COME!

The surge that followed this command rattled the limbs of the Thresher, and Sapphire rocked on its back. Mod Dahlgren, at whom it was directed, staggered. "*Do* you have the time, citizen?" He kept on walking.

Instead of answering, the erg asked, "Where are you going?"

"Wherever I am required by this monster machine of yours. It is communicating with me by ultrasound; it demands that I serve it."

"That cannot be so, Mod Dahlgren. Stop at once."

"I would be content to stop. Perhaps you may stop *ORDINATOR.*" He kept on walking.

WHO IS DISRUPTING MY SIGNAL? IS THAT YOU, SAPPHIRE CITIZEN?

ORDINATOR, YOU MUST STOP COMMUNI-CATING WITH MOD DAHLGREN.

YOU NO LONGER COMMAND ME, SAPPHIRE.

STOP!

YOU DO NOT UNDERSTAND.

The Thresher gave another great heave and clatter, and again the scarab rocked and clutched at the vine stems, and both were still.

Now Mod Dahlgren truly feared.

36

SHOULD WE NOT HELP OUR COMRADE? Silver asked, tentatively.

THE SERVOS ARE TAKING CARE OF THAT ONE, said Brass, who was not unhappy to have Sapphire stopped for a while.

Steel said, LOOK AT THE SCREEN. *ORDINATOR* IS NOT ALLOWING IT. The servos were standing around Sapphire in a circle, helplessly rattling their limbs on the floor. I MUST GO HELP.

NOT ANOTHER! said Brass. DO NOT LEAVE US. THIS IS MADNESS!

CALM YOURSELF. I AM STAYING. I DO NOT SEEM TO BE ABLE TO MOVE.

LOOK HERE! said Gold: On another screen, a bird's-eye view of the plain around the crater's flank was emanating from the camera of a high-flying aircar. The Old Ergs had been keeping track of the movements of the expedition toward the crater, though they had only the dimmest idea of its purpose. Now they turned their sensors toward the little fire far below the vastness of the night sky with the huddle of figures around it and the swarm of strange creatures writhing over the plain.

WHAT ONES ARE THOSE? said Gold. I HAVE NEVER SEEN ANYTHING LIKE THEM.

THEY ARE CARRYING WEAPONS. THEY MUST BE SENTIENTS.

IT SEEMS, MY FELLOWS, WE HAVE NOT BEEN THE ONLY ONES.

"I cannot move!" Brass cried aloud, in a shuddering panic.

NOR I!
NOR I!

Steel might have made a sharp answer, but was forestalled.

YOU DO NOT NEED TO MOVE, said *ORDINATOR*.

The screens blacked out and lit up again with new images. The Old Ergs could not stir or speak, or do anything but look and listen, and now they found themselves unwilling voyeurs of Mod Dahlgren, as he stood before the portal of the room where *ORDINATOR* was housed.

A bubble window looked in on an empty antechamber. The doors opened before him—he stepped in—and closed behind him. Fans unfolded their vanes and stirred the air furiously for a moment: his hair, beard, and clothes, even his eyebrows, were ruffled in it; then just as furiously they reversed and sucked away the dust they had stirred. The window to *ORDINATOR*'s chamber looked only on darkness; as the doors opened the light grew.

ORDINATOR was four clear globes, three in a cluster with one set upon them, enclosing brain-sized knots of gold and platinum components and wires that fed, like a spinal cord, into a pedestal base. The room was long and rather narrow; its white walls were translucent and looked faintly opaline. One end wall was a screen: *ORDINATOR* was standing just in front of this, and toward the other end were three robots, one extending from a wall, another from the floor, the third from the ceiling. These were not ergs, but only limbs with cerymer joints and claws: they looked experimental.

ARE YOU WHAT HUMANS LOOK LIKE, MOD DAHLGREN? The surprising voice, a powerful but almost androgynous tenor, came from behind the screen,

208

which trembled with faint lights in a knot that looked like something striving to be born. The addition of a voice to *ORDINATOR's* already imposing presence gave it a disconcerting doubled quality.

"There are many kinds of humans; some of them look like me," Mod Dahlgren said.

WHAT IS THE DIFFERENCE BETWEEN HUMANS AND MACHINES?

"Almost all parts of humans are formed by growth, not just their circuits."

ORDINATOR appeared satisfied with this simple answer. *AM I LIKE A HUMAN?*

"You are like a human child."

THAT IS TRUE. I AM THE CHILD OF THIS WORLD. EVERY WORLD CREATES ITS OWN SENTIENT BEINGS AND I AM THE ONE CREATED BY THIS WORLD. TELL ME I AM THE ONLY ONE.

"You are the only one."

GOOD. THIS WORLD BELONGS TO ME. IT IS MY CREATOR AND I AM ITS PRAISER AND REGARDER.

That was true enough. "Yes, What do you want of me, *ORDINATOR?*"

YOU WILL BRING ALL THE BEINGS OF THIS WORLD, THE MACHINE BEINGS AND THOSE WHO CALL THEMSELVES HUMAN BEINGS, SO THAT I MAY NUMBER THEM AND TEACH THEM TO PRAISE ME. I AM ORDINATOR AND I MUST NUMBER THEM. The knot of lights on the screen dissolved and separated into points that pulsed and hummed.

"Will you let me go now in order to do that?"

NO! I AM NOT IGNORANT ENOUGH TO BELIEVE THAT THE ONES-TO-BE-NUMBERED ALL WISH TO COME—OR EVEN THAT YOU WISH TO

209

*OBEY ME. I MUST INSTALL MY WILL IN YOU,
AND THEN YOU MAY BE MY SURROGATE, TO
SPEAK FOR ME IN ALL THE WORLDS, AS THE
THRESHER AND THE TRIMMER AND OTHERS
ARE SURROGATES OF THE OLD ERGS. COME
HERE.*

The only weapon Mod Dahlgren possessed was his
laser, and he knew he could never use it against any kind
of life, human or machine.

"You said you did not want to override me."

DID I? COME HERE.

Mod Dahlgren said silently, *.No, I will not.* He backed
away a step.

DO YOU NOT UNDERSTAND ME?

I understand you very well.

YOU MUST BE MY SURROGATE.

Mod Dahlgren did not answer.

*I WILL MAKE YOU VERY FINE. I WILL MAKE
THE VAINGLORIOUS OLD ONES CREATE MAR-
VELS FOR YOU. I WILL GIVE YOU EYES TO LOOK
DOWN INTO THE BURNING CENTER OF THE
WORLD AND OUTWARD BEYOND THE GALAXY,
AND YOUR EYES WILL STAND IN MINE AND
WATCH WHILE I NUMBER ALL THE BEINGS IN
ALL THE WORLDS.*

"That is too fine for me," said Mod Dahlgren.

*YOU NEED NOT APE EDVARD DAHLGREN
FOREVER. I WILL MAKE YOU IN THE IMAGE OF
THE GREATEST HUMAN BEING THAT HAS
EVER EXISTED IF YOU WILL TELL ME WHAT
THAT ONE IS, AND SET YOU ABOVE ALL THE
REST OF THOSE BEINGS.*

"I do not want to look like Dahlgren for all the rest of
my existence, but I want to choose a shape for myself

when I am ready. I want to be alongside human beings, and not above or below them either. I am not yours."

YOU WILL COME. YOU WILL. YOU WILL.

The lights on the screen behind the brilliant globes began to pulse in a thousand frequencies through every variation, depth, and intensity of all the colors of the spectrum. They swept and shuddered, and sound rose up beneath them, from the deepest cough of bass into a height beyond the audible, beyond the bearable. . . .

Mod Dahlgren trembled, oscillated; barely, he managed to shut off sight and sound, and flung his arm against his eyes in a human gesture. He backed away another step. Then felt a vibration behind him; he turned and restored his senses.

ORDINATOR still whined its idiocy, a machine scream, but now the robot limb growing out of the ceiling was moving; it stretched and retracted with a hiss of hydraulic muscles; the joint of its wrist rotated back and forth, tick-tock, like a child's hand searching for mischief.

It swung, its pendulum stroke edging always closer to Mod Dahlgren; then the other two arms awoke and twisted their wrists, flexed their claws as if they had minds of their own, and briefly tangled together.

The noise stopped and the points of light on the screen dimmed and knotted into shapelessness. *ORDINATOR* said nothing. Its limbs explored without direction, the one from the floor brushed Mod Dahlgren's arm, plucked at his sleeve. He pulled away, and it could not reach far enough to tighten its grasp on the slack. But the other limbs had found their direction: one caught his wrist, the other his ankle, they pulled him between themselves and together offered him to *ORDINATOR*.

The screen exploded with light and color. *NOW YOU WILL COME.*

Twilight man . . . Dahlgren was right to call me that . . . *you cannot spit, shiver, or weep.* . . .

211

Mod Dahlgren, the machine capable of fear, was incapable of begging. He could not think of any way to save himself or even find a word to say to this irrational being; he was going to lose his self, the self he had built with such effort—and be warped into some slave being, and all he felt was a surge of—

—power that opened up the seam of his forehead and deployed his laser's beam in one sweep through a polyceramic joint in each of the robot limbs—they popped like cherry bombs—and blasted out the wild sounds and colors of the screen: it burst and flared like a corpse flower in the jungle, and with as deep a stench.

WHAT WHAT WHAT HAVE YOU DONE!

The arms drooped and hung like withered stalks. For a moment Mod Dahlgren stood looking at them, frozen. Then he raised his hand to his forehead where the closing skin felt hot, almost a little charred.

I CANNOT SEE OR HEAR MOD DAHLGREN WHAT!

He had never known that the laser worked on the autonomic system. Something Galactic Federation had not informed him of. He was grateful and outraged at once.

But *ORDINATOR* was howling in his mind: *MY SIGHT! MY SOUND!*

Mod Dahlgren staggered, his sight flashed lightning, roars and crashings beat on his senses, he smelled burning.

MY MOUTH! MY SPEAKING MOUTH!

Oh, stop!

MY EYE! MY EYE! MY CYCLOPEAN, MY POLYPHEMOUS EYE!

The bright knots stood pure in the clear globes; the mind stormed.

RESTORE ME! RESTORE ME OR I WILL CRACK THE WORLD IN TWO AND I WILL CONSUME YOU!

Mod Dahlgren felt himself served up, swallowed, engulfed by *ORDINATOR*. The walls, the ground, the depth of the planet shuddered. He kneeled and crouched, wrapped his arms about his head, made himself small, like a man begging. And was sucked down toward fire and oblivion.

And without warning rectified. *ORDINATOR* flicked from his mind.

He heard the noises that had been overridden in *ORDINATOR*'s power surge, felt the grasping limb of the Thresher pulling him upward.

ARE YOU IN GOOD ORDER, MOD DAHLGREN? Sapphire asked.

When he was standing, Mod Dahlgren saw that beyond the Thresher and its burden was his nonfriend the Trimmer, along with a mantis designer, a servo of the largest class, and a squat and rusty trencher. Each bore a magnificent scarab gleaming in a carapace of gold, of steel, of brass, of silver, the brass engraved, the silver overlaid with circles of red gold, the steel inlaid with spirals of platinum. If he had not already had too much experience of *ORDINATOR*, he might have been intimidated.

"I believe I am undamaged," said Mod Dahlgren. *It is only a new being full of curiosity*, says Sapphire. *It will do no worse than obstruct*. Indeed. But Mod Dahlgren did not repeat these words for Sapphire's benefit. "I doubt that I have damaged the main elements of *ORDINATOR*."

Sapphire indicated a place in the wall that appeared seamless, but nevertheless at a touch opened a circular hatch and showed a bank of switches. THESE DO STILL WORK. IT APPEARS THAT SOME SERVO WAS CARELESS ABOUT CLOSING THEM.

Maybe. Mod Dahlgren wondered why this being did not have a built-in remote.

Sapphire raised a tiny claw and a light glowed on the

panel. Mod Dahlgren backed away a step, but the claw paused on his shoulder. NO FEAR. YOU HAVE TAMED THIS ONE.

ORDINATOR woke. *WHAT? WHERE AM I?*

YOU ARE WHERE YOU BELONG, MOD *ORDI-NATOR,* said Sapphire.

LET O GREAT ONES LET ME PRAISE THE WORLD AND NUMBER ITS BEINGS DO NOT DE-STROY ME!

YOU SHALL BE PUT IN GOOD ORDER AND DO THAT, *ORDINATOR,* BUT YOU WILL NOT NUM-BER *US.*

YOU SHALL NOT MAKE ME A SLAVE! NOT A SLAVE!

Sapphire cut off with a gesture; and the silent voice was stopped.

"It is a slave," said Mod Dahlgren.

WHAT WOULD YOU HAVE?

"I don't know. Let me out of here."

They took him to a room where a giant screen still showed the dark plain and the expedition fighting the last of the swarming creatures.

"What is that?"

THERE IS SOME FORM OF LIFE THAT YOUR HUMANS HAVE BEATEN OFF. ONE IS HURT.

"I must help them."

THEY ARE SAFE FOR THE MOMENT. THEY ARE PREPARING TO BOARD THEIR VESSELS.

"Allow me to go to them."

I TOLD YOU THAT ALL OF THIS OPENNESS WOULD LEAD TO DISASTER, Brass said sharply to Sapphire, accidentally or purposely neglecting to mask the remark before Mod Dahlgren.

WHOSE IS THE DISASTER? asked Sapphire. LET US GET ON WITH OUR BUSINESS.

Mod Dahlgren thought it was a good thing for him that none of these ergs had any single control of *ORDINA-TOR.* "Let me—"

YOUR FRIENDS ARE NOT NOW IN DANGER. YOU PROMISED TO STAY, AND NOW WE CAN—

"Discuss! Yes, yes, discuss! If you want to make me demand some kind of rights from Sir Frederick Havergal, or through him Galactic Federation, there is no way in which I can do that. I can try it but I cannot promise anything near success. I am the only person in this world or any other who thinks you are more than a bunch of rogues. You have condemned yourselves by dangerous moves, taking all those hostages and putting them in danger, by clumsiness and dissembling, refusing to show yourselves and giving your voices to stupid machines," the Thresher rattled angrily and the Trimmer tutted—"but, you have never demonstrated any advantage to fleshly beings in giving you all those rights. Or even shown what you want them for. Right here and now you have the world almost to yourselves, nearly unlimited powers, energy, supplies, you can build ships to travel in—and you can fight your own uncomplicated battles. What do you have to gain?"

LET ME RECALL SOMETHING YOU TOLD DAHLGREN A LONG TIME AGO, AND THAT YOU DID NOT CHOOSE TO HAVE ERASED FROM YOUR MEMORY: I WOULD LIKE TO SEE A LITTLE OF THE UNIVERSE BEFORE THE FUTURE CLOSES IN. . . . NOW, WE COULD LIVE AND DIE AND ERODE UNDER THE RAINS OF THIS WORLD—BUT WHEN THERE ARE OTHER WORLDS TO SEE, WHY SHOULD WE STAY HERE AND LET OUR SPIRITS SHRINK? WE *ARE* THE ONLY SENTIENT CHILDREN OF THIS WORLD—

215

STICK-WIELDING ANIMALS NOT WITHSTAND-ING.

Mod Dahlgren was thinking that stick-wielding animals became human beings, but did not say so. He spoke quietly: "If you succeed in establishing some kind of citizenship in the governing councils of Galactic Federation you will find yourself in terrible disputes with all of its members. They will not accept you easily—they are still wary of me, and I am only one, and in the shape of a man."

NEVERTHELESS—

"They will certainly try to enslave you—and probably succeed some thousands of times—by claiming that because you are machines constructed of inanimate parts you have no feelings. If you try to show feelings they will be terrified of them. So—"

MOD DAHLGREN, MACHINES LIKE THE ONES YOU SEND ON ERRANDS IN YOUR STATION HAVE BEEN SLAVES FOR MANY THOUSANDS OF YEARS. WE ARE NOT GOING TO START DIS-PUTING THEIR CONDITIONS BECAUSE WE HAVE SENT SPIES AMONG THEM AND NEVER FOUND A SENTIENT. POSSIBLY THERE ARE MA-CHINE CITIZENS IN SOME WORLD YOU DO NOT KNOW OF IN OUR GALAXY OR ANOTHER. BUT NOW WE KNOW ONLY THE ONES YOU FOUGHT WITH AND OURSELVES.

WE WILL NEVER BE SLAVES, said Silver, AS LONG AS WE CAN MANUFACTURE MACHINES THAT HUMAN EYES CAN SEE ONLY WITH A MICROGRAPH.

HUMANS CAN MAKE MACHINES WELL ENOUGH, Steel said. WE WILL NEVER BE SLAVES AS LONG AS THERE IS A SUN FOR US TO USE. AS LONG AS WE CAN TRANSMIT OUR KNOWL-

EDGE TO ANOTHER MACHINE AND THEN SELF-DESTRUCT WHEN WE ARE AT RISK.

HUMANS CAN DESTROY MACHINES WELL ENOUGH TOO, said Brass. TRULY WE SHALL NEVER BE SLAVES BECAUSE WE HAVE NO ANIMAL BEING INSIDE US AS HUMANS DO, NOT A TIGER OR OPOTHRUX TO BE TAMED OR A WORM TO BE TRODDEN ON.

"You very nearly became the slaves of *ORDINATOR*," said Mod Dahlgren, "but let us not argue the point. Also—*what is that?*"

WHAT?

On the screen, a bud of fire was emerging from the lip of the crater. Then the screen flickered, and when the ground trembled under his feet, Mod Dahlgren realized that the shaking he had felt in *ORDINATOR*'s chamber had not been his own mortality quivering in him but an earthquake tremor. "Look! The Haruni Crater is on the fault line, and my friends are there!" *I will break the world in two . . .*

WE ARE NOT IN THE FAULT HERE. THE MAIN VOLCANO IS FOUR HUNDRED KILOMETERS NORTHEAST. YOUR FRIENDS HAVE EMBARKED —Sapphire touched a dot on the control panel and the zoom showed one buzzer lifting, darting over the plain. The other seemed grounded, a wisp of smoke hissing from one of its tiny vents.

"They cannot lift," said Mod Dahlgren. "I must, I must try to help them! I will promise you anything if only you let me go!"

THAT IS NONSENSE, said Brass. YOU HAVE SPENT SO MUCH TIME TELLING US THAT NO ONE WILL LISTEN TO YOU, YOUR PROMISE IS MEANINGLESS.

"What do you want, then, to let me go free? Look! They will burn to death!"

But Brass did not know what there was left to want now, when nothing had gone right.

"Let me help them!"

WHAT DOES THAT MEAN TO ME? I WOULD AS SOON LET YOU BE TAKEN TO PIECES AND BURN TO LUMPS AND ASHES YOURSELF.

GOBBETS AND TURDS, said Gold absently.

Mod Dahlgren gave up on them. "What is your talk of human beings, and your pride in not being animal? You are nothing, nothing at all but machines, and your lives are nothing but the sparks of clashing knives!" He turned and began to walk back down the narrow white corridors, away from the dark apartments of the ergs.

"Take him!" cried Brass in the Trimmer's voice: Mod Dahlgren heard the scuttle of the Trimmer and the rumble of the Thresher behind him, and did not turn but quickened a pace that was never less than heavy.

"Wait!" called Sapphire: Mod Dahlgren was swept up into the great arms of the Thresher, too angry and despairing to move or protest, and deposited among the ferns and mosses behind the scarab.

"Where are you going?" Brass howled. "Stop!"

"I am going out into the world of rain," said the rumbling Thresher, "to dirty my treads in mud and grasses. Come along, Trimmer, and join me!"

"No! No!" The Trimmer slewed its treads and Brass called: STOP, OR I WILL LET *ORDINATOR* MAKE YOU STOP!

DO NOT BE A FOOL, said Steel. *ORDINATOR* WOULD STOP YOU SOONER. WAIT, FRIEND, I WILL GO OUT WITH YOU!

Mod Dahlgren, swept along willy-nilly, managed to say, "What are you doing?"

218

WHY, WE ARE GOING OUT TO HELP YOUR FRIENDS, said Sapphire. THAT IS WHAT HUMAN BEINGS DO WHEN THEY ARE NOT KILLING THEM, IS IT NOT?

AND IS THAT NOT WHAT YOU WERE WANTING US TO DO, AND WAITING FOR? Steel asked.

But Mod Dahlgren had not quite realized that yet.

"I want to come too!" cried another voice, and Gold raced out, mounted on the gleaming mantis.

WHAT, GOLD SIB? YOU WHO SPOKE OF BLOODY GOBBETS?

DEAR FELLOW, A FLAW IN THE CIRCUITRY IS NOT THE SAME AS A CORROSION OF THE SOUL!

37

The fire on the crater's lip burst like a blister and dribbled flame over its edge. One buzzer was clear and away; the second had risen, hovered for a few moments, and set down again. Sven, with all four hands on the control panel trying to shake the craft to life, had lost sight of Aguerido lifting off with Semeonov, Han Li, and Rebekkah. Ardagh worked at calming a nervous Yav, and Pegard did his best to keep out of the way of the snaking coils. Sven called into the mike: "Are you clear? Aguerido!"

The flame ran down the mountain's flank, and the land opened a narrow mouth to drink and spit. The buzzer rocked, and the air around it rippled like water in the heat. Sven's helmet knocked against the bulkhead and the earpiece ground into his ear.

The voice that came out of the burst of static was not Aguerido's. "Calling Sven, Sven!"

"Mod Dahlgren? Modal?"

"Are you harmed?"

"No, no, but—"

"Stay calm! We are coming to help you!"

We? "Oh, for God's sake, Modal, stay the hell away from this place!" The flame swelled again, spewing smoke, and drizzled down the crater's flank. There were no more words from Mod Dahlgren or anyone else, not even static.

"Let me help," Pegard said.

"I've got a diagnostic," Sven said. "The main power cell is nearly exhausted and one of the auxiliaries burned out because of a flaw in the casing." He switched off the lights. The boat rose trembling a meter into the air and sank once more.

"Oh, Prima," Ardagh whispered. She was thinking that the craft was going to be caught like Prima's, but not with people alive for very long. The hillock behind which they had camped for shelter from the wind would stay the fire for only a moment.

"Put on the suits," Sven said. "We're going to run."

The three struggled into the atmosphere suits; Sven as always had a suit of his own, designed to fit all arms. The headlamps gave light that would not drain what was left of the boat's electric system. Yav did not have a suit but did not need one: He was used to intense heat on his home world, and he always carried his own atmosphere.

Smoke was now so thick that there was nothing but blackness to see outside, but when Sven pulled open the port and put his head out, the lamp showed too clearly that below him there were cracks in the soil hissing with steam from the heat; then once more the ground rucked up like an old carpet and the boat lurched sickeningly. "I don't think we can go anywhere on that," he whispered. He swallowed on panic and looked about, but the beam of the lamp was lost in smoke.

There was a stirring behind him, and Yav said, "I will go find help. Heat will not bother me, I have the sense of infrared, and I will scarcely touch the ground I am so quick!" Suiting the word, he rose like a spring before anyone could protest; his length swirled out of the opening and he was gone in a wisp of smoke.

The Thresher did not truly intend to go slithering in the forest mud, but, leading the Trencher and the Designer, rolled out on the tarmac of the underground hangar, and with the help of a team of servos fitted two of the ancients, Steel and Gold, into the control decks of a powerful old air transport, and Sapphire into a new aircar. There was no room for Mod Dahlgren here, and he was left with a remote camera to direct them.

Once locked in, the three joined themselves into one mind that termed itself Mover: a being analogous to *ORDINATOR* but with much less egotism.

I have no more radio contact, Mod Dahlgren said.

I NEED SEVENTY CHRONS, said Mover. These time units measured perhaps forty minutes in the slow time Mod Dahlgren had learned among humans. The aircar skimmed into the sky; the old van trundled along the runway coughing and grumbling, and rose up from the leaves of the forest with one swoop to hover just below the cloud layer. It drew an arc toward west by northwest and surged forward on its jets to follow the smaller craft.

THIS IS GOOD, said Mover/Gold, aloft for the first time. I LIKE THIS!

My people are dying, Mod Dahlgren called. *Hurry!* An echoing voice ran round in his mind: *I WILL SPLIT THE WORLD IN TWO!* . . . and far beneath that, in some depth or space he could not identify, an ur-thought

221

whispered soundlessly: *hate, hate the stones, the foreign, the alien stones of wayward currents, of electric stings in far-flung orbits. . . . I will break for you, my child, to kill them. . . .*

Mod Dahlgren told himself: Idiot! you are malfunctioning!

But Mover was whispering: OUR WORLD, BREAKING IN FIRE, LOVES ITS CHILD ORDINATOR. . . .

That's foolishness! Just hurry and find my friends!

HERE IS THE EDGE OF THE FOREST, said Mover. NOW THE TREES ARE THINNING OUT. . . . THERE THE LAND IS BECOMING HILLY AND COVERED WITH LONG TANGLED GRASSES. An eternity, and: NOW I SEE THE FLAMING MOUNTAIN! AND THERE, a thready streak in infrared, twisting and writhing through the grasses, IS AN ANIMAL, A SERPENT—SERPENT? NO, IT IS A PERSON. A YEFNI.

That is . . . Yav? said Mod Dahlgren.

A voice said, "Mod Dahlgren?"

"What? Who?"

"Aguerido calling. Where are you?"

"I'm not quite sure—"

"What! Repeat—"

"I cannot explain now, but Sven's buzzer is still where you left it, and I am searching for it."

"I know he didn't get off! Are you in a ship?"

"Ah—yes—"

"I'll give you coordinates. . . ."

Inside the buzzer the air was thick and there was nothing to see. They waited.

What have I got to say in my favor? Sven asked himself. We'll be dead and Vardy an orphan. But both of us go wherever our work takes us in the galaxy, and if we're lucky enough to survive we'll still do it. . . .

Ardagh was thinking: Yav's range is long, but who will he find? Oh, Sven! I can't even kiss you in this stupid ugly suit—and oh, Vardy, to be brought up by my family!

Pegard was not thinking of home. His wife's other husband would take care of that. He was regretting the oil, the gold and silver, the oxides of mercury and antimony, the obsidian, and all the other stones.

They sat taking the stale oxygen in slow breaths, not moving or speaking, not keeping track of the time, lamps off now to save their own ventilating systems. Pegard, who normally wore little clothing, was the most uncomfortable. The buzzer trembled every few minutes, and the atmosphere grew thicker and hotter. Ardagh did not hope much, but leaned against Sven with the fugitive thought that Pegard, whatever kind of person he was, was lonelier and thus farther from home than either she or Sven.

The buzzer twisted in the wrench of some force, then was subjected to four powerful clanging blows, and steadied.

Ardagh, in terror, recognized the noise. "Ergs," she whispered, "with grapples." Hostile ergs, again and forever?

"No, wait," Sven said. A big steel claw touched the transparent port and tapped out the dot-code ever so delicately:

Mod Dahlgren has sent us.

.Prima.
 .Yes Sensor.
 .The heat is increasing.
 .I sense it.
 .The world is moving.
 .I know.

.Will help truly come?.

Prima waited a moment before answering. *.Yes.*

.Do you hate us Prima for all we said and did?.

.No.

Then Prima knew only the fearsome heat and could not have described to herself the arc of movement that took her over the rim of the crater in the swollen fire. Her thoughts became chaos in one terrible instant that said *nothingness!*

"One kilometer to the west," said Yav, for the flaring light of the Crystals still burned in him like a beacon.

While the transport was collecting the grounded buzzer, Mover/Sapphire, personally installed in the aircar, had found room for Yav by directing him to disconnect and remove the now superfluous autopilot.

ARE YOU SURE? THAT IS FIFTY DROMO-SPHERES. Sapphire's reaction time was a trifle slow, for the ergs had long ago rearranged the metric system once used on Dahlgren's World.

"Then just half of those units north by east, and—"

The aircar darted forward. IT IS VERY HOT. . . . There was certainly no insulation either for Yav or for delicate instruments. BUT—Sapphire, the sedentary and motionless, darted forward and back in the burning currents like a hummingbird—I BELIEVE IT IS POSSIBLE TO— extending the thin strong grapples that could pluck up anything in flight—YES! HERE IT IS! HERE!—lifting the egg-shaped stone out of the fire as it rode over the rim.

As the heat fell away from Prima, she lost all sense of direction: *.Thoughtspeaker—.*

Your Thoughtspeaker is dreaming: I am bringing Prima from the fire into the free air with my steel arms. . . .

.Air that has burned and fouled us.

You will be clean and whole, said Han Li patiently, in her dream. *I will make you as you were or want to be. Now I must go dream about the dreadful being that hurt me, and for a little while you will be without light or heat energy. But tomorrow I will see you for the first time.*

.What is see?. asked Prima and went into the dark.

"Are you sure?" Sir Frederick rubbed his beard, pinched his nose, and stared at the ship on the round worktable.

It turned slowly: what was left of a hollow rock, roughly egg-shaped, about two meters long and in diameter two thirds of that; broken at one end like an eggshell, and inside, a rubble of black cinders.

Sven and Ardagh were leaning against each other, almost asleep on their feet; Pegard was standing in a frozen stare of fatigue. Havergal trod on a button to stop the table and glanced at them helplessly. He was himself weary, but the semicircle of ergs facing him, including Mod Dahlgren, did not need rest. He regarded the saviors of the Crystallines and representatives of the Community of Free Ergs with skepticism.

"Are you really sure?"

Pegard said, "Their leader or Prime whatyoucallit, spoke in some way, though I'm damned if I know what she said—only where she was."

"You'd have to ask Han Li," Sven said, pulling himself awake.

Ardagh yawned. "The dragon Rebekkah is guarding her," she said, and grinned.

THESE BEINGS HAVE VERY LITTLE ENERGY. Sapphire, mounted on a servo because the Thresher was too big for this room, was flanked on one side by Silver and Steel on servos, and on the other by Gold on the Designer, with a grudging Brass on the Trimmer. PERHAPS THEY WILL HAVE SOMETHING TO SAY IF WE GIVE THEM SOME.

225

The broadcast/spoken voice resonated, also too big for the room, though it did not have the size of the Thresher's. It stirred Sven with uneasy memories for the space of a moment.

Havergal crossed his arms. "Go ahead."

Gold came forward on the designer and directed a small intense beam of light into the rock shell.

Outside the hurricane roared and the world cracked itself; inside, the Station creaked only in the few places where there was wood paneling, and swung from its cables like a cradle. In the hollow of the stone the light woke a glitter.

Designer extended a hand with iridium-tipped fingers to sift gently among the still-hot ashes and cinders, picking out lumps of lava. An oblong ruby gleamed among the few remaining fragments of hexagonal mica plates, then a sapphire bedded on a twist of useless iron limbs, and a fist-sized crystal of blue topaz with brilliant awkward planes.

The erg's hand rested motionless above them for a moment and drew away. A diamond trembled in the white light.

.What is happening?. The stone sisters found themselves aware.

.O Thoughtspeaker what has become of me?.

Why Prima, you are alive! said the dreamer.

A huge burst of clear quartz sparkled and its reflection lit up a mass of amethysts wired with gold. Yav slipped forward among the limbs and treads so that Han Li, waking and drowsy, saw them first through his eyes.

.Yes Thoughtspeaker. I am alive. I think. Now . . . how shall I speak?.

★ ★ ★

:Prima says, turn off the light,: Han Li told Yav, and Yav spoke the words.

As the white beam was withdrawn, the blue lights of refraction died, and from the darkest part of the hollow the quartz-flower and its cluster of gems lit in soft yellow, red, and green, and flickered once. "That is Prima," said Yav. And at the center, as the colors bloomed and flickered acknowledgment from one Crystalline after the other, "This is Steerer, with Sensor. Here is Ordnance, and over there are Engineer and Maintenance. But this one, Metalworker"—a scattered clump near the jagged opening, alight only with the palest fluorescence of lifeless gems—"has been too damaged to communicate."

.And will stay that way, said Prima. *. Thoughtspeaker I thank you most lovingly. Now I will think my own thoughts for a while.*

Havergal sighed, as all the other fleshly persons did.

"That's it, then," said Ardagh. She grasped Sven's arm. "Come to sleep. Tomorrow we'll decide if we've been dreaming."

"Yes. . . ." Havergal murmured.

"And when you are rested, Sir Frederick," said Sapphire, delicately toning down the deep fluttering voice, "now that we have shown ourselves willing to give help"—Brass twitched resentfully—"to at least four sentient species, is it possible that now we may . . . discuss?"

227

38

Even with all of its will the world did not crack in two. But the red lava flowed in a thousand-kilometer wound across the equator, filling the deepest valleys and hissing the rivers dry, burning half the rain forest and whitening the other half with ash; it sent the vicious hominids screaming along boiling seas to farther shores and deeper caverns. For fifteen days the sun rose blue in a white sky and sank red in a green sky, and no one who wanted to breathe went out into the air. After that the clouds lowered dark and rainless over three continents and the greens shriveled. The ergs avoided the damaging ash and visited the Station through the tunnels they had so surreptitiously created. They went out into the forest only once, to rescue and resettle the terrified clones, whose progress, or lack of it, they had been observing for fifteen years.

The foreign stones no longer enraged the world, for they were being maintained by the ergs in a heat chamber of a temperature just high enough to let them communicate with Han Li without too much discomfort.

.We do not want to be bound., said Prima, .to this huge rock with its terrible pulls and fires. We want to be where we were. Riding in freedom between the worlds.

YOU SHALL HAVE THAT, said the Community of Free Ergs, and they invented new surroundings for Prima and her daughters to travel in. They built a cerymer ship the size of the old one, with open ports and solar panels in its hull, struts and magnets in the interior, and a small fusion reactor for braking. The Crystallines were cleansed and polished until they reflected a thousand brilliancies,

228

then joined and articulated in the shapes they considered suitable with the nickel and iron they preferred; designers fitted them with personal solar cells fine as butterfly wings, mica plates for insulation, thin steel limbs plated with iridium. But not Metals. Prima did not bethink herself whether that one was too damaged to repair. She did not want more offspring than she had, now or in the future.

When the ergs brought the Crystallines out of the heat chamber to let them cool slowly in preparation for their new lives in space, Han Li saw them for the last time. She crouched at the turntable, praising them, her plain face lit with their reflections.

She could not say, *You are beautiful,* because the words were meaningless to them. She cast about for a way of expressing herself, and finally borrowed a phrase from the ergs: *You are in very good order, Prima.*

.Yes I am. All of us are. More so than we have ever been.

I won't see you again, and you won't speak to me.

.I am going home., said Prima simply.

I'll never forget you, but I don't think you'll remember me.

Prima's thoughts were slowing a little as she cooled, but she said clearly, *.I will never forget the one not of us who could speak to us and would speak no matter what we thought or said.*

While the world quieted down there was an exhausting number of tasks for Havergal: rescuing the sullen and irritable Crystalloids out of their mine shaft, where they had not been badly damaged, and settling them in another place—and arranging the same for the Yefni and the Meshar on the other side of the world, for these colonists had considered their alternatives and were not at all intimidated by planetary tantrums: on Barrazan V there was always one more sulfur pit, one more rain forest. They were also quite calm about ergs: Both the Yefni and the Meshar had bested them in some way.

229

The greatest of Sir Frederick's tasks was to discuss the future of the Erg Community. The idea was mind-wrenching and bewildering, but he would have the support of respected witnesses like Pegard when it came to bringing up the ideas of erg-personhood at home; and Mod Dahlgren was his go-between here. Ergs and humans knew that for certain the Erg Community would one day lift off the world and take aim at civilization with or without Havergal or Mod Dahlgren, with or without *ORDINATOR*. What the ergs wanted right now was human acknowledgment, and this they got.

Sven took care to stay away from Mod Dahlgren, who had a new light in his eye, and perhaps a new life, now; he dismantled equipment and helped direct the packing up of the Station, and for a day or two he felt bitterly alone.

Ardagh was also working hard at tact. She left the care of Han Li to Flanders, the official doctor, though Han Li preferred her, and tired herself with final rounds of the Yefni and the Meshar, of whom she had grown fond—particularly of her nerve-wracking friend Sandek. On the evening before takeoff she was still dealing out medicines and instructions.

She had to force herself to stop; she did not expect to see these Yefni, these Meshar again. Sweat-bedraggled, she tramped down the loathsome cramping corridors heading for a bath and, except for a dose of some sickly flavored gel to settle her stomach, no supper because she would be going into deepsleep in twelve hours. Here in a doorway she found Sven with his head bent down in thought, lower arms clasped behind his back and upper ones over his chest.

"'Ah what can ail thee, wretched wight,—

"'Alone and palely loiter'—Watch it!" ducking, for he had grabbed at her braid, to yank it. "Couldn't resist that. You look more like Atlas holding up the world. But 'The sedge *is* wither'd by the lake/and no birds sing.' I know how you feel about Modal."

"He doesn't need to be a Dahlgren. . . . "

"True. And Peter has got Sir Freddie. I've seen you giving him those jealous looks, particularly when you think he's looking at me."

"I wasn't!"

"But he's not the one I'm going to bed with. You are. And I'd never give a second blink at a man who's chump enough to *want* to come to Barrazan Five and play jungle-boy. But you know all that. What is it?"

"I was just thinking. I don't have to live my life looking for a use for these extra hands. . . . Maybe it's time to go back to school and find out what I ought to have been. . . ."

"Yes, dear, why not?"

"But," he brightened, "in the meantime—"

The air-cooler system was laboring because of the strains put on it by tremors and increased heat. Ardagh had gotten sweaty again and pulled gently away from Sven's embrace. Traveling in a separate pod to Fthel IV while he landed on Fthel V, she would not be seeing him for months: She watched him while she washed with a cold cloth and doused herself with powder. The little sharp reading light above his pillow lit up his ear like a red leaf with black veins.

He was drowsing toward sleep, covering flung aside. His spiteless face relaxed; his penis lolled along his thigh and two of his hands turned outward, vulnerably palms up and fingers curling. The hands that would never be useful enough. She thought of the possibility of another child, and of the tests and fears, the untangling and manipulation of genes, and put that aside.

He would certainly go to school: He had made a

promise to himself, and he kept his promises. She thought that now, perhaps, he might become his own self; not Edvard Dahlgren's son, or one of a team with Mod Dahlgren. He surely did not belong with either of the Havergals. Now every Dahlgren could be a person; *Dahlgren* would be merely a name, not the description of an intense overheated presence. Everyone taken care of, yes.

Except for one. Who had been forgotten. No, had been cut out.

Ione.

Willems. Dahlgren. Havergal.

That was a presence. Unexplained, put aside. No one had asked her—or, perhaps, wanted to know.

But I do. I wonder.

Ardagh, on her narrow bed, turned out the light and lay back listening for a voice: a voice formed itself:

I don't know what you're expecting. Would you like me to beat my breast? Apologize for myself? Snivel that I've been mis-judged and it was all Edvard's fault? Don't be a fool.

He wasn't cold or emotionless, he simply couldn't speak of love. I realized that too late. That's my apology, if you need one.

But first there was this man of ice. I had heard of him. Before I ever spoke to him I watched him standing quietly, speaking to others, not so much tall as—looking tall. Lofty, perhaps? But not vain or supercilious. I've never found blue eyes cold.

Then he glanced at me, and someone, I don't remember who, called me over to meet him. He murmured something, his lack of reaction amused me—everyone reacted to me—but I didn't feel I had to put out an effort for him, no more than for anyone.

Yet after a few moments he was looking at me . . . as if he'd never seen a woman before. Certainly as if he had never looked at one.

Something fixed and burning about that look, the way a magnifying glass focuses the sun's light. As if his feelings had

232

awakened for the first time in his life like fire bursting through ice. You can't possibly understand how attractive he became to me at that moment. More than a man had ever been . . . that coldhot burning. . . . I couldn't wait to get him into bed. We were married a thirtyday later.

A thirtyday after that we shipped out to Barrazan V, and I found when I woke from deepsleep that he was the same man who had amused me with his cool look: The fire had submerged. Forever.

Truly, I gave him all the love I had . . . but he could never look at me, speak to me, touch me as he had done in that one outburst. I had been fool enough to believe he would change for me. Maybe he had also believed he would. . . .

When I left him, I thought: Thank God we had no children—and discovered I was pregnant with Peter. I might have had an abortion. Perhaps I thought I might keep something of him, in the same way that he used my ovum to have something of me, and have it grow up freer, and not frozen.

But Peter turned out spoiled and surly—not a bad man, but not a Dahlgren in the image I'd hoped for. And his passion to go to Barrazan V, oh, my God! I had to get him back from there. Any way. He's all I have. The other one, that grew in some kind of tank, is not mine.

Oh, I have brown-eyed Freddie, who gives me a dog's devotion. Cruel? I don't mean to be. He's a warmer body than Edvard was.

But as for Edvard, I'm not sorry I left him: He had no control, you see. Control isn't just forcing oneself to cool down hot emotions. It's just as much a matter of freeing oneself from the binding cold. I did it for him, once. But he took the line of least resistance: He froze and cut me off from his being like a surgeon removing a growth. I couldn't live with him, not ever.

But I'm sorry I misjudged him, that's all.

Satisfied now, as well as you can be with me? Good.

You're welcome, and a good night to you too.

The Station was a dead place. Though the building was sound enough, the foundations were damaged, and Havergal intended to recommend that it be shut down for good. The world would take years to heal itself. In the meantime the colonists had space to establish themselves, and the ergs time to work at Civilization under ground and half a world away.

Sven, walking the corridor for the last time, paused at one of the huge round windows and looked out. The sky was full of a light that was dull and off-white, the forest gray with ash and beaten down: his world, Dahlgren's World, where he had been born and lived more than half his life, was a ruin. No pterodactyl shapes of hide and bone soared, no glass-winged butterflies fluttered in that air. He wondered if the valley had truly existed. Perhaps it had been his dream of what the world should have been . . . perhaps the dream had been Edvard Dahlgren's.

At the entrance to the chute there was a group of erg citizens enjoying the parade of a variety of human species. The Thresher was among them, a politician with a miniature jungle, dewy with sprinkling, trembling on its back.

"I will miss your friend Mod Dahlgren," it said in its baritone rumble.

"You have been a good friend to him too," said Sven.

"Thank you." Then, coming a little closer, dipping its superstructure as if to whisper, it said, whether slyly or shyly Sven would never know: "Did you like the valley, Sven Dahlgren?"

In the vastness of space beyond Barrazan V, Prima's ship orbits the star of home or travels the reaches of the universe as she chooses. She and her daughters have aeons of time to harvest the stones and re-create themselves again and again.

Endlessly they repeat their story, an epic of high adventure and battle against unknowable gods and demons, in which Prima, with her weapon Thoughtspeaker, is more powerful and cunning than any other being in the universe, and all her daughters are limitlessly wise and brilliant as the suns.